Laird's Curse

HIGHLANDER OF THE ISLES SERIES
BOOK 1

KATY BAKER

ARE YOU SIGNED UP FOR DRAGONBLADE'S BLOG?

You'll get the latest news and information on exclusive giveaways, exclusive excerpts, coming releases, sales, free books, cover reveals and more.

Check out our complete list of authors, too!

No spam, no junk. That's a promise!

Sign Up Here

www.dragonbladepublishing.com

Dearest Reader;

Thank you for your support of a small press. At Dragonblade Publishing, we strive to bring you the highest quality Historical Romance from some of the best authors in the business. Without your support, there is no 'us', so we sincerely hope you adore these stories and find some new favorite authors along the way.

Happy Reading!

CEO, Dragonblade Publishing

Chapter One

JENNA MACFINNAN ROLLED up the jeans and stuffed them into the bin bag with more force than was strictly necessary. The Spider-Man T-shirt went next. Then the socks. Then the boots. Then every other tiny scrap or reminder she could get her hands on. It didn't take long to fill.

When she was done, she tied it off, dragged it to the door, then picked it up and flung it with all her strength. The black bag sailed through the air and landed with the others by the gate with a satisfying thump.

With a huff, she whirled and scanned the room, looking for what else she could throw. Her eyes alighted on the pile of vinyl records stacked on the sideboard. She stomped over and picked up the nearest one. *The Who.* Seventies music had been one of *his* things. Along with dirt-bike racing and rock climbing.

Oh, and cheating on her, of course.

Grinding her teeth, Jenna cocked her arm to hurl the record out with the rest, then hesitated. It would be a shame to ruin such collector's items. They might actually be worth something and, let's face it, she needed all the money she could get right now.

An image flashed through her mind. *Getting home from work early. Pushing the door open. Pausing at the strange sounds coming from inside. Creak, creak, creak. A woman's cry. A man's grunt. And then... and then...*

With a bellow of rage, she picked up the stack of records, carried them to the door, and flung them out into the pile of garbage that had once been her life. Far from the satisfaction she hoped it would bring, the action only made her feel hollow.

So much gone. So much ruined.

She kicked the door closed, crossed the living room, and slumped onto the sofa. Drawing her knees in, she wrapped her arms around them and stared at nothing. Why did this hurt so much? Why did it feel as though somebody had taken a rusty knife and carved her insides out?

She felt tears coming again and dashed them away angrily. She would *not* cry over him. He didn't deserve her tears. Yet, try as she might, they fell anyway, running down her cheeks no matter what she did to try and stop them.

"Here," said a voice suddenly. "You've got snot coming out of your nose."

Jenna looked up to see two women standing over her. She'd been so engrossed in her misery she hadn't even heard them come in. They both had the same dark hair and green eyes she did—all the MacFinnan women had the same coloring—but one was older with her hair tied back into a severe braid while the other was only a few years older than Jenna herself with pink highlights running through her hair. It was the younger one who'd spoken, and she was holding out a handkerchief.

Jenna snatched it and blew her nose. "Don't you two know how to knock?"

The woman shrugged. "The door was open."

Jenna scowled. "What do you want?"

The older of the two sighed. "What do you think we want, Jenna? We've come to check you're okay. And by the looks of it, you most definitely aren't."

"I'm fine." Jenna said, waving them away. "Just fine. Go away and leave me alone."

They ignored her and sat down on the couch on either side. Her aunts, Rose and Elise, were not very good at abiding by her wishes, and she should have known they'd be over the moment they found out what had happened.

And, despite her protestations, she was glad they were here.

Rose, her eldest aunt, put her arms around her and drew her close. "It's all right, Jenna," she said soothingly. "It's going to be all right."

Jenna put her arms around Rose and cried. Elise, her younger aunt, patted her awkwardly on the back. "Is there anything we can do?"

Yeah, you can turn back time, so I never meet that bastard called Alex Carter, she thought. *How about that?*

She cried until her eyes were puffy and her face blotchy and all the while Rose and Elise waited patiently, neither saying a word, both just comforting her by their presence. But eventually, Jenna's tears ran dry. She drew a deep breath and pushed herself out of Rose's embrace. Her aunts watched her warily, as though wondering if she was going to have another outburst. Jenna wasn't entirely sure herself.

Rose patted her knee. "He wasn't good enough for you any-way. We always said that, didn't we, Elise? You deserve someone who's going to love you for who you are. Someone who respects you. Someone who doesn't spend all his money on his dirt-bikes or stupid records."

"Sure," Jenna murmured. "Where am I going to meet some-one like that?"

Rose pursed her lips. Instead of answering Jenna's question, she growled, "Alex Carter had better watch out. If I run into him, he won't know what's hit him! Tell you what, shall I put a hex on him? Make him come out in boils? Shrivel his manhood to the size of a peanut?"

Jenna snorted. "If only! But we all know you can't do that. Our powers can only be used for good, remember?" How often had she heard that growing up? She'd had so many lectures on the fact it was a wonder she didn't repeat it in her sleep.

"Who needs a hex?" said Elise with a shrug. "Just kick him in the balls and be done with it. Get him in just the right spot and his manhood *will* shrivel to the size of a peanut."

Despite herself, Jenna laughed. Her aunts always seemed to know what to say to make her feel better. Rose, the sensible one, and Elise, the wild-child, they balanced each other out and gave some much-needed stability to Jenna's life. Since her mother died, they'd been her rock, and she didn't know what she would have done without them.

She smiled and took each of their hands in hers. "Thanks, guys."

Rose smiled and Elise ruffled Jenna's hair like she'd done ever since she was a kid. "What's family for if not for times like this? And I *will* put a hex on him if you like, rules be damned. Or kick him in the balls. It's your choice."

Jenna shook her head. If anyone was going to put a hex on Alex Bloody Carter, it would be her. Shrivel his manhood to the size of a peanut? That would serve him right!

But Jenna knew she wouldn't. She didn't use her powers anymore, and she wouldn't break her promise now—not even for Alex Cheating Bastard Carter.

The MacFinnan women had always been witches, wielding abilities that had been passed down from mother to daughter. When she'd been younger, Jenna had used her powers to help her mother with small things: finding lost pets, predicting the weather, doing little healing spells, and so on.

But none of her powers—or that of her aunts—had been enough when it really mattered—when her mother had been diagnosed with cancer. Alongside the surgery and grueling chemo her mother had undergone, Jenna and her aunts had tried everything in their power to help, using every spell and incantation they knew. Nothing had worked. Her mother had slowly wasted away before Jenna's eyes, and when she went, the last of Jenna's faith in the MacFinnan magic went with her.

After that, she'd vowed never to use her powers again. No longer would she rely on something that had failed her so utterly.

What use was it really, anyway? There were drones and GPS for finding lost pets. There were apps for predicting the weather. And as for healing? Well, they'd all seen how that worked out.

So, although Rose and Elise thought her mad for giving up her gifts, Jenna had not touched her power for the last five years, and her life had been all the better for it. Until now. Until Alex Cheating Bastard Carter had torn it in half.

"What are you going to do about the house?" Rose asked suddenly. "Doesn't he pay half the mortgage?"

Jenna nodded tightly. She *really* didn't need reminding of that. "I'll be fine. I'll pick up more shifts at work."

"And you've got the money your mom left you. That should help," Rose added.

Jenna said nothing. She did *not* have the money her mom left her. That had gone into the deposit for buying this place and then fixing the myriad of things that had been wrong with it, but her aunts didn't need to know that. The truth was, without Alex's wages she was up a certain creek without a paddle, but she'd be damned if she was going to admit that. She *would* find a way out of the mess he'd landed her in, no matter what it took.

"Tell you what," said Elise, rising to her feet and pointing to the pile of Alex's things on the path and waggling her fingers theatrically. "How about we have a little bonfire? It's the least he deserves. When I split with Gary, I burned everything he'd left in my apartment. Made me feel a lot better, I can tell you."

"Don't go telling her things like that, Elise!" Rose said. "You'll have the police around here and Jenna being prosecuted for arson!"

Elise shrugged. "So?"

Rose frowned at her sister and then looked at Jenna. "I'll take Alex's things down to the second-hand store. If he really wants them, he can buy them back from there, can't he?"

Jenna nodded. "Okay. Thanks, Rose."

"Why don't you come and spend the day at my place?" Rose continued. "I'm making chutney. I've even roped Elise in to help."

Elise rolled her eyes. "Blackmailed is more like. Yeah, come, Jenna, and save me from a day of tedium."

Jenna smiled at their efforts to cheer her up. "Thanks, but I can't. I've got work later, and I promised Mrs. Turner I'd walk Bunny before my shift starts."

"All right," said Rose, patting Jenna's shoulder before climbing to her feet. "But you know where we are if you need us."

"Sure."

Her aunts walked to the door, and Elise turned at the threshold and waggled her fingers again. "And if you change your mind about that hex on Alex The Bastard, be sure to let me know."

Jenna gave a soft laugh. "You better get out of here before I decide to take you up on that offer."

They left and Jenna sighed at the sudden empty silence that filled her home. She felt a little better, a little more determined, after their visit. After all, she was Jenna MacFinnan, wasn't she? She was from a long line of strong women who'd never let a man ruin their lives. She was *not* about to be the first.

She grabbed her laptop and opened it, balancing it on her lap. Logging into the coffee shop's timetabling system, she scrolled through, looking for overtime. She'd already booked as many extra shifts as she could, but was hopeful there might be more available. If she was going to keep the house, she needed every extra penny she could get.

But there was nothing. All the extra shifts had already been taken. She fired off a quick email to Brenda, her boss, practically begging her to let her know if anything came up. Sickness. Home emergencies. Anything that might give her a few extra hours. She didn't hold out much hope, and even if she did get extra shifts, she knew it wouldn't be enough to stave off the bank that was already on her back over the mortgage arrears.

She felt that hot well of despair rising up inside her again. Damn it! She chewed on her lip, staring unseeing at the screen. What could she do? There must be something.

She clicked on a file on her laptop, then stared at the document she'd been putting off completing. She'd hoped it wouldn't come to this. Now she realized she had no choice.

Taking a deep breath, she began typing into the document, trying to ignore the two words printed across the top.

Words that read, *Loan application.*

Chapter Two

THE SAND CRUNCHED under his boots as Arran MacLeod walked along the beach. It was a fine day, with the sun high in a cloudless blue sky and a gentle breeze coming in off the sea, sending his blond hair waving out behind him like the tendrils of the kelp beds that dotted the coastline.

Aye, it was a fine day, a rare thing for this early in the season on the Isle of Skye, but Arran barely noticed. His mood did not match the weather. It was as dark and threatening as the winter storms that rolled in from the Atlantic and battered the island with rain and fury.

His entourage had waited at the head of the beach, letting their laird come out here alone, which was a wise decision on their part. He was in no mood for company, and the gaggle of guards and advisors that had insisted on accompanying him would only have made his anger worse.

He stopped and stared out at the bay. It was even worse than he'd imagined, even worse than his breathless scouts had reported at first light this morning. The twelve fishing boats lay in remnants along the shore, some half out of the water, others listing in the waves. All destroyed. All soon to become wrecks on the seabed. But worse than this was the sight of the things that bobbed in the water beside the ruined hulks.

Bodies.

Bloated and already attracting the attention of gulls and other scavengers, the remains of the fishermen floated like bits of discarded wreckage, some drowned when they tried to flee their boats, others hacked to pieces when they'd tried to defend them.

Arran's hands curled into fists. He ached to hit something. Anything. He needed to vent the fury that bubbled inside him like molten metal. Yet there was nothing on which to vent his rage. The raiders were long gone, back to whatever infernal hell they'd come from.

It was only April, early in the raiding season, and Arran's stomach tightened with dread at the thought of what the summer—and calmer waters—would bring. How would they hold off the raiders when they came in force? If he couldn't even defend this bay, how could he defend the rest of Skye? How could he keep his people safe?

Something caught his eye on the beach, and he knelt to pick it up. It was a wooden disc, no bigger than a coin, carved on one side with angular runes, on the other with a trident. Arran recognized it immediately. He'd seen many such tokens before.

So. These raiders were Norse, and this was a token one of them had dropped into the sea to beg the favor of their gods. Seems it had worked.

He straightened, gazing out at the softly sighing waves stretching to the horizon, hand tightening around the Norse token. He was laird of the Clan MacLeod of Skye. It was his duty to keep his people from harm, but he'd failed them. The weight of guilt settled around his shoulders, heavier than any mantle.

He was descended from a long line of proud MacLeod chieftains who had given their sweat and tears—their very lives—to protect Skye. But he was so much *less* than his ancestors had been. He was chieftain of a failing people whose courage and resilience were gradually being eroded by the endless waves of attackers who showed not the slightest pity or mercy.

It should *not* have been this way. He should have found a way to stop Skye's ancient magic from failing. But he hadn't. For years, the protective barrier that guarded the island, keeping Norse, Irish, and English raiders from their shores had been weakening, and he'd been powerless to stop it.

Now, it had failed completely, and the attacks had doubled, then trebled, turning the spring and summer months into one long hellish battle, with his warriors riding from one part of the island to another responding to every raid, but never quite getting to any of them in time.

He sank to his knees, staring out at the waves. All looked calm. And yet, he could well imagine the chaos, the terror and the carnage that had been visited on this tranquil bay only a few hours ago.

After all, he'd seen it often enough.

He'd been little more than a boy when his father had died and he'd been made chieftain. Just seventeen years old, he should have been looking forward to finding a wife and raising children before the trials of the lairdship were thrust upon him. But raiders had taken his father and elder brother long before their time, and so the burden had fallen on his young shoulders. He'd done his best to bear it, giving everything he had to his duty, giving up thoughts of a wife, a family, in his determination to serve his clan. But it hadn't been enough.

What would his legacy be? he thought bitterly. He had no children to follow him, and it was perhaps just as well. What would they inherit? A barren, half-dead island where a handful of desperate people clung on to their meager existence?

He closed his eyes and whispered a prayer to the gods of the sea who had once protected this place.

Please help my people. Please send me a way to keep them safe.

He didn't expect an answer. After all, every other prayer he'd uttered had gone unanswered, and the plight of his people had only gotten steadily worse. So his eyes flew wide in shock when a sudden wind sprang up, howling down the beach in a maelstrom, whipping sand into his eyes and turning the waves into a thrashing white froth.

He climbed to his feet and staggered back a few paces, flinging his arm up to protect his eyes against the stinging sand. The waves grew fiercer, crashing against the shore and battering what remained of his fishing fleet. Then a huge wave reared up, taller than the rest, taller than Arran, frothing and seething like a living thing.

Arran squinted into its green depths and felt his stomach tighten in fear. There was something inside it. A figure stood in the middle of that wave, a silhouette against the green water.

The wave toppled over, crashing onto the shore with a roar and drenching Arran with freezing spray. When the water receded, it left the figure behind.

It was a woman. She stood at the water's edge, young and shapely, with a flowing pearlescent dress covering her feminine curves. Hair the color of ripe corn fell to her waist and seemed to wave and move of its own accord, like sea grass. But it was her eyes that drew him the most. They were large and oval-shaped—and entirely silver.

Ice slid down Arran's spine. He reached over his shoulder and drew his claymore in a rasp of steel. Clutching it before him with both hands, he faced the stranger.

"Who are ye?" he demanded. "What do ye want?"

The woman did not reply. She stared at him with her silver eyes until, finally, she nodded as though satisfied. "There is no need for that," she said, gesturing at the sword. Her voice had a strange musical note to it and reminded Arran of nothing so much as water bubbling over rocks.

He did not lower his sword. "I think I'll keep hold of it all the same if ye dinna mind."

"Ye dinna need to fear me, Arran MacLeod."

"How do ye know my name?"

She laughed, a bright sound like rain tinkling on the ocean. "It wouldnae be much good coming to speak to ye if I didnae know who ye are, would it? I heard yer prayer, lad."

Lad? She looked younger than him. And what did she mean

by that last statement?

"Ye… ye heard my prayer?"

She took a step forward, and Arran noticed that her feet left no impression on the sand. "I did. It was heartfelt and carried with it some of the power of the old ways. It's a long time since I felt such conviction. And so I came."

"Who are ye?"

"Dinna ye know me? My name is Lir."

Arran's heart skipped a beat. Oh, yes, he knew her. His childhood had been filled with tales of Lir and others like her. She was the Guardian of the Isles, so the tales went, and in times past, rituals and ceremonies had been held in her honor at the summer and winter solstices. Mariners still prayed to her, hoping to win her protection whenever they embarked on a voyage. She was a goddess of the sea, as beautiful and capricious as the ocean. So the tales said. But they were only tales, weren't they?

"That's… that's… not possible."

"Isnae it? If ye didnae believe, then why did ye pray?"

He didn't have an answer for that. Still holding his claymore protectively in front of him, he said, "What do ye want?"

Something like irritation flashed in those silver eyes. "The first thing I want is for ye to stop waving that bit of iron at me. Put it down, Laird MacLeod. I willnae speak to ye while ye hold it."

He suddenly got the impression that although she might look younger than him, she was, in fact, very, very old. He felt like a boy being scolded by his tutor. Reluctantly, he sheathed his claymore in the scabbard across his back. He felt vulnerable without its reassuring weight in his hands, but what could a sword do against a goddess anyway?

"That's better," Lir said, giving him a beaming smile. Her hair floated and swayed as she walked towards him, and it took all his courage not to back away.

She halted an arm's length away and looked up at him. She was not as tall as he was—not many people were—and so she had to crane her neck, but even so he suddenly felt that *he* was the smaller of the two, a child facing a giant.

"Aye," she said softly. "I see it in ye. Ye have the courage to do what is necessary to save yer people."

"I'll do whatever ye ask of me," Arran blurted. "If it sees my people and my island safe."

She raised an amused eyebrow. "Dinna be so quick to agree, my laird. Ye may live to regret it."

"I dinna care. I vowed to keep my people safe. Just tell me what I must do."

"There is only one way. Ye must restore the magic that once protected Skye."

Arran sagged, hope leaking out of him like a burst waterskin. "That's impossible. Skye's magic was woven by a MacFinnan spellweaver, and that line died out long ago."

"Did it?" Lir asked. "Are ye so sure, my laird?"

"I'm sure." After all, he'd scoured not only Skye, but Barra and Islay and even the mainland, searching for any trace of a MacFinnan spellweaver. He'd found none, and as the last of his scouts had returned empty-handed, the last of his hope had died.

"They're gone," he growled, anger in his voice now. "They've been gone for over a century, so dinna waste my time."

"So impatient, my laird," Lir said with a faint, mocking smile. "So sure, and yet so blind."

"What do ye mean by that?"

"I mean that things are not always what they seem. Ye, of all people, heir to an ancient magic and guardian of many secrets, should know that. Ye didnae find any MacFinnan spellweavers in *this* time. But that doesnae mean that they are gone entirely."

She gestured behind Arran, and he turned to see an almost perfectly circular pool in the rocks behind him.

He was certain that rock pool had not been there a moment ago. Lir stepped up to the pool and stared into its depths. Hesitantly, Arran joined her. It was deep, far deeper than any rock pool had a right to be, so deep he couldn't see its bottom.

There was none of the seaweed, small crabs, and other things he might expect to see. Instead, it looked like a clear, bottomless blue hole that led to… what?

"The MacFinnan line didnae die out," Lir said. "The power of the spellweavers resurfaced again, but far into the future. If ye wish to save yer people, ye must travel to the future, find a MacFinnan spellweaver, and convince her to travel back here with ye to restore the magic."

"Travel to the future? That's impossible."

"Ye are good at saying that," Lir replied, making a tutting sound. "Look closer, my laird."

Arran found himself leaning forward, staring into the blue depths of the pool. As he did so, it began to change. Images appeared deep below the surface, strange, alien images that made no sense. He saw tall buildings, far taller than any of the castles or spires of Alba. He saw strange metal boxes on wheels moving at incredible speeds. He saw more people than he'd ever seen in one place before, bustling along smooth streets lined with glass-fronted buildings and many-colored lights.

"What is that place?" he breathed, looking at Lir with awe.

"That is the future. The place to which ye must go if ye wish to save Skye."

The image in the pool began to change, and this time he saw a woman. Close to his own age, she had long hair the color of midnight. He couldn't see her face clearly, but she was sitting on the porch of a building with her knees drawn up to her chest.

"Is that her?" Arran asked eagerly. "Is that the woman I need to find?"

"Aye," Lir replied. "What is yer choice, my laird? Will ye accept this task?"

"Gladly," Arran said with a nod. He didn't even have to think about it. He would take *any* chance, no matter how small, no matter how insane, if it gave him even a tiny hope of protecting his people.

Lir cocked her head and regarded him with her strange eyes.

"Aye. I chose well in ye, Arran MacLeod. But know this. This will be different to any battle ye have yet faced. It will be harder. Darker. Are ye ready for that?"

No, he wasn't. He wasn't ready for any of this. But he met Lir's stare head on.

"I'm ready."

"Then jump into the pool. Remember, ye canna force her to come back with ye. That must be her choice. Ye must find a way to convince her, my laird."

"I'll find a way," he said more confidently than he felt. How would he convince a woman to travel through time just to help him?

He stepped up to the edge of the pool, his boots scraping on the rock. Lifting his gaze, he looked out over the bay one final time, taking in the remains of the fishing boats bobbing in the swell and the horrific sight of the bodies floating next to them. He'd find a way. He had to.

Pulling in a deep breath, Arran MacLeod jumped into the pool.

Chapter Three

"BUNNY!" JENNA SHOUTED. "Here, girl!"

She always felt faintly ridiculous shouting that name. "Bunny" was no bunny at all but a great big slobbery Great Dane who belonged to Mrs. Turner, Jenna's neighbor. Since Mrs. Turner had a hip replacement a little over a month ago, she'd been unable to walk Bunny and so Jenna had volunteered for the job. After all the home-cooked meals and delicious cakes that Mrs. Turner had showered her with over the years, it was the least Jenna could do.

Bunny came ambling along the path, taking her own sweet time to catch up. For such a big, powerful dog, she was incredibly lazy, and Jenna was pretty sure she'd be perfectly happy snoozing on Mrs. Turner's couch all day given the choice.

"Will you hurry up? Anyone would think you don't want to go for a walk!"

Bunny gave a huff as if she understood every word, sniffed Jenna's hand, and then trotted off along the path that hugged the edge of the lake. It was a lovely spot, with the lake looking like a polished silver coin on such a sunny day as this. The evergreens that bordered the lakeshore whispered in the light breeze and a family of geese paddled along, keeping pace with Jenna and clearly wondering if any food might be forthcoming.

Jenna breathed deeply and did her best to push her worries

out of her mind and concentrate on the beautiful day. But it was hard. So hard. No matter what she did, her thoughts kept returning to Alex's betrayal and her money worries. Her future, which only a week ago had seemed bright and full of promise, had turned into a murky wasteland which she could no longer see a path through.

Oh, hell. What was she going to do?

Bunny suddenly gave an excited bark and went pelting down to the water's edge, sending mud flying. Jenna sighed. Again? Seriously?

"Bunny!" she shouted. "Are you ever going to learn? It doesn't matter what you do, you are *not* going to catch one of those geese!"

But the dog ignored her, dancing around the lake's edge like some excited puppy, tail whipping from side to side, and back end wriggling madly. She barked again, a loud yip that was entirely too high-pitched for such an enormous beast.

Jenna let out an exasperated groan. "Fine! Have it your way. You're going back on the leash."

She took the leash out of her pocket and marched down to the water's edge, only to halt in surprise when she realized it wasn't the geese that Bunny was barking at. It was something… else. There was a strange disturbance out in the lake, perhaps thirty feet or so from where she was standing. The water had begun to move, turning slowly like a whirlpool. The area wasn't large, perhaps a few feet across, and the water around the anomaly remained perfectly still and smooth.

Jenna frowned. What on earth?

As she watched, the whirlpool began to spin faster, whipping the water into a frenzy of froth and tiny white waves. Then all of a sudden a spout erupted from it with a whoosh, only to fall back to the lake's surface in a shower of silver droplets. When the spout dissipated, the whirlpool was gone, but something else had been left in its place.

A man.

Jenna's eyes widened, her jaw dropping. What the hell? Where had he come from? The man was floating on his back, arms and legs spread-eagled, with his eyes closed as though unconscious. Golden blond hair floated around his head like some sort of halo.

"Hey!" Jenna shouted. "Hey! Are you all right?"

The man's eyes flickered open and he rolled over, sinking under the water for a moment before coming up again, gasping and spluttering.

Shit!

Jenna waded into the shallows. "Hey! This way!"

The man struggled weakly towards her. When he was close enough, she grabbed his shirt and helped to haul him into the shallows. He collapsed, half-in, half-out of the water, gasping for breath.

Jenna crouched next to him. "Are you hurt? Should I call an ambulance?"

"Not hurt," he gasped. "Just… help me up."

He struggled to his knees, then braced one hand against the muddy bank for leverage. Jenna got her shoulder under his other arm and supported him as he pushed unsteadily to his feet. God, he was heavy! It was only when he was finally standing that she realized how big he was. Well over six feet, with wide shoulders and powerfully muscled arms, he was built like a boxer or a football player. And what the hell was he wearing? Some kind of strange, tartan wrap thing hugged his torso and then fell in folds to his knees where it was met by knee-high boots of soft leather.

"You okay there?" she asked, looking up at him.

Startling blue eyes met hers, as bright as the summer sky above. "Aye, I'm fine now. Just a wee bit dizzy from crossing over is all." His blond eyebrows pulled down into a frown. "She could have warned me it would near drown me."

Crossing over? What was he talking about?

"Are you sure you don't want me to call an ambulance? You don't look so good."

"I am well, lass," he rumbled. "But I thank ye for yer help."

He had a deep, rolling burr to his accent and she guessed he must be Scottish. The tartan was a bit of a giveaway too, of course. He laid a big hand on her shoulder and then pushed away from her support. But he'd not taken more than two steps when he staggered suddenly. Jenna darted forward and got her shoulder under his arm again to steady him.

"All right, big man," she said. "If you won't let me call you an ambulance, you'll at least come home with me and let me take a look at you. You clearly aren't fine and no wonder either. Come on. It's not far."

He didn't protest as she began walking back towards her house, and leaned heavily on her for support. Bunny trotted along at Jenna's side, tongue lolling and head tilted to the side, clearly intrigued by this newcomer into her world.

By the time they reached the back door of her house, Jenna was breathing heavily and sweating. It had been hard work getting him here despite his protests that he could walk unaided, thank you very much. Yeah, right. If she'd stopped supporting him she suspected he'd have fallen flat on his face.

She kicked the back door open and managed to bundle him through into the kitchen and help him to one of the chairs at the table. He slumped down heavily, the chair creaking alarmingly under his weight, and leaned forward, bracing his elbows on the table. Bunny seated herself in front of him, tail wagging from side to side.

"My thanks, lass," he rumbled. "It seems I'm weaker than I thought."

"Really?" Jenna replied, crossing to the sink. "You don't say. Here, drink this."

She held out a glass of water which he took in shaking hands and began to sip. Slowly, he began to look a little better. His lips were no longer blue, and a blush was starting to creep across his cheeks. But still, perhaps she ought to just take a look—

No! she told herself fiercely. *I'm not doing that. Never again, remember? If he needs healing, he can see a doctor like everyone else.*

The man finished the glass of water and placed it on the table. He looked over at her with a wry smile. "I dinna suppose ye have anything stronger? Whisky, perhaps?"

"You supposed right." She filled the kettle and put it on the stove. "I'll make us some coffee. Although, I think I might have some tea around here if you'd prefer?" He *was* British, after all.

"Tea?" he asked, in his rumbling voice. "What is this thing?"

She snorted. "Oh, right. You don't have it in Scotland, I suppose?"

"Not where I'm from, lass."

"Fine. Whatever. Coffee it is then."

She didn't have the energy or inclination to argue. She would make him a coffee, let him dry off, and then send him on his way. She would have done her good deed for the day, and what happened to him after that was none of her concern.

He watched her as she worked. He was, she noticed, shockingly attractive with his sculpted features, wide blue eyes, and blond hair. She scowled. So what? In her experience good-looking men were not to be trusted, Alex being the perfect example of that.

She turned around and focused on the coffee while he started petting Bunny. The big dog seemed to have taken a liking to him and rolled onto her back for a belly rub.

"How did you end up in the lake?" she asked without turning around. "Were you kayaking? Fishing? If you've capsized your boat, there's a guy who looks after the place who I can call to go salvage it for you."

"Nay lass, I dinna have a boat."

"Then, what? You were just out there swimming?"

She remembered the strange whirlpool she'd seen and then that huge spout of water. It had almost been as though… as though the water had coughed him out from somewhere.

"Something like that," he muttered.

She finished making the drinks and pushed his mug across the table towards him. He took a sip, making a face that told her exactly what he thought of it. She didn't sit but leaned against the kitchen counter, fingers curled around her own mug as she watched him rubbing Bunny's belly. He was so big that he seemed to dwarf her tiny kitchen and despite herself, she couldn't stop her eyes from tracking along the contours of his well-defined body, so obvious beneath the wet clothes clinging to his skin.

"I'm sorry," she said. "But I don't have a change of clothes to lend to you." Aunt Rose had taken Alex's clothes away and even if she hadn't, there wouldn't have been anything to fit this guy.

He waved her apology away. "Ye have already done more for me than I could have wished for. Ye have my gratitude, lass."

His blue eyes met hers, and Jenna felt a faint flush creep up her cheeks. She took a sip of coffee to cover it. "It's nothing. I wasn't about to let you drown, was I?"

"Well, ye have my thanks all the same." He cleared his throat. "And I, it seems, have forgotten my manners. I havenae even introduced myself." He scraped back his chair and rose to his full impressive height before giving her a courtly bow that would have looked ridiculous on anyone else but for some reason seemed to suit him. "My name is Arran MacLeod, laird of the MacLeods of Skye. Pleased to make yer acquaintance."

"Laird?" she asked. "What's that? Some kind of lord?"

"Aye. I am chieftain of my clan."

"Nice to meet you too, chieftain of your clan," she said. "I'm Jenna. Now tell me, what was a Scottish laird doing in the lake outside my house?"

"I was sent here by the goddess Lir to seek aid for my people. I'm looking for a MacFinnan spellweaver."

Jenna's mug smashed as it hit the kitchen floor, splashing coffee all over her shoes.

"Damn it!" She crouched and began picking up the pieces of broken crockery, using the movement to cover her sudden shock.

A MacFinnan spellweaver? How did he know that term? Nobody was supposed to know about her and her aunts. The

MacFinnans had been persecuted as witches in times past and as a result, they'd kept their powers carefully hidden. But now a man dressed like he belonged in some historical reenactment came looking for one? And what had he said? He'd been sent by a goddess?

"Here, let me help." He took a step towards her but she flung up a hand to stop him.

"I can manage!"

She picked up the bits of broken crockery, slung them into the bin, and then stood with her hands resting on the countertop, back to Arran MacLeod, staring out of the window. Just when she thought her day couldn't get any worse. What had she done that was so bad the universe had decided to crap on her like this?

"Lass?" he said from behind her. "Jenna? Are ye all right?"

His voice rumbled across her skin like a warm breeze, deep and soothing.

"Fine," she lied. "I'm just fine. Now, if you're dry and you've finished your coffee, you'd best be on your way. I have to get ready for work." She suddenly wanted him gone, wanted him out of her house, out of her life. She didn't need this complication.

She heard the soft tread of his boots as he came to stand behind her. "Have I offended ye, lass?"

She whirled. "No, you haven't offended me, just—" She cut off as she realized how close he was, not six inches away, staring down at her with those deep blue eyes of his. She swallowed thickly. "But I think you'd better go now."

He studied her face and his eyes suddenly narrowed. "Wait," he breathed. "I know ye. Ye are the one in the vision Lir showed me. I recognize ye now!"

"Don't be stupid. We've never met before." Vision? What vision?

"Ye said yer name was Jenna," he said softly. "Jenna MacFinnan. Am I right?"

She pushed past him and went to stand on the other side of the table, putting some space between them. "Yes, I'm Jenna

MacFinnan, and I'm also very busy. So you need to leave now."

He shook his head. "I canna do that, lass. I need yer help."

"I've already told you, if you need to retrieve your boat from the lake, there's a—"

"I need ye to come back through time with me to save my people."

Jenna stared at him. "I beg your pardon?"

"The goddess Lir sent me from the year 1497 to bring a MacFinnan spellweaver back through time with me. Only yer magic can save my people."

He was clearly insane. "If you expect me to believe that—"

"I'm telling the truth, lass. The lake ye dragged me from? That was the portal Lir sent me through. Ye are a MacFinnan spellweaver—surely yer powers can tell ye I speak the truth?"

His blue eyes were alight with something like hope, and his voice sounded so earnest that Jenna paused. He really believed what he was saying. Either he was completely mad or... or... he was telling the truth.

She hadn't touched her power in years and had no wish to do so now, yet she couldn't deny that there was something very odd about the way he'd arrived here, not to mention the way he was dressed. All right. Just this once. Just a tiny bit.

Slowly, reluctantly, she opened herself up to her spellweaving magic. It was like opening the drapes on a sunny morning and the world suddenly sprang into sharper focus, revealing things that were normally hidden. The first thing she saw was the strange displacement that surrounded Arran MacLeod like the shimmering optics of a rainbow. It hurt Jenna's eyes to look at, and she knew immediately what it was.

A distortion of time.

Arran MacLeod was most definitely not of this time, which explained his strange appearance and his strange clothing. What it did *not* explain was how he thought she could help him, or why she would want to.

She disengaged her power, and the world faded to normal. "I'm sorry," she said, striding to the door and holding it open for him. "I can't help you. Now please leave."

"Will ye not even hear me out?" he replied. "Will ye not even hear what I've come all this way to say?" There was an edge to his voice now, one that sounded like anger.

"I've heard enough. I'm not the person you're looking for, and I can't help you. Now go, before I call the police."

He studied her. Warring emotions shone in his eyes. Anger, yes, and something else. Desperation? He was an imposing sight standing there like that, all six-foot-something of him with his huge shoulders and raptor's glare. But she wouldn't be intimidated. If he tried anything, she would kick him in the balls like Aunt Elise had suggested.

His fists clenched and she tensed, expecting some kind of outburst, but then his shoulders relaxed. "I can pay," he said finally. "Name yer price."

ARRAN WATCHED JENNA MacFinnan closely. She opened her mouth as though to speak—to tell him to go hurl himself in the lake most likely—but then closed it again. He took this as a good sign. Since his offer of payment she hadn't refused him outright nor tried to throw him out of the house.

Lir had told him that he couldn't force the spellweaver to come back with him, and that he had to find a way to persuade her. For a moment, when she'd refused to help him, he'd considered picking her up, slinging her over his shoulder, and bodily marching her back to the lake, whether she willed it or no.

He was so desperate to help his people that he would have done it had his conscience and common sense not stopped him. He'd never manhandled a woman in his life, and he wasn't about to start now. And besides, this was a woman who could most likely toss him through the air like a leaf in a breeze if she chose to.

So he'd resorted to the only tactic he could think of: a deal. He'd pay whatever she wanted if she would agree to help him. He'd happily hand over what was left of the MacLeod wealth if that's what it took. Wealth could be replaced. Lives could not.

Still, she said nothing, and he read skepticism in her wide green eyes. He couldn't blame her. In his present condition he hardly looked the chieftain of a once-prosperous clan, did he? Neither had he brought any coin with him in order to make such a bargain.

He yanked the chieftain's torc from around his neck and tossed it onto the kitchen table. It landed with a heavy thunk. "Here, I will give ye this for starters. It's gold. Worth a pretty sum even in yer modern age I would image."

The lass's eyes widened. The torc was a heavy, braided circle of metal, with its terminals carved into the semblance of snarling sea-wolves with garnets for eyes. The torc had been the symbol of the chieftains of the MacLeods since time beyond measuring, passed down from chieftain to chieftain. It pained him to give it up. But that was naught compared to the pain of seeing his people suffer. What was one lump of gold compared to that?

Jenna cleared her throat. "Yes," she said, her voice barely above a whisper. "That would be worth a fortune."

"And there's more where that came from," he said, pressing his advantage. "I will pay ye a king's ransom if ye can save my people."

She swallowed. He couldn't quite decipher the expression on her face. Hopeful and despairing at the same time, as though she was being pulled one way and then another.

She was not what he'd expected, this MacFinnan spellweaver. She was beautiful, that was for sure, with her lustrous black hair, bright green eyes, and a smattering of freckles over her face. Confident too, if the way she'd waded into the lake to help him and then brought him back to her dwelling place was anything to go by.

And yet she seemed... fragile. There was a shadow in her

eyes and he'd yet to see her smile. He got the feeling that she didn't do that very often.

"So, lass?" he pressed gently. "What do ye say?"

Her eyes moved from the torc on the table, to his face. Arran held her gaze, refusing to look away, and for an instant they stood like that, staring at each other.

Then the lass turned away. "I'm sorry," she said. "But you've got the wrong person. I may be a MacFinnan, but I'm not a spellweaver. Not anymore. I'm not the person you need."

"I think ye are. Lir sent me to ye."

"Then she got it wrong! I can't help you. Now please leave." Her expression had gone blank, shutting away whatever she was feeling behind an expressionless mask. She strode to the door and held it open for him.

He ground his teeth in frustration. He had come all this way, traveled through the layers of time for this woman. He could *not* go home empty-handed. "Listen, lass. I—"

"Just go!" she yelled. And then more softly, added, "Please. Just go."

The anguish in her voice stopped any further protest. "All right," he breathed in defeat. "All right."

He picked up the torc, its weight feeling as heavy as the despair that settled in his stomach. He'd failed. This had been his last chance, and he'd failed. He walked to the door and paused as he reached her. She did not look at him, but stared straight ahead.

"Thank ye for the coffee." He gave the giant dog one last scratch behind the ears, then walked down the porch steps and onto the path that would lead back to the lake.

He heard the door close behind him.

Chapter Four

JENNA WATCHED ARRAN MacLeod walk down the drive and then turn onto the path into the trees. She hugged her arms around herself, trying to tell herself that she was glad he'd gone. What he'd asked her to do... It was ridiculous! Go back in time with him? Use her powers to restore some ancient spellweaving she'd never even heard of?

Yes, she was glad he'd gone. So why did she feel so shaky? Why did she feel like a coward?

Her eyes strayed to where the gold torc had lain on the kitchen table. Arran had been right—it would be worth a pretty penny. Maybe even enough to pay off some of the mortgage arrears. Certainly enough to get her a bit of breathing space until she could figure something out.

And all she had to do to get it was break her vow and use the powers she had lost faith in long ago.

No. She wouldn't do it. She couldn't do it. She would find the money another way.

She sighed. This was turning into one of those days where she wished she hadn't bothered getting out of bed.

"Come on," she said to Bunny, who was standing in the doorway staring in the direction Arran had gone. "Let's get you home."

Clipping on Bunny's leash, she took her down the street to a grateful Mrs. Turner, then hurried home. She had to get ready for work. The last thing she wanted to do was be late and get into trouble with her boss. She wasn't likely to be given the overtime she needed then, was she?

But as she hurried up the steps and onto her porch, her phone beeped. Digging it out of her pocket, she opened the message that had just appeared, and read it. It wasn't very long, just a few simple words, but they spelled the end of Jenna's hopes.

Your loan application has been declined.

Jenna stared at the words, fighting back the sudden tears that stung her eyes. The dark wave of despair she'd been holding back ever since she'd found Alex in bed with that blonde woman rose up and threatened to drown her. She took deep, steadying breaths, but it didn't help. She felt suddenly as if a giant pit had opened in front of her feet and if she took another step, it would swallow her.

She was going to lose her house. She was going to lose everything.

There is more where that came from. I will pay ye a king's ransom if ye can save my people.

A tiny chink of light opened in the darkness, like a firefly in a dark room. It was a crazy choice, but it was the only choice she had. Hurrying down the steps, she took off along the path to the lake.

She just hoped she wasn't too late.

In fact, she wasn't. Luck, it seemed, was on her side for a change. Running at full pelt, she spotted Arran on the trail ahead and managed to catch him before he reached the spot on the lakeshore where she'd first found him.

"Wait!" she cried. "Wait!"

He turned and she saw a flicker of surprise cross his face as he spotted her. He stopped walking and waited.

Jenna puffed up to him and doubled over with her hands on her knees, trying to catch her breath.

"What is it, lass?" he asked. "Is something wrong?"

She held up a hand. "Just... give... me... a... minute." She gulped in great whooping breaths and then finally straightened. "This fee you're willing to pay. How much exactly did you have in mind?"

He frowned, his forehead creasing. "I thought ye said—"

"I know what I said! How much are you offering?"

He studied her for a moment. "I can offer ye one hundred gold lions."

Jenna thought about this. She had no idea how much that equated to in modern money but with the price of gold these days, she guessed it was a fair amount. Enough to pay off her mortgage arrears? Probably. And more, if she was lucky.

She took a deep breath and then stuck out her hand. "All right. You've got a deal."

Arran looked at her hand but didn't take it. "So... ye will do it?" Despite his size and seeming confidence, there was an odd vulnerability in his voice as he asked the question, as though he wanted to hope but didn't dare let himself.

Jenna nodded tightly, not quite able to believe she was doing this. "I'll do it. Do we have a deal?"

"Aye, lass," Arran breathed, his blue eyes flashing. "We have a deal." He reached out and took her hand, his big hand dwarfing hers. She could feel the strength in his grip, and the callouses that marked his palms. Whatever else he was, this laird of Clan MacLeod was a man used to physical labor.

"Good," she said with a nod, shaking his hand. "That's agreed then."

"Aye," he replied. "It is."

He did not release her hand and stood for a second just staring at her. There was a faint dusting of stubble on his chin and Jenna found herself wondering stupidly if they had razors in the fifteenth century. Or toothbrushes. Or soap. Or a million things she took for granted. Oh, heck. She hadn't really thought this through, had she? Perhaps she ought to go back home and pack a few things—

"This way, lass. We must hurry."

Before she could say a word, he released her hand and strode off along the path. Jenna trotted behind. She ought to be asking questions, finding out as much as she could about the strange place she was going to and the task she'd be doing when she got there, but all such sensible considerations were pushed out of her head by the craziness of what she was about to do.

Had she really just agreed to go back in time with some strange guy in order to fix some magic she didn't know the first thing about? What had happened to her promise never to use her magic again? What had happened to her determination to live a normal, sensible life?

Alex happened, she answered herself. *The mortgage arrears happened. My normal, sensible life going down the toilet is what happened.*

Arran strode along in silence, his gaze fixed on the path ahead. He was getting some strange looks from the dog-walkers they passed, and Jenna wasn't surprised. After all, it wasn't every day that you passed a hulking Highlander dressed in a tartan plaid that covered him to his knees and left his muscled arms bare for all to stare at, was it? But Arran barely seemed to notice. Didn't notice or didn't care.

They finally reached the spot where she'd pulled him out of the lake. A few ducks were paddling around by the lake's edge looking for food but there was nobody else in sight, for which Jenna was profoundly grateful.

She looked around. "So what now?"

Arran strode down to the water and looked back, holding out his hand. "Now we go in."

Jenna took one look at the cold, dark water stretching out ahead of her, and felt her stomach twist with apprehension. "In there?"

"Aye, lass. It's the portal."

Oh, bloody hell. She reached out, gingerly taking his hand, and allowed him to lead her into the water. It was bitterly cold and she gasped as it reached her ankles, then her knees, then her thighs.

What was she doing? If her aunts could see her now, they'd think she'd lost her mind. Perhaps she had.

For his part, Arran didn't seem to feel the cold at all, and strode into the lake with all the confidence of someone who was born to water. In only moments, it was so deep that Jenna felt the bottom disappear and found herself swimming awkwardly, following Arran as he moved with confident strokes out towards the center of the lake. He turned to wait for her, treading water easily, and Jenna struggled up to him, trying to ignore the cold that seeped through her clothes and right into her bones.

"What now?" she gasped.

Even as she said the words, she felt something grab her ankles and begin to pull her under. She screamed, terror exploding through her, but then Arran was there, wrapping his arms around her and pulling her against his hard, muscular chest.

"Take a deep breath and dinna fight it. Close yer eyes. Trust me. I will keep ye safe."

Jenna sucked in a deep breath and clung onto Arran as she felt herself yanked into the dark, freezing water. It took everything she had not to panic, not to try and claw her way back to the surface, to hold her breath and close her eyes as he'd instructed. Arran's arms tightened around her and the solid feel of him, hard and unmovable like granite, was the only thing that kept her from screaming as they went down, down, down, into darkness.

It was over in a heartbeat. Jenna's lungs hadn't even begun to strain for air when the blackness suddenly retreated, light appeared above, and then the two of them broke the surface with a whoosh. Jenna drew a great breath, gasping in lungfuls of the sweet, clean air.

She felt Arran give a powerful kick, and he pulled her over to a shelf of barnacle encrusted rocks. Jenna grabbed hold of a rock and shook her head, trying to clear the clinging threads of wet hair from her face.

"Are ye all right, lass?" Arran's voice was so deep she felt it vibrating right through her chest.

With a start, she realized he was still holding her and that she was pressed against him, his wet clothes doing nothing to hide the hard ridges and contours of him.

Heat flooded her cheeks. "I... um... yes... I'm fine."

If he noticed her embarrassment, he didn't show it. He nodded as if satisfied and then released her. Despite herself, Jenna found herself a little disappointed as he moved away from her, grabbing a rock and then hauling himself up to sit on the lip.

She glanced around. She seemed to be in some sort of rock pool. It wasn't large—perhaps five feet across, and encircled by boulders covered with barnacles and seaweed. Wherever she was, this was clearly not the lake anymore. She could hear the sound of waves crashing nearby.

Arran climbed to his knees on the rock shelf, water cascading off him, then held out a hand. Jenna took it and allowed Arran to haul her out of the pool and onto the rocks that circled it. Jenna's legs felt a little wobbly, so she sat on one of the rocks while she caught her breath.

The rock pool nestled among tumbled boulders at the back of a beach where gentle waves lapped the shore of a horseshoe bay. Bobbing in the waters of the bay were the burned-out remains of boats in all shapes and sizes.

Oh God, she thought. *I'm here. I'm really here. I'm in fifteenth century Scotland.*

The enormity of the situation crashed in on her with the power of a tidal wave. She leaned over and deposited her breakfast all over the rocks.

ARRAN BREATHED DEEPLY, savoring the salty sea-air that told him he was home. He glanced at the sky, trying to determine how much time had passed while he'd been in the future. The sun was lower in the sky than it had been but he didn't know if this was the same day he'd left or another. Lir had been pretty sketchy on the details of how time travel worked. What he did notice was that the floating bodies had been removed, for which he was grateful.

He looked around for the goddess, expecting her to be waiting for him, ready to explain what to do next, but there was no sign of her. Climbing to his feet, he padded down to the water's edge, trying to ignore the way his guts twisted at the sight of the broken hulks of his fishing fleet.

"Lir!" he shouted, his words swallowed by the pounding waves. "Lir!"

There was no response. The goddess, it seemed, had done all she was willing to do. Now it was up to him and the spellweaver.

He turned at a sudden sound and found the lass doubled over, retching into the sand.

"Lass?" he asked in concern, striding towards her.

She retched again and then wiped the back of her hand over her mouth. "I'm fine," she muttered. "This is my first attempt at time traveling. Guess you have to get used to it. Like jet lag."

The tales of MacFinnan spellweavers passed down through Arran's clan spoke of women of immense power and wisdom who could turn you into a toad as soon as look at you. This raven-haired beauty spewing her guts into the sand was not what he'd envisaged at all. She seemed so... normal. Younger, and certainly more attractive than he'd expected.

What did *you expect?* he asked himself. *Some wizened old crone with a cat?*

Jenna wiped her mouth then climbed shakily to her feet.

"Can ye walk?" he asked her. "Or would ye like me to carry ye?"

She gave him a flat look. "I can walk just fine, thanks. Where are we going?"

He nodded in the direction of the dunes that rose behind the beach. "My keep. It's around ten miles that way."

"Ten miles? And I suppose it's too much to ask to call a cab, hey?"

"A what?"

She shook her head. "Nothing."

He led the way as they climbed the dunes, picking the easiest path between the tussocky grass and shifting sand. Jenna puffed along behind him, letting out a string of curses that any Highland warrior would have been proud of as her boots sank into the soft sand. Finally, they reached the top.

Arran put his hands on his hips and looked out. He loved the view from here. The Isle of Skye stretched out before him, a landscape of sparkling lochs and undulating moorland, rising up to snow-capped mountains in the distance. The land was a part of him as much as much as he was a part of it, and he would do anything to safeguard it. Anything.

"Wow," Jenna said, coming to stand by his side. "So that's Skye, huh?"

"Aye."

"And I'm really here? In the fifteenth century?"

"Ye really are."

"My aunts will never believe this."

"And neither will my people when I show up with a MacFinnan spellweaver. The looks on their faces will be something to behold." He squinted at the sky, trying to gauge the time. "Come. It's getting late, and we've a long way to go if we want to get back before dark."

They set off inland, leaving behind the beach and the wreckage of his fleet, and took the northern road, a well-trodden track that snaked its way towards the island's interior. He set a steady pace but was careful not to go too quickly, mindful of Jenna's earlier bout of sickness. Although, he reflected, as she paced along at his side, she seemed to be doing just fine. There was a rosy blush to her cheeks and her eyes sparkled with curiosity as she looked around, taking everything in. The wind sent her cloud of dark hair streaming out behind her, and with her odd twenty-first century attire of billowing coat and red boots, she looked like some kind of warrior queen out of an old tale.

Aye, this MacFinnan spellweaver was not what he'd expected at all.

She looked at him suddenly and he glanced away quickly, embarrassed to have been caught staring. He cast around for something to say, some way to fill the silence.

"So... um... yer aunts," he said at last. "They are spellweavers too?"

She nodded. "Yep. Both stronger than me. You would have done better enlisting either of them to help you."

"I dinna think so," he countered. "Lir led me to ye for a reason."

"So you said. I'm not sure how much I like the thought of being chosen by a goddess."

"Me neither. In my experience, it's always best to remain beneath the notice of those who wield power. But desperate times call for desperate actions."

Her expression turned pensive. "Desperate times, eh? Does that have something to do with all those burned ships?"

Arran's stomach clenched. "Aye," he growled. "It does." He didn't want to talk about it right now. He was cold, tired, and hungry and wanted nothing more than to get back to his keep where there would be food and a roaring fire waiting.

But Jenna did not take the hint. "What happened?"

"Raiders," he said gruffly. "Stealing and killing and burning. That's what happened."

He was saved from having to explain further by a sudden shout from up ahead. "My laird! There ye are!"

He halted as a group of mounted men came riding down the trail and pulled up their horses in front of them.

"Damn it, Arran!" Their leader, a huge man with blond braids and a hook nose, glared down at him from atop his prancing mount. "Where the bloody hell have ye been, cousin? When ye disappeared on the beach we thought you'd been taken! We've been scouring the whole bloody island for ye!"

"I didnae 'disappear' as ye put it, Mal," Arran replied. "I had something important to take care of."

Seeing Jenna, the men behind Mal broke into leering grins and began elbowing each other in the ribs.

"Seems our laird found something to distract him!" one of them called.

Arran strode up to the man and unceremoniously yanked him from the saddle. Grabbing his tunic in both fists, he shook him and snarled, "This lass is no 'distraction', Sean MacLeod! She is a MacFinnan spellweaver come to aid us, and ye will show her the same respect ye show to me! Is that clear?"

Sean swallowed thickly, his eyes darting between him and Jenna. "Aye, laird. My… my apologies."

Arran released him and studied his men. They were staring at Jenna with wide eyes, a chorus of awed murmurs rippling through the air.

A MacFinnan spellweaver!

We're saved!

But they died out, surely?

Jenna said not a word but licked her lips nervously as she looked around at the men, clearly a little rattled by this greeting.

Mal was the first to regain his composure. He bowed to Jenna from his saddle. "Welcome to Skye, my lady. We are at yer disposal." He turned to Arran. "There is quite the tale in this I suspect, cousin."

"Aye, there is, but it's telling can wait until we're all safely back in Dun Tabor. Sean, double up with Mal. I will take yer horse. Hamish, Dougal, ride to the keep and warn of our arrival."

As the men scrambled to obey, he turned to Jenna. The earlier rosy hue to her cheeks had faded and she looked a little pale. "We'll move more quickly by horse. Will ye consent to ride with me?"

She blinked. "What?"

"Will ye consent to ride with me?"

"Um… I suppose so—"

"Good." Without further ado, he bent and lifted her into his arms. She gave a surprised shriek as he hoisted her into the saddle and then swung up behind her.

"Wait! I didn't know you meant—"

"Yah!" He nudged the horse into a canter.

The lass squawked and was thrown back against Arran—something he didn't mind one bit. She felt warm and inviting where she touched him and her scent—something akin to sandalwood—made his nostrils tingle and a pleasant warmth steal through him.

The next moment, she grabbed hold of the saddle horn and clung on for dear life, pulling herself forward until she was half slumped over the horse's shoulders, her eyes squeezed closed.

"What's wrong?" he asked, puzzled.

"What's wrong?" she cried. "Isn't that obvious? Make this thing slow down!"

He did as she asked, pulling on the reins until the horse slowed to a trot. Yet this only seemed to make things worse as the lass bounced around like a sack of turnips, not swaying with the horse's gait at all.

"Aargh!" she cried. "I think my bones are getting shaken loose!"

He slowed the horse to a walk. "It will take longer to get home at this pace."

She peeled her eyes open, loosened her death-grip on the saddle horn, and slowly pushed herself upright, sitting rigidly and being careful to keep a gap between them.

"You know what? That's a risk I'm willing to take."

The wind picked up, sending her hair billowing out behind her and making it tickle Arran's chin. It was not an unpleasant feeling, and he found himself wishing she would lean back against him again.

Stop that, he chided himself. *It's been too long since you had a woman if you're having such thoughts about a MacFinnan spellweaver!*

He schooled his patience as they plodded their steady way along the trail. There was none of the usual banter among his men as they rode, caused in no small part by the atrocities they'd seen on the beach today but also, no doubt, by the presence of the woman riding with them.

Everyone knew that MacFinnan spellweavers were not normal women. Possessors of formidable powers and strange gifts, they were more akin to witches or seers, and anyone with an ounce of sense was wary around them. He caught his men casting covert glances at her and then looking away quickly when she noticed.

For her part, Jenna said nothing, but her head swiveled from side to side as they rode, taking in the craggy landscape they passed through. Was this as strange for her as it was for him and his men? Or was time traveling all in a day's work for her?

Finally, Dun Tabor, the ancestral home of the MacLeods of Skye, came into view. It was an impressive sight, even if he thought so himself. A tall, imposing keep, it was built into the side of a rocky hillside, with a winding causeway leading up to the gates. High, round towers rose at all four corners and pennants snapped in the breeze. A loch spread out from the keep's knees, and clusters of houses were nestled in terraces below the keep and around the loch's shore.

He felt a flush of pride as he looked out at Dun Tabor. His home. The place he loved more than any other in all the world. With the sparkling loch at its base, the craggy hills behind, and the thick forests of pine, alder, and birch that cloaked the hills to east and west, it was a beautiful spot that never failed to take his breath away.

And it was under threat. If they failed, if Jenna was unable to revive the magic that protected Skye, all of this would be lost. An image formed in his mind's eye. Smoke billowing. The houses and crofts burning. Dun Tabor's gates broken, its towers nothing but skeletal ruins reaching into the sky.

No, he told himself. *That will not happen. While there is breath in my body and blood in my veins, I will not let Dun Tabor fall.*

At the sight of the keep, some of his men let out delighted

whoops and cries of triumph. He understood their excitement. They had survived another day and made it home to their families. In these troubled times, that was the best any of them could hope for.

As they began passing through Dun Tabor village, people stopped what they were doing and came to line the road, calling out greetings and well-wishes. There were many faces he knew, some he didn't, but he waved and called out greetings and bantered good-naturedly with them all the same, letting his people see him relaxed and in control, as they needed their laird to be.

The curious glances at Jenna were many and his men moved into a circular formation around his horse without Arran having to ask them, shielding Jenna a little from the prying eyes and prying questions that Arran waved away without answering.

"They all seem to know you," Jenna observed in a quiet voice.

"Aye," he replied. "I've led them for ten years now. My father was chieftain before me, and my elder brother should have followed him. But they were both killed in a raid so the title passed to me."

She glanced over her shoulder at him, her eyes large and shining with compassion. "I'm sorry."

"Dinna be. It was a long time ago and although I canna say I ever wanted the lairdship, I've found peace with it. After a fashion." He wasn't sure he was being entirely truthful. Aye, he'd found acceptance of a kind, but that didn't mean it didn't chafe at him.

They wound their way up the causeway to Dun Tabor's open gates and clattered through into the bailey where they pulled their horses to a halt. The messengers he'd sent on ahead had obviously reached the keep in good time as it seemed the whole of the household staff had turned out to welcome their laird home.

Welcome me, he thought dryly. *Hardly. It's the MacFinnan spell-*

weaver they've come to welcome.

The household was arrayed in two lines in front of the keep's doors, the soldiers, farriers, kennel masters, and stable hands in the row behind, with the steward, chamberlain, cook, and household servants in the front row. His mother stood in the middle of the front row as well, wearing her best dress and the MacLeod plaid draped across her shoulders.

Arran swung down from the saddle, handing the reins to one of the stable boys. "Bring the mounting block to help the lady dismount," he instructed the lad.

"Aye, my laird," the lad replied, running off in the direction of the stable.

But Jenna didn't wait. Grabbing hold of the saddle horn, she swung her leg over the horse's back in a most undignified manner and then slid ungracefully to the ground. Her knees buckled and she would have fallen had not Arran darted forward to catch her. He set her safely on her feet.

"Thanks," she muttered, looking up at him.

He found himself staring into her bright, clear eyes before clearing his throat and stepping back. "I... um... ye are welcome."

Arran's mother stepped forward and executed a perfect curtsey. Despite her advancing years and the gray that now lined her once auburn hair, she was still a vigorous woman. When she smiled, he saw the glimpse of the beauty she had once been. But the death of her husband and eldest son had taken its toll on Lady Rosaline MacLeod and now she rarely smiled.

"Welcome to Dun Tabor, my lady," she said. "I'm Rosaline. A delight to meet ye." She glanced briefly at Arran, her eyes full of questions. No doubt he'd get a grilling later, but she was too well schooled in courtesy to ask anything in front of Jenna.

"My lady?" Jenna replied. "I don't think I've ever been called that before! It's just Jenna. And wow. Your place is amazing!"

"That's very kind of ye to say, my lady. Jenna. Will ye come inside? I've had a room made up for ye and food prepared. Ye must be tired after yer… um… journey."

Again that glance from his mother that promised a thousand questions later. Arran sighed inwardly. Jenna wasn't the only one who was tired. It had been a challenging day, and Arran would love nothing more than to shut himself in his study in front of a roaring fire and enjoy a tankard or two of ale in solitude. Little chance of that. His mother would not be the only one with questions, and he knew he'd be up late trying to explain everything.

"Go with my mother," he said to Jenna. "Get some rest. We'll begin work in the morning."

"Right. Okay," she said, looking slightly unsure. Then she smiled at Rosaline. "Lead the way."

Arran watched as Jenna left with Rosaline. She paused at the doors to the keep and looked back. Their eyes met across the distance, and damn him if he didn't feel a strange stirring inside. Then she was gone.

"Is she really a MacFinnan spellweaver?"

He turned to see David, his steward, standing at his elbow, staring after Jenna. "And is it true she's come to save us?"

Arran stifled a sigh. "Aye, it's true."

Mal joined them and whistled under his breath. "Bloody hell, ye dinna do things by halves do ye?"

"What do ye mean?"

"This morning ye swore ye would find a way to stop the raids. This afternoon ye ride home with a MacFinnan spellweaver. I dinna think ye could have caused more of a stir if ye had ridden home having grown horns and a tail."

It was true that an excited hubbub filled the bailey—the kind of enthusiastic clamor that had been missing from Dun Tabor for many a month. His people were talking among themselves, gesticulating at the door through which Jenna had gone, and shooting him awe-filled looks.

Ah, damn it. Perhaps he'd underestimated the impact that bringing Jenna might have on Dun Tabor. MacFinnan spellweavers were a legend on Skye, most people assigning them the status of myth, and now here he was riding through the gate with one of them. No matter. The lass would do what he'd brought her here to do, he would pay her the agreed fee, and she would go home. Then Dun Tabor could go back to life as usual.

Life as usual? he thought. *I'm not sure what that is any more.*

What would he do with his time if he wasn't constantly scouting his lands, fighting off invaders, or training his warriors? Perhaps he would finally have time to settle down, find a wife, and give his mother those grandchildren she was always badgering him about.

"Ye are going to have to tell them something," Mal said.

"Eh?"

Mal nodded at the people filling the bailey. "Ye are going to have to tell them how it is ye have returned with a MacFinnan spellweaver and where ye found her. If ye dinna tell them something, then ye can be sure the gossips will and before ye know it, the whole island will be abuzz with wild tales and outlandish rumors."

Arran found himself reluctant to talk about his encounter with Lir and his subsequent trip through time. It was uncomfortable to think about, and part of him still couldn't quite believe it had been real. How could he expect his people to understand something he didn't understand himself? But Mal was right. He needed to tell them something if he didn't want tongues wagging with all sorts of mischief.

"Fine. Tell everyone the laird will be attending the evening meal tonight where he'll address them."

Mal clapped him on the shoulder. "I'll put the word out. I look forward to hearing yer tale."

Aye, Arran thought, as Mal walked off. He had quite the tale to tell. Question was: would it have a happy ending?

Chapter Five

J ENNA TOSSED AND turned on the bed, trying to get some rest. Rest? Ha! Chance would be a fine thing. How was she supposed to rest when a million thoughts were chasing each other through her head like startled rabbits?

She'd tried closing her eyes but every time she did she saw Arran's face in her mind's eye saying *you will restore the magic and save my people.* She'd tried pacing up and down in her room to tire herself out but all that did was bring her close to the window through which she could see the Highlands of fifteenth century Scotland spreading out. That made things worse. She'd tried mantra meditation to clear her mind but each time she did, her mantra just turned into a slew of voices.

Sorry, your loan application has been denied.

Ye will restore the magic and save my people.

You are too good for Alex anyway. He didn't deserve you.

Aargh!

She thumped her fists onto the bed, staring up at the underside of the canopy that covered it. It was a huge four-poster affair, easily big enough to sleep four people and just about the most luxurious bed she'd ever seen. The same went for the room she'd been given. Although "suite" would probably be a more accurate term as there were three rooms in all.

Aside from this large, lavishly furnished bedroom, there was a sitting room that boasted a fireplace large enough to stand in, dark wood furniture polished until it gleamed, and a rug so thick that her feet sank into it whenever she stepped on it. Finally, there was even a smaller chamber that housed another fireplace with a large metal tub seated in front of it that she guessed was this era's equivalent to a bathroom.

It was not at all what she'd expected from a fifteenth century Scottish castle, but then, she had to admit, she hadn't known *what* to expect. She knew next to nothing about Scottish history, or the Highlands, or the people who lived here.

It doesn't matter, she told herself. *You're just here to do a job and then you'll be going home with enough money to end your troubles.* And, if she was really lucky, she'd return to the exact same moment she'd left so nobody would even notice she'd been gone. Yes, everything would work out fine, she was sure of it.

Buoyed a little by this reasoning, she drew a deep breath and let it out again, feeling a little steadier. She frowned and cocked her head as she heard noises from somewhere deeper into the castle. The hubbub of many voices. And… singing? And was that even a bit of music?

It sounded like somewhere in the castle people were enjoying themselves. And she'd not been invited? Humph. Lady Rosaline had instructed three maids to take care of her and there was a little bell-pull by the fireplace that she could tug if she needed anything, but what Jenna most needed right now was a little company.

Didn't Arran realize that she needed to talk to him if she was going to figure out exactly what she was supposed to do to fix this place? Didn't he realize that staying cooped up in this room—comfortable and lavish as it might be—would drive her crazy?

No, clearly he did not.

Fine. She got up, strode to the door, and pulled it open. A long corridor stretched off in both directions, shiny wooden doors like her own along the walls. Lady Rosaline had explained that these were the guest quarters and from the silence, Jenna guessed she was the only guest right now.

The hubbub from below was louder out here in the corridor. She could make out laughing, the clink of glasses, and the sound of a stringed instrument being played. Pulling her door closed, she headed down the corridor, reached the elegant stone staircase, and made her way down it.

At the bottom lay a grand entrance hall. To her right stood a large wooden door, slightly ajar. It was from here that the sounds were coming. Firelight and warmth spilled around the edges, warm and welcoming. Taking a deep breath, Jenna strode to the door, pushed it open, and walked in.

She found herself in a huge, vaulted hall. It was lit by firelight from the roaring fire at one end and by hundreds of candles set in wheel-shaped chandeliers hanging from the ribbed ceiling. Long tables filled the room, and the benches were full of people eating, talking, laughing, and singing. In one corner a man was playing on a fat-bellied guitar-like thing and singing a merry tune in a language Jenna didn't recognize. Gaelic, perhaps?

A woman sitting nearby suddenly noticed Jenna standing in the doorway and urgently elbowed her companions. A murmur spread through the room and the laughter, chatting, and singing died away. All eyes turned to her. Even the musician, noticing he'd lost his audience's attention, fell silent.

Jenna licked her lips nervously. Oh heck. Perhaps this hadn't been such a good idea. She was reminded of those scenes in old Westerns where a stranger walks into a bar and it all goes quiet. Only this time, *she* was the stranger.

"Um," she said, forcing a smile. "Hi."

She heard the scrape of a chair being pulled back, and a tall figure rose from a table at the far end of the room. Arran. He couldn't be mistaken for anyone else with his broad shoulders and honey-blond hair gleaming in the firelight.

"My lady," he said, his deep voice carrying across the hall. "Is all well?"

"Um. Sure," Jenna replied. "I just heard the party and thought

I might join you. Sounds like you're having fun."

A murmur of surprise went around the room. Arran shared a look with Rosaline who was seated next to him, then cleared his throat.

"We would be honored." He gestured for a servant to bring another chair and place it between his and his mother's. "Please, come and be seated."

Jenna swallowed. "Right. Thanks."

Many pairs of eyes followed her as she made her way awkwardly around the outside of the hall to the seat Arran had indicated. She couldn't quite decipher the expressions on people's faces. Not hostile but not exactly friendly either. More like… nervous? But why would she make them nervous? *She* was the one who'd been pulled hundreds of years out of her time and was in a room full of strangers. What did *they* have to be nervous about?

Arran didn't look particularly comfortable at the sight of her either, truth be told, but he held out the seat for her like some genteel lord all the same. She nodded her thanks as she sat between him and his mother. Arran resumed his seat and waved over a teenage youth dressed in the colors of Clan MacLeod.

"Food for the lady."

The lad gulped, gave Jenna a nervous glance, then bobbed his head and scurried away. Arran reached for a jug and poured a golden liquid into a pewter goblet which he held out to Jenna.

"Drink?"

She took it carefully and gave the liquid a long sniff. It wasn't wine, as she'd been hoping, but it didn't smell like beer or whisky either. "What is this?"

"Mead," Arran replied. "The finest in the Isles. We get it from Holy Island. The monks there make the best mead in all the known lands."

"Holy Island?"

"Lindisfarne. In Northumbria."

"Oh." Jenna hesitantly took a sip. The drink was sweet and,

much to her surprise, rather pleasant. She took a big gulp, enjoying the warm feeling of it sliding down her throat and settling into her stomach. "You know what? That's not half bad."

The big, hook-nosed man whom she'd met earlier—Mal, was it?—who was seated to Arran's right, gave a hearty laugh and winked at Arran. "I think the lass is going to fit right in!" He raised his cup to Jenna in salute. "Drink to yer heart's content, lass. There's plenty more where that came from!"

Mal's warm welcome settled her nerves a little. She grinned and raised her goblet in a toast, then downed the rest of the mead. Almost instantaneously, a servant refilled it.

"Is yer room to yer liking, my lady?" Lady Rosaline asked from Jenna's other side. "If not, I'm sure we can arrange—"

"Are you kidding? My room is amazing! Seriously, it would give any swanky hotel a run for its money. And it's Jenna, remember, not 'my lady'."

Rosaline smiled. "I'm pleased to hear it, my lady... um... Jenna. We wish yer stay with us to be as comfortable as possible. It's the least we can do to repay what ye are doing for us."

Jenna nodded, although Rosaline's gratitude made her a little uneasy. She wasn't sure she deserved it. After all, she'd only come here because she was getting paid. She looked out at the sea of people filling the tables. Most had gone back to their conversations and the musician had begun playing again, but even so, she noticed plenty of covert glances aimed in her direction. Each time, she spotted the same look in their eyes as Rosaline had. It wasn't nervousness she realized suddenly. It was... gratitude. And hope.

Oh hell, she thought. *These people expect me to save them. What if I can't?*

She hadn't used her powers in years. What if she'd come all this way only to let them down?

Her thoughts were interrupted by the serving lad bringing her a platter, which he placed on the table in front of her. The platter was piled high with roasted meats, vegetables in various sauces, and a big pile of some kind of flat bread. Jenna stared. She was supposed to eat all this?

"Er… thanks," she murmured to the serving boy.

He flushed scarlet, gave a sketchy bow, and fled.

Jenna looked around for some cutlery but didn't see any. "Um. Is there a knife and fork?"

"Here." Arran reached to his waist and pulled his belt-knife, handing it to her handle-first.

Jenna took it gingerly and looked around, seeing that other people were also using knives to eat with, spearing food on it like a fork. She guessed it was probably an honor to be given the chieftain's knife to eat with, but she would much rather have a spoon. She speared a piece of beef in gravy and stuffed it into her mouth.

The meat was delicious, falling apart on her tongue like melting butter. Whatever else this place was, lacking in hospitality it was not.

Everyone else was digging into the food, nobody waiting on ceremony or paying her any mind at all. Good. Jenna dived into the meal, allowing the simple act of sharing a meal with others to dispel some of her unease. She might be hundreds of years from home, but no matter where you were, it seemed some things didn't change.

As she ate, she listened. Arran was in conversation with Mal, discussing deployment of warriors and debating the best way to keep the settlements on the tip of the island in contact with Dun Tabor.

Garrisons? Forts? Relay stations? They sounded like a people at war.

"It's hardly conversation fit for the dinner table, is it?" Lady Rosaline said suddenly.

Jenna turned to the older woman. "I'm sorry? What?"

Rosaline nodded at Arran. "No matter how many times I tell him, he *will* insist on discussing such things at the most inappropriate times." She sighed. "I tried to teach him courtly manners.

In that, I'm afraid I've failed badly."

Rosaline's affection for Arran was obvious from the way she looked at him, but her exasperation too. It was, no doubt, the way her aunts looked at her. It seemed the push and pull of familial relationships was another thing that didn't change, no matter where or when you found yourself.

"Oh, I don't think you did too badly," Jenna replied, taking another sip of mead. "He's been nothing but a gentleman since I arrived." She remembered the feel of Arran's hard chest against her back as they'd ridden here and colored slightly.

"Well, I'm glad to hear that," Rosaline said. "Although I suspect ye are merely being polite." She swiveled in her seat until she was facing Jenna and took hold of her hand. "I will say this in case my unruly son forgets to: thank ye. I know how ye came to be here and I canna imagine how difficult it must be to leave not only yer home but yer time as well. So, on behalf of Clan MacLeod and everyone on Skye, thank ye."

Jenna shifted uncomfortably. "I... er... no problem," she muttered.

Rosaline patted her hand and then returned to her meal. Jenna covered her discomfort by taking another sip of mead. She'd already finished two cups, and the sweet drink was going down very well. A little *too* well, actually. Her thoughts were starting to feel a bit fuzzy and there was a comforting glow burning in her stomach.

As the meal wore on, the people of Dun Tabor seemed to forget her presence—for which she was profoundly grateful—and the racket grew gradually louder until the sound of the musician was almost drowned out by people talking, shouting, arguing, and laughing.

Jenna looked around as she ate, trying to work out who everyone might be. Closest to the high table where she sat with Arran and Rosaline, the benches were filled with rowdy men who were busy getting drunk, laughing, and making ribald jokes at each other's expense. From their size and the way they were dressed—the same plaid wrap as Arran and with daggers at their belts—she guessed they were his warriors.

Slightly farther away sat a group of men and women dressed in plain but well-made clothes. A few of them bore silver brooches on their shoulders carved into different designs: a book, a hammer, a set of weighing scales, and Jenna wondered whether these were the household staff and those brooches signified their occupations. She considered asking Arran, but he was still in conversation with Mal, ignoring her entirely.

Farthest away from the high table, the benches were filled with an assortment of people. Men, women, children, young and old, and Jenna guessed these were from the local village or else visiting the castle. The cacophony of sounds and smells— laughing, swearing, singing, wood smoke, food, sweat—was a little intoxicating.

And a little overwhelming. She took another sip of her mead.

"I need the privy," Mal announced loudly. He climbed to his feet, weaving unsteadily.

Rosaline glared at him. "Malcolm MacLeod! What have I told ye about manners?"

"Oops, my apologies, Aunt." He gave a shaky bow. "If ye will excuse me, I have... business to attend to." He wobbled out of the room.

"Sorry about him," Arran said, turning to Jenna. "But my cousin has resisted all my mother's attempts to tame him."

Jenna raised an amused eyebrow. If he thought Mal was bad, he'd clearly never been down to Jenna's local bar on a Saturday night.

"Oh, I don't know," she said, waving a hand. "I think he's kind of charming."

Arran snorted. "Charming? Did ye take a whack on the head during the journey here, lass? That is *not* a word I would associate with my cousin. Loud, aye. Uncouth, aye. But charming? Not so much."

Jenna laughed. "I'll tell him you said that."

Arran gave a lopsided smile. "Too late. I tell him all the time."

They fell silent, both watching the proceedings in the hall. Jenna took another sip of mead.

"I know this must be difficult for ye, lass," Arran said at last. "And everything must seem strange, but it willnae be for long. Tomorrow, after ye have fixed the magic, I will take ye home."

Jenna choked on her mead, spraying it all over her lap. "I'm sorry? Did you just say tomorrow?"

Despite the amount of mead he'd drunk, Arran seemed not in the least affected by it. His gaze was still as piercing, his posture still as rigidly in control. The firelight reflected off his hair, making it look like burnished gold as he stared at her.

"Aye. Once ye've restored the magic, we can use the tide pool to take ye home again."

"Just like that? Do you think I can just click my fingers and fix everything? It's a little more complicated than that!"

His eyes narrowed. "But ye said—"

"I know what I said! And I'll do everything I can to help you, but it's not as simple as you seem to think. I can't just wave a magic wand. It will take time. There are things I need before I can even begin."

Annoyance flashed in his bright blue gaze. "Like what?"

"Like figuring out how the magic was made in the first place. Like learning everything I can about the spellweavers who created it. Like figuring out why it failed and what I need to do to revive it. Do you know the first thing about what you're asking?"

"Nay," he growled. "I dinna. Which is why I'm paying *ye* handsomely to know about it instead. Are ye saying ye canna do what's needed after all?"

"Are you listening?" Jenna snapped. "What I'm saying is that I'm going to need some *time* and you are going to have to be patient. I would love to waggle my fingers, say 'abracadabra', and then be on my merry way, but that's not how this works." She jabbed a finger in his direction. "So I'm afraid you're going to be stuck with me a while longer. Okay?"

Arran glared at her. He opened his mouth as though for an angry retort but before he could speak, Jenna spotted Rosaline out of the corner of her eye. She was giving her son a stern look of disapproval. Arran glanced between Jenna and his mother and then snapped his mouth shut.

"My apologies," he said, not sounding apologetic at all. "Of course ye shall have everything ye need. We have a library here at Dun Tabor, and I will ask Brother Merrick to find everything he can on the MacFinnan spellweavers. Tomorrow, I will show ye the island." Rosaline caught his eye again and Arran coughed. "That is, I will show ye the island if that is agreeable to ye."

Jenna nodded. "Fine. So now that's sorted, pass me that jug of mead will you?"

Chapter Six

"MY LADY?"

"Go 'way," Jenna mumbled, turning over and burying her head in the pillow.

"My lady, it's time to get up."

Jenna ignored the voice. Perhaps it would go away. But then she heard the sound of the drapes being pulled back and light flooded the room, spearing into Jenna's brain like jagged shards of glass.

"Aargh! Are you trying to kill me?"

She pried her eyes open and found herself staring up at the underside of her bed canopy. Damn it. So yesterday hadn't been a dream then? She really was here in fifteenth century Scotland?

With an effort, she struggled into a sitting position. Her head pounded like someone was whacking it with a rolled-up newspaper, and her mouth tasted like something had crawled into it and died. Jeez. How much mead had she drunk last night? Too much, if her pounding head, grainy eyes, and roiling stomach were anything to go by.

A red-haired young woman who she guessed must be a maid hovered by the bed, wringing her hands and looking nervous.

"What time is it?" Jenna groaned.

"Past dawn, my lady."

The way she said the words suggested she considered this to

be late, but "past dawn" was still the middle of the night as far as Jenna was concerned. Outside, the sky still held the pink blush of sunrise. Oh, hell. Did people always get up at this hour here?

Jenna flopped back down onto the pillows. "Wake me in a few hours."

The maid shifted her feet nervously. "My apologies, my lady, but the laird has requested yer presence. He says ye are to go riding today?"

Jenna let out a long sigh. It seemed this place was determined to torture her. She pushed herself up, swung her legs around, and balanced on the edge of the bed. She was, she realized, fully clothed. She had hazy memories of Rosaline helping her back to her room last night, but beyond that, everything was blank.

She gripped the bedstead as her stomach roiled and her head spun. "Do you have any water?"

"Water? Nay, my lady," the maid replied. "It isnae safe to drink the water. We have ale, though." She crossed to the table by the cold fireplace on which sat a covered tray and a large jug. She poured something into a small pottery cup, then held it out for Jenna. "Here, my lady."

Jenna took it gingerly and sniffed the liquid inside. It was indeed ale. She looked at the maid and gave a sheepish grin. "Well, you know what they say about hair of the dog? Bottoms up!" She downed the cup in several long gulps and was pleased to discover that "ale" was only a loose term and the liquid was so weak that it likely contained hardly any alcoholic content at all. It was more like drinking beer flavored soda.

"Thanks," she said, holding out the cup. "I needed that."

The maid took it and then crossed to the table. "If ye are ready, I've brought some breakfast for ye."

"What's your name?" Jenna asked.

The woman bobbed a curtsey. "Ingrid, if it please ye, my lady."

"Well, it's very nice to meet you, Ingrid. And it's Jenna, not 'my lady'. Sorry if I'm a bit grouchy. I'm feeling a little... delicate."

Ingrid smiled. "Aye, ye were singing when ye came back last night."

"Singing? Really?"

"Aye. Some song about a reindeer with a red nose? And ye wouldnae let me undress ye. Ye were asleep the second ye lay down."

Jenna groaned. "Oh. Sorry about that too. I've not exactly made a good first impression, have I?"

"Lady Rosaline says ye are a breath of fresh air, and I agree with her."

Jenna looked at Ingrid, surprised. "She does? You do?"

Ingrid cleared her throat, suddenly embarrassed. "Um, if ye would like to bathe, I've brought hot water up for ye."

Yes, she would very much like to bathe. Tottering to her feet, she followed Ingrid into the bathing room to find that, sure enough, the metal tub was full to the brim with steaming water. Some large cloths for use as towels hung on a rack by the fire and there was even a bar of lavender-scented soap in a little tray. Jenna breathed in the scented steam, allowing it to clear her head a little.

"Would ye like me to help ye bathe?" Ingrid asked.

Help her bathe? Why on earth would she need help with that? "Er, no," Jenna replied quickly. "I'll be fine."

"Then I'll be in the next room. Call if ye need aught."

The maid left, closing the door behind her, and Jenna wasted no time in stripping off and sinking into the tub. It was a little too hot, but Jenna put up with it, allowing the water to soothe her muscles and ease her aching head. She lay back, putting her head on the rim of the tub, and considered her predicament.

She'd promised Arran that she could fix the magic her ancestors had placed around this island. Both he and Rosaline, and all the people she'd met so far, seemed to think she was some kind of savior. So, no pressure then.

Aunt Rose would know what to do. Or even Aunt Elise. But Jenna hadn't used her magic in five years. What if she no longer knew how?

What had she been thinking? She was going to fail. She was going to let these people down, go home empty-handed, lose her house, and—

Stop it!

She took a deep breath, closed her eyes, and reached inside herself for her magic. She felt it immediately, like a ball of glowing energy deep within her. Tentatively, carefully, she began to channel it. Only a tiny amount, hardly anything really, but guided it out into the bath water, using it to cool the water a little. To her utter astonishment, it worked.

She let the magic go. She was breathing a little heavily, not from the exertion, but from the shock of contact with her magic after all these years, and the deluge of memories and emotions that touching it sent through her.

Her mother lying pale and motionless on the hospital bed. Tears on the faces of her aunts. A dark, hollow feeling inside as Jenna realized how powerless she was.

Never again, she had vowed that day. Never again would she rely on a magic that had betrayed her. Now here she was, breaking that vow, and she was shocked by how easily it had come to her, like an old friend eager to welcome her back.

Jenna scrubbed herself down with the lavender soap, washed her hair as best she could, then reluctantly climbed out of the bath and toweled herself down. She eyed her pile of clothes. She did *not* relish the thought of putting them on again. They were mud-stained and unpleasant-looking, but she'd not brought a change of clothes with her. She *knew* she should have gone home and packed.

But she needn't have worried. The door opened and Ingrid stuck her head through. Jenna yelped and wrapped the towel around herself.

"I heard ye get out of the bath," Ingrid said, completely un-bothered by Jenna's embarrassment. "And knew ye would be wanting a change of clothes. The laird has sent some up for ye."

Oh, he has, has he? Jenna thought, wondering exactly what Arran would know about how twenty-first century women dressed.

Pulling the towel tight around herself, Jenna followed Ingrid back into the bedroom and looked around for a clean pair of jeans, shirt, and underwear. She didn't see any. What she *did* see was a long flowing burgundy dress laid out on the bed, some kind of underskirt, and what Jenna could only describe as a corset.

She looked at Ingrid. "You've got to be kidding, right? You can't expect me to wear that!"

"The laird sent it up for ye especially. He said he would like ye to wear it."

"Oh did he? Well, I'll wear just what I please, thank you very much. I reckon if I wiped my jeans down, they'd be just fine—"

"He said it was important that ye blend in when ye go about the island."

Jenna paused. "Blend in? Why? Everyone knows who I am and where I come from."

"Everyone in Dun Tabor knows," Ingrid corrected. "But the people in the outlying villages dinna. And the laird says it might be best if ye dinna stand out to any enemies."

Enemies? Jenna swallowed thickly. What enemies could she possibly have?

The raiders, she thought, remembering the burned-out ships she'd seen yesterday.

"All right, fine," she said, running her hand along the arm of the dress. She had to admit it *was* beautiful. Made from a fine satin but with velvet panels on the bodice, it would no doubt look amazing on Ingrid or Rosaline. But on her, she suspected it would look nothing short of ridiculous.

"Wonderful!" Ingrid said, clapping her hands together. "Then I will help ye dress!"

It turned out that, despite her protestations to the contrary, Jenna most definitely needed Ingrid's help to get into the dress. It was a complicated affair with many layers that had to be followed in order, and then a set of hooks up the back of the dress that she couldn't reach by herself. By the time she was finished, she was feeling irritable and her headache was worse. Did women in this time have to put up with this every day? How did they stand it?

When she was finished, Ingrid stepped back and looked Jenna over. "Oh, my," she breathed. "Ye look like a princess."

"Really?" Jenna asked, looking down at her arms hidden in the dress's long, bell-sleeves and the way the dress flowed over her hips and fell to the floor in waves. "I feel like one of those frilly plastic women you put over a toilet roll."

Ingrid blinked, uncomprehending, and Jenna waved a hand. "Never mind. Well, I suppose we shouldn't keep the laird waiting."

"Would ye not care for some breakfast first?"

Jenna eyed the steaming tray. The smell coming from it made her stomach turn. "You know what? I think I'll skip breakfast."

ARRAN PACED THE bailey with barely concealed impatience. Where was she? Was she going to keep him waiting all morning? As lord of this castle, he was used to everyone working to his timescales and wasn't accustomed to being kept waiting. He didn't like it one little bit.

"Ye are going to wear a furrow in the stones if ye aren't careful," observed Mal.

He was standing a few feet away with the horses, arms crossed over his broad chest, an eyebrow raised in amusement. Arran bit back an angry retort. Snapping at his cousin was unlikely to make the lass appear any quicker.

"Too bad for the stones," he muttered.

With a sigh, he stopped pacing and ran a hand through his hair. His eyes felt grainy and his limbs heavy from lack of sleep. He hadn't slept well, although this was nothing new. It seemed he'd not had a decent night's sleep from the moment his father and brother had died and the lairdship had fallen to him.

Yet he felt more out of sorts than usual this morning, full of impatience and irritability, when he ought to be full of hope and enthusiasm. After all, hadn't he gone into the future and found a MacFinnan spellweaver? Hadn't he convinced her to come back here with him and fix the magic that would save them? He'd done everything Lir had asked of him and now, surely, there was cause for optimism?

So why did he feel so surly this morning?

Jenna MacFinnan's face flashed into his mind. In truth, much of his sleepless night had been spent thinking about her, no matter his efforts not to. There was something about her…

Of course there is, he told himself. *She's going to restore the magic and save Skye, so of course you would be thinking about her.*

Aye, that must be it. It was most definitely *not* that lustrous hair of hers, or those deep, intelligent eyes, or that fiery temper, or the way she stood up to him like nobody else did. It was most definitely none of that.

He glanced at the sky. The sun had crested the horizon, a brilliant red orb in a cloudless sky that promised a glorious day to come. And the lass was missing it. He'd been up for two hours already. What was keeping her?

He growled under his breath and was just about to march back into the keep to find her when the door opened and Ingrid came to stand on the top steps, followed a moment later by Jenna. The two women paused and looked out into the bailey, taking in the fresh morning air.

Arran stopped in his tracks. Jenna hadn't seen him yet, and she and Ingrid shared a word or two and then a soft laugh. The sound of it sent a strange ripple of… something… right through Arran's body. It was as beautiful as the trilling of a robin on a winter's day. She was, he noticed with satisfaction, wearing the dress he'd sent up for her. Just as Rosaline had said it would, the dress fitted Jenna perfectly, accentuating all her feminine curves and the deep burgundy color only highlighted her glossy black tresses.

"Shut yer mouth, my laird," Mal said sardonically. "Or ye may catch flies."

Arran cleared his throat and gave his cousin an annoyed glance.

Jenna and Ingrid came down the steps and Arran went to meet them. "Glad ye could join us." He winced as the words came out sharper than intended and sounded slightly sarcastic. "I… er… trust ye slept well?"

Jenna pulled at the neck of the dress as though uncomfortable. "Fine. I slept just fine. Thanks for asking." Her tone was stilted and formal and, was Arran imagining it, or did she look a little pale?

"Well, if ye are ready, we had better be going. We have a lot of ground to cover today."

He led Jenna over to where the horses were waiting. Bran, his huge black gelding, pranced and snorted as Arran approached, wanting attention. Arran reached up and patted him on his sleek neck.

"Easy, boy," he murmured. "Ye'll be getting a run soon, I promise."

He moved over to the smaller white mare, Sunflower, that Mal had been holding. Taking the reins, he led the horse over to where Jenna stood, eyeing the horses suspiciously.

"Can ye mount unaided, or should I have a mounting block brought?" he asked.

"Eh?"

"I said, can ye mount unaided, or should I—"

"I heard what you said. But it sounded like you expect me to ride that thing."

Arran glanced at Sunflower. The docile mare was drowsing, head hanging down while she waited patiently. "Aye, I expect ye to ride 'this thing,' whose name is Sunflower, by the way. How else do ye expect to tour the island today?"

Jenna glanced at Sunflower. "Um. I don't know how to ride. I thought that was pretty obvious yesterday."

"I thought that was just because ye were disorientated from the trip through time."

"Nope. Disorientation had nothing to do with it. Before yesterday, I'd never ridden a horse in my life."

Exasperation rose up in him. "Then why did ye agree to come riding with me today? In case ye havenae noticed, this isnae yer time, and here we get around by our feet or by horse."

"Yeah, I noticed!" she snapped back. "But I thought you might have a carriage or cart or something I can ride in."

"Lass, if we took a cart to tour the island, we wouldnae be back at Dun Tabor before harvest!"

"Well, how was I supposed to know that?"

She glared at him and Arran glared right back. From the corner of his eye he saw Mal, Ingrid, and the rest of his men watching this exchange with wide-eyed fascination. It wasn't often they heard somebody speak to their laird in such a fashion, but this infuriating lass from the future had no fear of him and was not intimidated by his rank in the least.

It was irritating and refreshing in equal measure. He took a deep breath and let it out slowly, trying to calm his annoyance.

"Then ye will have to ride with me," he said in as polite a voice as he could manage.

She hesitated. "With… you?"

"Aye. Bran is easily strong enough to take the pair of us."

Jenna looked up at the enormous gelding, and her face paled. "On that?"

Despite himself, Arran laughed. "Aye, on that. Come, I'll introduce ye. He willnae bite."

With a dubious expression, Jenna walked over to Bran. She tentatively held out her hand and the big gelding gracefully arched his neck, lowered his nose, and sniffed her hand. Jenna let out a delighted laugh and then patted him on the end of his fuzzy nose. The big horse snorted softly, his eyes closing.

"See? He's a big softie really, and I think he likes ye."

Jenna gently stroked the white stripe that ran along Bran's nose. "He's beautiful."

As are ye.

The thought flashed through Arran's head before he could stop it. He blinked, suddenly caught off balance. Where had that come from?

He turned to Mal. "Take the men and patrol the coast as far as Ransay. Make sure none of the raiders have decided to hole up in the caves out there."

Mal frowned. "But I thought we were riding out with ye?"

"That willnae be necessary."

Mal's bluff face folded into a scowl. "Willnae be necessary? Are ye serious? With what happened yesterday? Those raiders—"

"Will be long gone by now. They wouldnae be foolish enough to loiter around the same area."

"And if ye are wrong?"

Arran clenched his jaw. "Then I will deal with it. Or do ye think yer laird is so weak he needs the protection of ten men wherever he goes?" His tone was low and full of threat, but Mal didn't back down.

"I'm sure my laird is more than capable of looking after himself, but he will have our guest with him, willnae he? Can my esteemed laird guarantee the lady's safety?"

Arran ground his teeth. He knew he was being reckless sending his men away and the sensible thing would be to allow them to accompany him and Jenna on a tour of the island. But he suddenly didn't feel sensible. He felt stifled, constrained, and wanted, just for a little while, to be free of the shackles of being the laird. And he wanted to be alone with Jenna.

"Dinna concern yerself with the lady's safety," he growled. "I willnae let harm come to her." And, truth be told, he doubted a MacFinnan spellweaver would need any protection from him.

Mal scowled for a moment longer, but then inclined his head. "As ye wish."

Arran nodded and turned to where Jenna was petting Bran. "Ready?"

She shrugged. "As I'll ever be."

"Good." He put his hands around her waist and lifted her into Bran's saddle.

She yelped in surprise and gave him a murderous scowl. "Will you stop doing that? A little warning next time, please?"

"Aye, my lady." He hid a grin as he got his foot into the stirrup and swung up behind her, settling his weight into the soft leather saddle. Reaching around her, he gripped the reins and then nudged Bran into a walk towards the gates.

Jenna clung onto the saddle horn, leaning forward so she was almost draped over Bran's neck, and looking so ungainly that Arran had to stifle a smile.

"Straighten up, lass," he instructed her. "Let yer weight settle through yer hips and sway with the movement of the horse. Ye will soon find yer balance."

"Easy for you to say," she muttered. But she did as he instructed, pushing herself upright while still holding onto the saddle horn. It brought her close to Arran, her back only an inch or two away from his chest, so close he could smell the scent of lavender soap on her.

Without looking back, he guided Bran through the gates of Dun Tabor and out into the wilds of Skye.

Chapter Seven

THIS WAS NOT what Jenna had in mind when she'd agreed to a tour of the island yesterday. Although, to be honest, she didn't really know *what* she'd had in mind. Yesterday had been such a blur, and there had been so many thoughts swirling around in her head that she could have agreed to anything.

Still, she reflected, as they moved at a sedate walk down the gravelly road that led from Dun Tabor's gates and through the village, it could be worse. The morning was bright and sunny, with a pleasant breeze blowing in from the sea, bringing with it the scent of sea salt and helping to clear Jenna's headache a little.

And, she had to admit, being this close to Arran MacLeod wasn't too bad either. True, the man was rude and taciturn, but there was something solid about his presence that helped her relax. He'd said he'd keep her safe while she was here, and Jenna instinctively knew he meant every word.

Despite the ridiculously early hour, the village was already busy as they rode through. She heard the clinking of metal coming from somewhere as a blacksmith worked, the bleating of sheep as a shepherd worked his herd with his dogs on the hill next to Dun Tabor, the chatter of women as they crouched by the stream, washing out bedding. It all seemed so… normal. But for the wild setting and the rustic houses, it could have been any morning anywhere where people were busy going about their day.

Yet as they rode through the village, the villagers stopped what they were doing to watch her and Arran pass. While many called out greetings to their laird, many of them stared in awe at Jenna and she heard the whisper go around, "There she is! The spellweaver!"

Jeez, she thought. *What exactly did my ancestors do to make the locals react like this?*

She felt uncomfortable under their scrutiny, like a goldfish in a bowl, and she felt the weight of their expectation settle on her shoulders like an iron coat. She did not want to let them down.

She was relieved when they left the village behind and began passing through wilder country, empty of people but for shepherds with their flocks up on the hills. The sea sparkled in the distance in every direction, looking like a carpet of shiny sapphires under the spring sun. The vales and hills were a kaleidoscope of green and purple, and Jenna felt her breath hitch with the beauty of it all. If she didn't know better, she could be fooled into thinking that this was a tranquil, bucolic place of peace and quiet beauty. But she did know better. The tranquility hid a dark truth, the evidence of which she'd seen only too clearly in the burned-out boats yesterday.

They rode in silence, and Arran didn't bother to explain where they were going although he seemed to have a destination in mind. They were traveling northeast as far as Jenna could tell, through a craggy landscape of small lochs and heather-covered hills, with stone-and-thatch crofts scattered through the wide landscape.

"Where are we going?" she asked finally.

"Ye said ye wanted to understand the magic, did ye not?" Arran answered, his voice a deep rumble that reverberated through his chest. "So I'm taking ye to where it begins."

No other explanation was forthcoming. Jenna shifted awkwardly in the saddle. Her backside was beginning to ache. Although they moved at nothing more than a fast walk, she'd already decided that she did not like horse riding. It was uncomfortable and slow and she was sure she would have bruises covering her buttocks come the end of the day.

"So," she said, trying to think of something to fill the silence. "This is Skye, huh?"

"Aye," he breathed, his warm breath tickling her ear. "This is Skye, and a more beautiful place ye willnae find in all creation." There was pride in his voice. She glanced over her shoulder and saw him looking out over the landscape with a gentle expression on his face. It made him look less stern, younger, and even more good-looking. The bright sunlight caused his eyes to shine a deeper blue than the tidal pool they'd jumped in yesterday, and from the bronze hue of his skin, she guessed he spent most of his time outside. Oh yes, he was definitely attractive, this taciturn Scottish laird. Which brought up another question.

"Are you married?"

He stiffened. "Why would ye ask that?"

"It's just that I met so many people last night at the feast, but I don't remember meeting your wife. People marry young in this time, don't they? So I just assumed you'd have a wife."

"Ye assumed wrong. I dinna have time for such things."

The way he said it suggested he didn't want to discuss this anymore. Well, what she'd discovered of him so far suggested that he didn't want to discuss much of anything. Not to be deterred, Jenna tried a different tack. "Your mom seems nice."

"Aye," Arran replied stiffly. "She does well running my estate."

Jenna laughed. "That's not what I meant!" God, he was so straight-laced and stuffy! "I meant she's *nice*. I like her. Although, she seemed kind of... sad."

Arran shifted uncomfortably. "These are difficult times."

Jenna sighed, an image of the burned-out ships flashing through her head. "I know. Who are these people who keep attacking you?"

She felt Arran shrug. "Pirates and raiders. Skye lies in a strategic position close to the mainland's rugged coast and within striking distance of Ireland. With so much coastline to protect, we are easy pickings for those who wish to make a living from killing and thieving. There have always been raids, from the mainland, from Ireland, from Iceland and Norway. But the magic always repelled them and kept us safe. Perhaps because of that, we grew complacent and when the magic failed, we weren't prepared. That complacency cost my father and brother their lives, and the lives of many of my people. I willnae make the same mistake again."

His voice was hard and tinged with regret. His hands, where they gripped the reins had curled into fists and, as if sensing his master's anger, Bran began to snort and stamp.

Arran eased his grip and leaned forward to pat the gelding's neck. "My apologies, lad," he murmured. The movement brought him so close to Jenna that his arms brushed hers and his chest touched her back. She held herself rigid until he settled back, not liking the sudden rush of heat that went through her at his touch.

What was wrong with her?

They rode in silence after that while Jenna mulled over what she'd learned. The deaths of his father and brother had obviously hit Arran hard, and she began to understand a little more of what drove him and why he'd been willing to travel all the way to the future to find a way to help his people. It was a rare person who would risk so much for others.

The sun had risen to mid-morning and the day had turned hot and sticky by the time Arran announced they were nearing their destination. They had been climbing steadily up the craggy sides of a glen when he suddenly pulled the horse to a halt and pointed.

"There."

Spread out ahead of them was an otherworldly landscape of undulating, cone-shaped hillocks interspersed with huge boulders and scattered with small lochs that glittered like coins under the sun. The hillocks were blanketed with gnarly trees from which curtains of moss hung down like old men's beards. In the center of it all rose a huge square of sandstone which looked for all the world like some fairytale castle.

Jenna's breath caught. The place had an ethereal, almost mystical beauty to it. And it thrummed with power.

"What is this place?" she breathed.

"Bail Nan Cnoc," Arran said softly. "The fairy glen. And the heart of Skye's magic."

"Let me down."

Without a word, Arran swung out of the saddle, then reached up and lifted Jenna down. As her feet hit the ground, she stumbled and Arran had to put out an arm to steady her.

"Are ye all right, lass?"

She looked up at him. "Fine. I'm fine. Don't you feel that?"

She'd stumbled because the moment her feet touched the earth she'd felt… something. There were tremors in the ground, but it was no earthquake or landslip; rather it was the thrum of power, deep within the earth and echoing up through the layers of soil and rock.

Arran cocked his head. "Feel what?"

"I'll take that as a 'no'." Jenna crouched, placing her palms flat on the mossy earth and closing her eyes. Her palms tingled. She'd never felt anything like it. There was power here, raw and primal. The life energies of the land lay just below her fingertips, golden lines of energy that vibrated with a frequency that matched the ball of power that nestled inside herself. It sang to her. She found herself swaying with it, becoming one with it—

"Jenna?"

A heavy hand settling on her shoulder snapped her out of it. Her eyes sprang open and she looked up to see Arran frowning down at her, a perplexed expression on his face. She climbed to her feet and pointed at the castle-like rock rising out of the valley.

"There," she said. "That's where it comes from."

Without waiting for Arran, she began walking. After a moment, he caught up with her, leading Bran by the reins. The trail was not easy and beneath the carpet of grass and springy moss, the ground was humped and ridged, eager to catch an unwary foot or hoof. Huge boulders in a variety of random shapes and sizes dotted the landscape as if they'd been tossed there by a giant in a fit of rage.

Jenna picked her way with care along the vale's base, skirting around the edges of a small, tear-shaped loch and then through a thicket of twisted rowan trees. The hanging moss stirred slightly at her passing, a faint whisper rippling through the air, so gentle as to be almost beyond hearing.

Glancing behind, she saw that although Arran followed close behind, his shoulders were hunched and tense, his face a little paler than usual. Even Bran seemed wary, snorting and rolling his eyes as he followed his master. It seemed she wasn't the only one affected by this place.

Finally, the rowans pulled back and they found themselves at the base of the outcrop from which the square of sandstone rose. It reached up into the sky, taller than anything around it, and Jenna had to tilt her head back to look up at its summit. Thorny bushes grew out of the rock's sides, and she could see old bird's nests in its cracked and pitted surface.

The place had a feeling of antiquity about it, as though she was looking at the exposed bones of the earth itself, old beyond time.

"Stay here," she instructed Arran. "I'm going to go closer."

He frowned but didn't argue as she made her way to the base of the rock and laid her hands against the rough sandstone. The shock that ran through her hand almost made her snatch her hand back. It reminded her of the time she'd touched an electric fence when out walking with her mother as a child. There was a kick and then a rush of sensation that ran right up her arm and into her chest.

If she'd wanted proof that Skye's magic was real and wasn't just folklore or superstition, this was it. The island was *alive*. The power beneath her fingers pulsed like a heartbeat, golden and shining in her mind's eye.

In her time, in the twenty-first century, whatever magic had once been in the earth was weak and fading. People had forgotten the old ways, had forgotten the forces of nature that had once governed people's lives, and now there were only a few hidden places where the magic remained strong.

But not here. Here it pulsed with a vibrancy that took her breath away and made her heart soar. It was so primal, so pure, so… so… alive.

The MacFinnan spellweavers of the past had *not* created the magic that protected Skye, she realized. They had merely *molded* it. They had used their own powers to shape it to their will and employ it to protect the people who lived here.

Perhaps she could do the same.

Closing her eyes, she reached down into the core of power that swirled in her chest and reached out with it to the magic that thrummed through the rock. It was like stepping into a whirlpool. Her consciousness was suddenly grabbed and she was sent spinning, spinning away into the void, into ropes of shimmery golden power that crisscrossed Skye in an intricate web.

She struggled to keep hold of herself, to stop her consciousness being fragmented by the awesome elemental powers that buffeted it. But slowly, she brought the clinging threads of her being together.

How? she asked Skye. *How do I help you?*

She traveled farther along the web of power and saw that many of the links were broken, dark sections in an otherwise sparkling golden maze. At the cardinal points of the net she saw points of swirling energy that locked the protective magic in place. Some shone brightly, alive and vibrant, but others glowed dully, like the dying embers of a fire. It was these points that were linked to the dark strands of the mesh.

Allowing her consciousness to drift closer to those dark strands, she probed them with her magic, trying to weave them back together, trying to make the magical web whole. It didn't work. Her magic merely dissipated into the void and evaporated like smoke.

Damn it, she thought stubbornly. *There has to be a way.*

She poured more of her magic into those dark strands, feeling it flow out of her in a rush. Weakness began to flood her limbs. Still, she didn't stop. There was too much riding on this for her to give in. The people of Skye needed her, and she needed Arran's payment if she was going to get home and fix her life. So she gritted her teeth, reached deep inside herself to the magic that had lain dormant there for so long, and used it to weave a skein of golden threads across the dark strands of the magical web.

Or, at least, that's what she tried to do. Her repairs held for perhaps a few seconds before they snapped and dissipated into the darkness.

In frustration, she pushed her consciousness ever closer to those dark holes in the magic. If she could just figure out—

But she moved too close. Suddenly the void reached out to grab her and she was falling down, down, down into darkness.

ARRAN DID NOT like this place. Oh, he respected it of course, and as laird of this land he observed the expected rituals at midsummer and midwinter, but it still unnerved him.

If he closed his eyes, he fancied he could almost hear whispers just beyond hearing and feel the thrum of energies far beyond his ken. The place made him feel small, like he was some insignificant speck in the mighty cosmos and that compared to the powers that slumbered here, his life was as fleeting and ephemeral as a butterfly's.

He shifted uneasily, stroking Bran's nose, and watched Jenna. What was she doing? Not a lot, it seemed to the naked eye. She was standing close to the rock, both palms pressed flat against its rough surface, with her eyes closed. She hadn't moved or spoken a word for the last ten minutes, although her eyelids fluttered as though she were dreaming.

He considered asking her what she was doing but then thought better of it. It was probably not wise to interfere with a MacFinnan spellweaver when she was doing... whatever it was she was doing.

Suddenly her lips parted and she let out a tiny gasp. Then she collapsed, puddling onto the ground like a puppet whose strings have been cut.

A shot of alarm went through Arran and, dropping Bran's reins, he ran to her side and knelt next to her, his knee sinking into the springy turf.

"Lass?" he asked urgently. "Jenna?"

She lay on her back, limbs splayed at awkward angles, her eyes closed. She had gone pale. No, worse than pale. She had lost all color, and there was a faint blue tinge to her lips. A rime of frost had formed across her eyes, her long eyelashes sparkling with silver. He pressed a hand to her face then snatched it back when he found her skin was as cold as ice.

With a muttered curse, he ripped off the brooch that held his plaid at his shoulder, pulled the garment off, and quickly wrapped it around her, tucking it close like a cocoon. She flopped around like a doll as he worked but she didn't wake.

The alarm turned to a spike of fear that turned Arran's insides cold. "Lass!" he called, shaking her shoulders. "Wake up!"

She did not respond. Hand shaking slightly, he pressed his fingers against the icy skin of her neck and was relieved to find a pulse, although it was weak and fluttering like a trapped bird. He looked around, searching for anyone who might help them, but they were alone. Except for Bran, there was not another living thing in sight.

"What have ye done to her?" he shouted at the towering face of the rock. "What have ye done?"

His fear gave way to anger. Anger at his helplessness. Anger at whatever had done this to her. Anger that it was he who had brought her here and caused this to happen in the first place.

He had no idea how to help her. Battlefield wounds he knew how to deal with, but this? This was far beyond his expertise. He had to get her back to Dun Tabor, and fast.

"Hold on, lass," he muttered as he scooped her up. "Hold on."

He hurried over to Bran and draped the unconscious lass over the saddle while he mounted. Once in the saddle, he rearranged Jenna's inert form until she was sitting in the saddle leaning against him, with her head lolling back against his chest. She didn't stir the entire time and despite the plaid that now wrapped her, he could feel the cold from her skin seeping into his chest.

He ignored it. The urgency boiling in his gut would have to be enough to keep him warm. Clamping one arm firmly around her waist and holding the reins with the other, he kicked Bran into an urgent gallop. Perhaps responding to his master's mood, or perhaps just eager to get out of this unsettling place, the gelding needed no prompting, and little guidance from Arran.

At a breakneck pace they sped along the base of the glen and up onto the trail that led south to Dun Tabor. He knew galloping at this pace was reckless but he also knew he had no choice. Jenna was a dead weight against him, her head lolling with the movements of the horse, and he was sure he could feel her slipping away from him inch by slow inch.

No, he said to himself. *I will not lose her!*

With this determination burning in his veins, and pushing Bran to his very limits, they reached Dun Tabor in less than half the time the journey had taken them this morning. He thundered through the village, Bran's hooves sending up sprays of mud, Arran bellowing at people to get out his way, and then clattered through the gates and into Dun Tabor's courtyard, not stopping until he pulled a sweating and lathered Bran up outside the doors.

Seeing his urgency, several of his men came running, including Mal, back from his scouting mission.

"What is it?" Mal asked. "What's wrong?"

"Take her," Arran barked.

He handed Jenna down to Mal, jumped to the ground, and then took her back.

"What happened?" the big man asked.

Arran ignored the question. Carrying Jenna up the steps, he yelled over his shoulder, "Fetch the healer! And send my mother and Ingrid to Jenna's room immediately!"

Not waiting to see if he was obeyed, he shouldered the doors open, hurried across the entrance hall, and then took the steps two at a time. At the top, he ran along the corridor of the guest wing and kicked open the door to Jenna's room.

Ingrid looked up from where she was fluffing the pillows on the bed. "Oh, my lord!" she cried, putting a hand to her chest. "Ye startled me—" She cut off as she spotted Jenna, her eyes going wide. "My lady! What happened?"

Arran laid Jenna on the bed, then tucked her under the blankets, pulling them tightly around her.

"Get a fire going and bring extra blankets," he snapped at Ingrid. "She's freezing!"

Ingrid jumped to obey and in only moments he heard the snap and hiss of flames behind him. He dragged a chair over to Jenna's bedside and sat, pressing a hand against her forehead. It was still icy cold.

Ingrid hurried over, bearing extra blankets she had taken from a chest, and threw them over Jenna. The girl's face was almost as pale as Jenna's.

"What's wrong with her?" she asked.

Arran shook his head. "I wish I knew."

Hurried footsteps sounded in the corridor outside and then his mother burst in accompanied by Martha, one of the keep's healers. She was a no-nonsense matronly woman with dark hair tied in a plaited coil at the back of her head who had tended to Arran's scrapes and broken bones ever since he was a boy. He was still a little afraid of her even now.

Martha took one look at Jenna laid out in the bed and snapped, "Everyone, get out of the way! Let me see my patient."

Arran left Jenna's side reluctantly, moving to stand beside his mother. Rosaline had an anxious expression on her face, and she was chewing on her bottom lip.

"What happened?" she asked in a low, worried voice.

"I don't know," Arran replied with a shake of his head. "She just… collapsed."

His stomach roiled with anxiety as he watched Martha inspect Jenna. The healer pressed her fingers against Jenna's pulse points, hissing at the icy touch of her skin, peeled back her eyelids to look into her eyes, gently probed Jenna's head with her fingertips, and pried Jenna's mouth open to look at her tongue. Next she peeled back the blankets and ran her hands down Jenna's arms and legs before gently feeling her abdomen and then lastly pressing her ear against Jenna's chest to listen to her heart.

Finally, she pulled the blankets back and straightened. "There's nothing wrong with her as far as I can tell," she pronounced, turning to Arran. "No signs of injury or disease. Whatever has caused this malady is something internal, something beyond my ken."

"That's it?" Arran snapped. "That's all ye can say? Why willnae she wake? What can be done to help her?"

Martha met Arran's furious gaze with a stern one of her own. "She is a MacFinnan spellweaver," she said softly. "And she touches powers far beyond yer ken or mine. There is something of that going on inside her, and neither ye nor I can do anything about it. She will either wake or she willnae. Keep her warm. That's all we can do."

She squeezed Arran on the shoulder. *She will either wake or she willnae.* The words cut through him like daggers.

"Leave me," he said into the sudden, heavy silence.

"My son, Jenna must not be left alone. Perhaps I should—" began Rosaline.

Arran spun on the three women. "I said leave! *I* will stay with her."

Martha looked as though she was about to argue, but perhaps sensing the storm within Arran, she wisely did not. "Come get me immediately if there is any change."

Arran nodded tightly and watched as they left the room. When the door closed behind them, he lowered himself into the chair by the bed and leaned forward, brushing a stray strand of hair out of Jenna's face. She looked peaceful, like she was only sleeping, but for the ice that had gathered in her lashes.

He wrapped his fingers around hers, ignoring the icy touch of her flesh. Her hand felt small and delicate in his big, ungainly paw.

"Come back, lass," he whispered. "Come back to me."

Chapter Eight

JENNA STOOD BACK from the bed while the medical staff rushed, shouting instructions and counting the beat while the doctor performed CPR.

And all the while there was the long, continuous beep of the heart monitor, and everything that meant.

But the doctors still worked, refusing to give up, even though Jenna knew it was pointless. Couldn't they see that her mother was gone? Couldn't they see that the spark that gave her life had fled?

There seemed to be a hole in Jenna's chest, a deep, dark hole into which she was falling and when she glanced down, she was surprised to see her chest whole and unmarked. How was that possible? Her heart felt it like it had torn out of her, so how come she was standing here, still breathing, rather than bleeding out her life onto the pristine white tiles?

You can't go, Mom, she thought. *I need you.*

And then the hole in her chest swallowed her up and she was being swept away into the darkness. The hospital room, the doctors, the lifeless form of her mom were all torn from her and there was only inky blackness wherever she looked and she was tossed and turned like a pebble in a flood, rushed along in a tide she couldn't see, hear, or feel.

She would have screamed if she had a voice. She would have

tried to fight her way clear if she had arms and legs. But there was nothing to grab onto, only a cold dark sea of... nothing. Then light ahead. A small point of light like a candle flickering in a dark room. She rushed towards it and it grew larger and larger until she found herself standing on the porch of her house.

It was a lovely summer's evening and a bottle of wine was tucked under her arm and a large pizza clutched in her hand. After all, it was payday and she and Alex deserved a treat didn't they? She'd even managed to get off work a little early so they could spend the evening together.

She pushed the door open and walked into the hall, halting as a strange sound came from deeper inside the house. Creak. Creak. Creak.

Puzzled, she put down the wine and the pizza and padded through the house, halting outside the bedroom door. The sound was coming from inside. Creak. Creak. Creak. And other sounds as well. Grunts. Sighs. A woman's moan.

She pushed the door open and stared at the scene within. It was Alex, tangled up with a blonde-haired woman on the bed. On *their* bed. The woman shrieked as she spotted Jenna and scrambled to pull a sheet over her nakedness.

"Shit!" Alex hissed. "Jenna! I thought you were at work. I—"

She didn't hear the rest of the sentence. She spun on her heel and walked away, out of the house and along the track that bordered the lake. And her heart, already torn out of her chest, was shredded into a million pieces that blew away on the breeze.

The blackness took Jenna again and this time she didn't fight it. She didn't care. Why should she bother? What was left for her? So she raced along in the dark, suffocating tide, utterly alone, just herself and cold, empty dark.

Except, she realized, she was *not* alone. Not quite.

Something had hold of her. Something strong and unyielding, something that brought a flare of warmth into the cold darkness. Then a voice spoke.

"Come back to me, lass."

The voice was familiar, although she couldn't quite figure out who it belonged to. It reminded her of open skies and pounding waves, of swaying trees and purple hills. It was deep and warm and so very alive in this endless dark. She latched onto that voice, allowed it to slow her headlong rush into the void.

"Come back to me."

Where was it coming from? There. She located its source in the darkness and began moving towards it. As she did, the darkness began to recede, becoming first an indistinct gray, then white, then a spectrum of colors, until finally, finally, it shattered around her in a kaleidoscope of rainbow droplets.

Jenna opened her eyes. The red and gold brocade of her bed canopy met her eyes. She blinked, giving her brain time to catch up, then slowly turned her head.

Arran MacLeod was sitting close by her bed, hunched over in the chair, head propped on one hand as he drowsed. His other hand was clasped around hers. This, she realized, was the touch she'd felt in the void. His voice was the one she'd heard, calling her back.

She experimented with using her body. First she wiggled her toes, delighted and surprised when they did what she told them. Then she flexed the fingers of her free hand and turned her head from side to side. Everything worked. She felt tired, but that would pass in time. Considering how close she'd come to losing herself in the magic, she'd been lucky. She would not be so stupid again.

Her gaze fell on Arran. He looked more peaceful than she'd seen him before. His blond hair cascaded to his shoulders in messy waves and his face was free of the lines of care and worry that normally marred it. His broad chest rose and fell gently with his breathing.

She squeezed his hand. "Hey."

Arran snorted and startled awake, looking around wildly, as though expecting an attack. His gaze settled on her and his eyes widened.

"Ye are awake!"

Jenna smiled sheepishly. "Seems that way."

"Ha!" Before she could say more, Arran leaned forward, got his arms under her, and wrapped her into a hug, practically lifting her from the bed.

Jenna squeaked in surprise, taken off guard by his obvious relief. What was this? She hadn't even thought he *liked* her. His arms were strong and reassuring, his warmth a delightful sensation after the cold dark of the void. She found herself wrapping her arms around him in return and burying her face in his shoulder, allowing herself to be comforted by his stalwart presence.

He released her and sat back, looking a little embarrassed. "My apologies," he rumbled. "I shouldnae have done that. It's just... I thought..." He ran out of words and scrubbed a hand through his blond locks.

Jenna grinned. "It's all right. I could get used to waking up to that."

Arran smiled wryly and a little thrill went through her. When he smiled, Arran MacLeod was stunningly good-looking.

"How long have I been asleep?"

"Yesterday afternoon and all last night."

She blinked in surprise. "What? And you've been sitting here all night?"

He shrugged. "Ye gave me quite the fright, lass. I thought I was going to lose ye." He cleared his throat. "That is, I thought *we* were going to lose ye. What happened?"

"I was bloody stupid is what happened," she replied, shaking her head. "Pushed too far and let myself get swept away by the magic. I've never felt anything so strong as the power in Bail Nan Cnoc."

Arran nodded. "Our legends say that it's the most powerful place in all the Isles and is the reason the protective magic could be laid in the first place."

"It's definitely where it originates from. It's... incredible. I could see the magic spreading out across the island like some vast golden net. But it's broken. There are holes in it. And I let one of those holes suck me in. A rookie mistake. My aunts would be furious. You have *no* idea how many times they've lectured me on the dangers of magic."

"Yer aunts sound like my mother. If I had a copper for every time she's chewed my ear off over something or another, I would be richer than the king himself."

Jenna laughed softly. "Families, eh?"

"Aye, families."

He met her gaze, his eyes dancing with mirth, and Jenna found she could not look away. There was something in that deep blue gaze that drew her in, a rarely glimpsed depth of warmth and longing behind the usual stern façade that sent a tingle down the back of her neck.

Arran cleared his throat. "Did ye find what ye needed? Can the magic be restored?"

"I think so. The magic is concentrated on cardinal points. I think the spellweavers who originally created the spell anchored the magic into keystones. If we can find all these keystones, I think I'll be able to repair the magical net."

"Then all the resources of Clan MacLeod are at yer disposal. What do ye need?"

"You said you had a library? I'll need everything you have on the original spellweaving and also as many maps of the island as you can get your hands on."

"Ye shall have it. I will tell Brother Merrick ye are coming and that he is to help ye find what ye need."

Jenna flung back the covers and swung her feet over the edge of the bed. "Then let's get going."

"What? Now?"

"Why not now? There's no time like the present is there? The sooner I get to work, the sooner I can get the magic fixed." *And the sooner I can get paid and go home.*

"Ye've had quite the ordeal, lass. Perhaps ye should rest a

while longer."

"I don't need rest. I'm fine." Now that she had a clue as to how to proceed, she was eager to get on with things. Lying in bed was not going to help anyone. And, besides, she didn't want to risk any more dreams of Alex or her mother.

She grabbed one of the bedposts and used it to lever herself to her feet. A wave of dizziness went through her and she staggered, clutching the post with both hands.

Arran was on his feet in an instant. One of his hands went beneath her elbow, steadying her. "I really think ye should rest a while longer, lass. And besides, Martha will have both our hides if she comes in here and finds ye gone."

Jenna had no idea who Martha was but she wasn't about to be dissuaded. "She can't have our hides if she can't find us, can she? Come on, I need to stretch my legs."

Arran sighed. "Are all MacFinnan women as stubborn as ye?"

Jenna snorted. "Oh, you have *no* idea, my friend," she replied, thinking of Aunt Elise. "No idea."

"This way then." He opened the door and held it for her.

Jenna inclined her head in thanks and then preceded him out the door. The corridor outside was wide enough for them to walk side by side, with a wine-red runner down the center and tapestries softening the austerity of the bare stone walls.

"Thank you by the way," Jenna said suddenly.

Arran glanced at her. "For what?"

"For bringing me back."

"Ye dinna need to thank for me for that. Ye gave me one hell of a fright when ye collapsed. Getting ye back to Dun Tabor was the only think I could think to do."

She shook her head. "I don't mean that." How could she explain that she'd been lost in a void of loss and heartache? That she'd been unable to find a way free until she'd heard his voice and felt his touch? "I just mean... I just mean, thanks for being there, I guess."

His eyes found hers. "Ye are welcome, lass."

Jenna felt her cheeks flush and looked away. "So," she said. "This library of yours. Is it far?"

"On the far side of the keep, away from the kitchens and the risk of fire. My grandfather founded the library. He was a scholar more than a warrior. As the youngest of three brothers, he was destined for the monastery but fate had other ideas. Both his brothers died before he did, and he ended up as clan chief in their stead. So, rather than the life of prayer and study he'd prepared for, he found a life of war and bloodshed instead. The library, I think, was his way of trying to hang on to that life he'd wanted."

There was something wistful in Arran's tone and she suspected there was more than a little of his grandfather's story entwined with his own. It seemed these fifteenth century Highlanders had little choice over their own lives and were often at the mercy of the vagaries of fate.

Their progress through the castle was slow. Not because Jenna had any more dizzy spells or because she felt unwell, but because they were stopped every few yards by someone who wanted to pass on awed greetings and words of gratitude to the "great spellweaver" or because they needed to speak to their laird about something.

Arran listened to them all with infinite patience, giving everyone that stopped him his complete attention, as though for that moment, they were the most important person in the world. Jenna began to understand why his people seemed to love him. He had a sincerity about him that put people at their ease and, despite his sometimes-gruff exterior, nobody seemed wary of approaching him.

He was nothing like Alex. Alex was a sales manager at a car dealership and had been smooth, full of himself, and utterly charming. Everyone had liked him. Everyone had wanted to be in his orbit. And yet, now she thought about it, there had been a shallowness to Alex's interactions with others, as if his sincerity was only skin deep. Not so with Arran. She could see in every interaction with his people how much he cared for them and how much they cared for him in return. With the surface-level interactions she was used to in her own time, she wasn't entirely sure what to make of it.

Finally, they reached an age-darkened oaken door, set with riveted bands of iron. Arran glanced at her, took hold of the round iron handle, and heaved the door open. Even with Arran's bulk behind it, the door swung open slowly, revealing how thick and heavy it was—another precaution against fire, Jenna guessed.

She followed him into the space beyond and stumbled to a stop, mouth falling open. She wasn't sure what she'd expected of a fifteenth century library, but it was most definitely not this. Hexagonal in shape, it filled one of the keep's towers, with mezzanine wooden galleries circling the tower's hollow interior, stretching up as far as Jenna could see. Zig-zag staircases led from one level to the other, and each level was filled with shelves of books and rolled scrolls.

"Wow," Jenna muttered. "Just… wow."

"You like it?".

"Like it? This place is incredible! It must have taken years to collect all these books."

"Aye," he agreed. "My grandfather's life's work. My father carried on the tradition and collected books and scrolls from all over Europe. Many are ancient Greek or Roman but we even have some rumored to have been saved from the great library in Alexandria, although I'm not sure about the truth of that." He pointed to a long wooden table that had been polished until it gleamed. "When I was a child, I spent many an hour sitting right there, being tutored in all sorts of things. Philosophy. History. Latin. Back then I thought all the knowledge in the world must be contained in this library and that if I stayed here long enough, I could learn it all."

There was a wistful note to Arran's voice and she wondered what kind of child he'd been. Like his grandfather, he'd not expected to inherit the lairdship. Like his grandfather, had he wished for a scholarly life among his books and scrolls before the role of leader was thrust upon him?

"My laird!" said a voice. "I didnae expect to see ye today."

A skinny man dressed in a long brown robe belted with a piece of rope came hurrying towards them, carrying a pile of books which he put down on the polished table.

"Good day, Brother Merrick," Arran greeted, inclining his head slightly. "This is Jenna MacFinnan, and she needs to see every bit of information we have on the spellweavers who originally placed the protective magic around Skye."

Brother Merrick turned to look at Jenna. Clearly a monk, he was bald but for two fluffy tufts of hair that perched above his ears like storm clouds. He squinted slightly, and Jenna guessed he was near-sighted from looking at his books all day. He broke into a wide, gap-toothed smile.

"Ah! So ye are the MacFinnan spellweaver I've been hearing so much about! I'm delighted to make yer acquaintance, my dear." He grabbed both of Jenna's hands in his and pumped them vigorously. "Honored that ye would deign to visit my humble library! Honored, I say! And perhaps, while ye are here, ye could answer some questions for me? I'm sure ye have knowledge which could answer some of the most pressing scientific questions of our time. For example, was the Venerable Bede correct in his surmise that the pull of the moon is responsible for the movement of the tides?"

"Merrick," Arran warned in a low voice. "Yer studies will have to wait. We need that information urgently."

"Of course! Of course!" Merrick said, looking a little sheepish. "I'll find what ye are looking for, although it will take some time to go through everything we have on the spellweavers. There is rather a lot, I'm afraid."

"Then leave everything else ye are working on and assist Lady Jenna with whatever she needs."

"Aye, my laird," Merrick said, rubbing his hands together with delight. "It would be an honor."

"And be sure to—"

Arran cut off mid-sentence as a loud clanging noise suddenly started sounding from the bailey outside.

"Damn it," he murmured. "That's the warning bell." He turned to Jenna. "I have to go. Merrick will see that ye have everything ye need."

"But what—" Jenna began.

"I have to go!"

Without another word, he spun on his heel and ran from the library.

Chapter Nine

THE CLANGING OF the warning bell didn't let up, ringing through the castle like a banshee's wail and bringing Arran's warriors running. Some burst out of the great hall, half-eaten food clasped in their fists, some came clattering down the stairs, hastily strapping on weapons, and as Arran stepped into the courtyard, he saw others streaming from the training ground, the stables, the guardhouses.

They gathered around Mal who stood in the middle of the bailey bellowing orders, his voice only just audible above the racket emitting from the bell tower.

Arran ran up to him. "What news?" he yelled. "What's happened?"

"Raid in progress at Tollman's Gate."

Arran went cold. "The same ones who hit the fishing fleet?"

Mal shrugged. "We dinna have any details. Only that Tollman's Gate is calling for aid."

Arran turned to survey his hastily assembling warriors. They all knew the drill by now and had responded in quick time the moment the warning bell began to sound.

"Warriors of Clan MacLeod!" he bellowed, his voice carrying over the noise of the bell. "We ride to relieve Tollman's Gate! It seems the bastards that destroyed our fleet are back! How about we go teach them a lesson that will have them terrified to set foot on Skye for the rest of their lives?"

An almighty cheer rumbled around the bailey and many of his men drew their claymores and brandished them in the air, the sunlight reflecting off their bright blades.

Grooms and pages came running, leading horses that had been hastily tacked. The stable master led Bran over to Arran and held him steady while Arran swung into the saddle and grabbed the reins. One of the pages held up Arran's claymore which he strapped across his back and then his longsword which he belted to his hip.

Yanking on the reins, he pulled Bran around to face the gates. As he did so, he caught sight of his mother, Ingrid, and some of the other women of Dun Tabor standing on the steps, their faces pale with worry. He didn't have time to speak to them. Instead, he rose in his stirrups, drew his claymore one handed, and bellowed, "We ride! Ride for Tollman's Gate!"

Then, slamming his claymore back into its scabbard, his set his heels to Bran's flanks and the horse sprang forward at an urgent gallop. Arran led his men out of Dun Tabor, a long column of horsemen flowing behind him like a river in full spate.

They thundered down the road from Dun Tabor's gate and through the village, the villagers crowding the side of the road and cheering as they passed. But Arran took no pride or comfort in their show of support. He did not feel like cheering. Instead, his gut churned as though it was filled with hissing snakes and a sick sense of dread settled on him.

He and his men had arrived too late to stop the attack on his fishing fleet. They would *not* be too late today. He could not, *would* not, allow it.

He led the charge at a blistering pace, trusting Bran to keep his footing, hardly taking notice of the landscape as they sped the ten or so miles along the coastal road towards the southern settlement of Tollman's Gate. He scanned the sea as they rode, looking for any sign of ships. There were none. Whoever these attackers were, they must have come around the southern tip of the island in an effort to evade detection.

In that, at least, the raiders had failed. Arran had set up a warning system, with a series of strategically placed watchtowers set on high ground where they had a good view of the sea, with access to a series of fast-horsed messengers that could bring the news of attacks to their nearest garrison or to Dun Tabor itself. It had not been enough to save the fishing fleet, but maybe, just maybe, it would be enough to save Tollman's Gate.

Finally, they rounded a headland and came in sight of the settlement. Tollman's Gate was a prosperous village protected from the worst of the weather by a series of rocky islets that dotted the coast in this part of Skye. The settlement had become important for both trade and feeding the island due to the abundant shellfish that could be found in its relatively shallow waters. And this, no doubt, was why the raiders had chosen it as their next target.

Two ships, Norse by the look of them, were anchored in the bay, with several smaller boats pulled up on the shingle beach. Inland, backing onto the base of a craggy hill, lay Tollman's Gate itself. A wave of attackers ringed the settlement and the bellow of men and the clash of steel could be heard even at this distance. But unlike the fishing boats, Tollman's Gate was not undefended.

At Arran's command, the settlement had been fortified by a deep ditch and rampart up which an attacker would have to scramble while being attacked from above. He'd left a small garrison of trained warriors here as well, and every able-bodied man in the settlement had been trained to use a bow.

That training was in evidence now as a cloud of arrows rained down from the rampart. Some found their mark, embedding themselves in throats or limbs, but most thudded harmlessly into the round wooden shields that the attackers held above their heads. The defenders of Tollman's Gate seemed to be holding their own though, and only a few of the raiders had made it over the rampart and these had been swiftly dealt with.

But this state of affairs could not last. The raiders far outnumbered the defenders and, as Arran watched, he could already see gaps springing up in the defender's line, and attackers hurrying to take advantage.

"Mal, yer men take the left flank, Angus, ye take the right," Arran bellowed. "The rest of ye, with me!"

His men peeled off to right and left while Arran led the charge in the center, straight up the road that led to Tollman's Gate's fortifications. He drew his longsword, nudging Bran to the greatest speed the horse could muster, and felt his lips pull back from his teeth in a feral snarl. A cold fury burned in his gut as his eyes swept over the sea of attackers. Here were the men who thought it their right to take what they wanted, to kill and pillage, and shatter the lives of Arran's people.

He would make them regret their arrogance.

He heard a high, wild screaming sound, and realized that it was coming from his own throat, a vocalization of all the fury and helplessness that had dogged him for months.

He slammed into the raiders without slowing, scything left and right with his longsword, feeling it bite into flesh and bone, and sending a spray of iron-tasting blood across his face. Bran fought too, kicking and bucking, and staved in the head of a man coming at Arran from the left.

All became chaos. All became a seething melee of bodies and blades, of shouting and screaming, of the stink of blood and voided bowels. His men moved to his left and right, cutting and parrying with their longswords and trying to drive a wedge through the attackers to reach the defenders on the fortifications.

But the raiders weren't just mindless barbarians. They too were well trained, and seeing Arran's tactics, they quickly pulled back and formed a shield wall with their interlocking shields, thrusting long spears between the gaps, designed to negate the advantage of the horses.

Arran growled in frustration, pulling Bran around in a circle, looking for a way through. As he did so, a hooked blade caught the hilt of his longsword and yanked him out of the saddle. He slammed into the mud and had an instant to register a blade swinging at his face. He rolled away as it slammed into the mud where he'd been lying and then kicked the man who wielded it in the knee.

The man grunted in pain and staggered, giving Arran enough time to climb to his knees and draw his claymore from across his back, which he held in a two-handed grip.

The man facing him was huge. Taller and broader even than Arran, he wore a sleeveless leather vest that showed off his tree-trunk arms, light linen trews, and soft knee-high boots. His long hair, matted and knotted, was hung with all kinds of charms: bones, twigs, feathers. On one arm he carried his round shield while with the other, he brandished his hooked blade.

"What are you waiting for, islander?" the man rasped in a guttural voice. "An invitation?" His accent was clipped, with a slight emphasis on the ends of words. Aye, definitely Norse.

Arran didn't answer the taunt. He'd been in enough fights to know when an enemy was trying to bait him, and the last thing he needed to do against this brute was lose his concentration. So he kept his stance, treading warily to his right, eyes fixed on his opponent. The man moved the other way and they began circling each other like predators.

Around him, Arran was dimly aware of the battle beginning to turn, of the defenders of Tollman's Gate opening the barricade and storming out to join Arran's men, but he had no time to spare for them now.

"Who are ye?" Arran asked the giant. "What do ye want here?"

The big man grinned, revealing white teeth that had been sharpened to points. God's blood. What kind of man was he?

"I?" he said. "I want nothing. My master though? He's another matter."

Arran said nothing, but continued circling, assessing his opponent's weaknesses. From the way he moved and the way he carried his weapons, it was clear he was well trained.

"Who is yer master?"

He did not expect an answer and had in fact only asked the question to catch his opponent unawares. Before the sentence was even finished, he dashed forward, swinging his claymore in a flashing arc that would have taken the man's head had it connected. The man threw up his shield and sword to block the blow and that's what Arran was waiting for. He adjusted his swing slightly, taking it above and away from the shield, allowed its momentum to carry it around and down, and then reversed the slash, bringing it low and slicing through the man's legs.

At least, that's what *should* have happened. But the man moved like lightning. As Arran's blade came down, somehow the man's blade was already there to meet it and the two blades slammed together with enough clanging force to send a jolt up Arran's arm and into his shoulder.

"Oh, you are good!" the man crowed. "My master was right about you!"

He was grinning manically, as though this was the most fun he'd had in a long time. Now that they were so close, Arran saw that the man bore a strange design inked into the side of his neck, an interlocking design of three spirals, with an angular rune above it.

"Who are ye?" he growled. "What do ye want?"

The grin widened. "You can call me Ingold. And what do I want? Nothing. But my master? Oh, he only wants your island is all."

With a grunt, Arran shoved the man away and attacked again, his sword moving in a blur of motion. Ingold parried everything Arran threw at him, the grin never leaving his face. Arran was soon sweating and blowing, but he did not let up. All the rage he felt, all the guilt and pent-up frustration came pouring out of him, at last finding a focus in this grinning madman.

The clang of steel on steel filled the air, along with the stink of sweat and the rusty tang of blood. He could hear his own labored breathing and his heartbeat thundering in his ears, but this was inconsequential against his need to end this leering fool.

He began pushing Ingold back, away from the ramparts around Tollman's Gate. He spared a quick glance for his men. The raiders were being inexorably surrounded. It would soon become a blood bath.

As if sensing this, the grinning man looked around, eyes narrowing as he surveyed his forces. Arran seized his chance, springing forward and swinging his blade in a series of lightning ripostes aimed at Ingold's ribs. The man deflected them all and Arran's frustration mounted. How could such a massive man be so fast?

Then, so suddenly it took Arran off guard, Ingold disengaged, lowering his weapon and backing away.

"Njord sends his regards! And sends his thanks for keeping his island warm for him!"

"This is *my* island!" Arran snarled.

The inked man laughed. "Not for long! Do you think your witch can save you? She can't! This land belongs to Njord. You just don't know it yet!"

Then he turned and ran, putting his fingers to his lips and whistling as he did so. The rest of the raiders battled their way free and fled, sprinting in a disorderly rabble towards the beach where their boats waited. Arran's men set off in pursuit, but Arran didn't join them.

A ball of ice seemed to have formed inside his belly. *Do you think your witch can save you?*

Jenna. The raiders knew about Jenna. And that meant she was in danger.

He slammed his claymore back into its scabbard and looked around for Bran. The warhorse was standing over by the entrance to the rampart, reins trailing. He'd lost his saddle in the melee and his flanks were crusted with dried sweat but his neck still arched gracefully and there was fire in his eyes as he shifted and stamped at two of Arran's men who were trying to calm him.

Arran put his fingers to his lips and whistled. Bran's ears

pricked and swiveled towards him, then he came trotting over, whinnying in greeting. Arran reached up and patted the horse's sweaty neck.

"Ye did well, boy," he murmured. "But I've got one last favor to ask of ye and then I promise ye can spend the next few days eating carrots and lazing in yer stable. How does that sound?"

As if he understood every word, the horse snorted and bobbed his head. Grabbing the reins, Arran vaulted on the horse's back, gripping with his knees.

"Mal is in charge here," he shouted to Tollman's Gate's defenders. "Do as he tells ye."

"Where are ye going, my laird?" one of them cried.

"To Dun Tabor. I have urgent business there." Patting Bran on the neck he said, "One last run, boy. Run home like the wind, Bran. Like the wind."

Nudging the horse's ribs, he urged him into a gallop towards home. Towards Jenna.

Chapter Ten

"**H**ERE YE GO!" Brother Merrick said enthusiastically, thumping down another load of books on Jenna's table. "I think ye'll find plenty about the spellweavers in these."

Jenna stifled a groan and forced a smile. "Thanks, Merrick."

"Dinna ye worry, lass, there is plenty more where they came from." He shuffled off, humming to himself.

To be honest, Jenna was beginning to regret asking to see everything that Dun Tabor had on the spellweavers. There was a *lot*. Books and scrolls already covered the desk and Brother Merrick had taken it upon himself to dig out every last scrap of information, no matter how obscure. Jenna had been reading for hours already—using a steady stream of magic to translate the Gaelic, Latin, and Old English they were written in—and so far she'd found nothing useful. They were all handwritten, some with beautifully decorated pages, but her head was starting to hurt from trying to decipher the tiny, ornate writing that most of the authors seemed to favor.

She thumped shut the latest book and pushed it away with a sigh. Most of what she'd read was nonsense. So far she'd learned that MacFinnan spellweavers could turn themselves into birds and fly away over the sea, how they regularly slayed giants, and protected Skye by calling up fearsome sea monsters that would swallow ships whole and destroy any fleet intent on attacking the island. She might not understand the magic that protected the island, but she did know one thing: sea monsters were definitely *not* it.

Stretching her arms over her head, she yawned hugely. Rosaline, who was sitting opposite her, gave a sympathetic smile.

"Not found aught yet?"

Jenna shook her head. "Not unless you count how one of my ancestors battled a dragon atop Bail Nan Cnoc or punished a wicked lord by turning him into a giant fish. Honestly, this is more folklore than history."

"Folklore is how we make sense of lives," Rosaline said. "It's how we remember where we come from, and how we orient our place in the world." She smiled ruefully. "Although, I must admit, those stories aren't much help when ye are trying to conduct serious research."

Jenna nodded. She'd been surprised when Rosaline had volunteered to help Jenna with her research, and even more surprised when she'd taken to it with almost as much enthusiasm as Brother Merrick. There was more to Arran's mother than met the eye.

"You sound like you've done this kind of thing before."

"Aye," she replied. "In my youth I was something of a scholar. These days keeping my errant son out of mischief and running this place leaves little time for aught else."

Jenna could well imagine. Although Arran was the boss and everyone deferred to his wishes, in the short time she'd been here Jenna had come to learn that it was Rosaline and her army of helpers who actually ran the place.

"Tell me more," Jenna said, propping her chin on her hand. "What did you study?"

"Oh, anything and everything," Rosaline replied, waving her hand. "I was the younger daughter and escaped the rigorous training in how to run a household that my elder sister was subjected to. As a result, I was allowed to indulge my insatiable curiosity. I was tutored in history, philosophy, languages—

everything I could get my hands on. I was what ye would call a 'bookish' child. While my brother and elder sister rebelled against everything our tutor tried to teach us, I lapped it up. My father even sent me to Paris for a while where I learned scribing and arithmetic. Except for when Arran and his brother were born, it was the happiest time of my life."

She sighed wistfully, and Jenna had a sudden image of a young, eager Rosaline rubbing shoulders with the scholars and thinkers of Renaissance Paris. It was no wonder she looked a little wistful.

"How come you ended up here?" Jenna asked. "We're a long way from Paris."

Rosaline shrugged. "My father arranged a match for me with the heir to the lairdship of Clan MacLeod. So I came here and here I've stayed."

It all sounded rather clinical to Jenna. Rosaline's father arranged the marriage? What about how Rosaline herself felt about it? "Didn't you have any say in the matter?"

Rosaline laughed lightly. "No more than a horse at market would have a say in who it's sold to." Jenna was surprised to detect no trace of bitterness in the words, just calm acceptance. "It is the way of the world," Rosaline continued. "And a woman's lot in life. It wasnae a bad marriage. My husband was courteous and treated me well and his father had a love of books that matched my own. He gave over care of this library into my keeping and I've been adding to the collection ever since."

That explained how the collection had grown so huge. But Rosaline's words troubled her. The way of the world? A woman's lot in life?

It was most certainly *not* the way of Jenna's world and would most definitely *not* be her lot in life. She'd already been hurt by one man, and she was never, ever, going to let any man have that kind of power over her again.

"So all of this," she waved vaguely, indicating the space around them. "Is part of Scotland, right? So how come the king hasn't helped you against the raiders? That's how things work in this time isn't it?"

Rosaline laughed softly. "Ye touch on matters of politics that are as tangled as an unwound ball of yarn. Clan allegiances change as quickly as the tide, and Skye has been pulled one way and then the other over the years. But we are closely allied with the Donalds of Islay, and Jamie Donald, the current chief and Lord of the Isles is our liege lord. As for why they dinna help us? I'm sure they would if they had men and resources to spare, but Islay and Barra are as beset by the raiders as we are." She shook her head and sighed. "I'm afraid we are on our own."

Jenna reached over and clasped the older woman's hand. "Not on your own. I swear I'll do everything I can to restore the magic."

Rosaline squeezed her hand and smiled. "I know ye will, my dear. Ye have a kind heart and a bright soul. Not many people would be willing to do what ye have, to leave behind yer family, yer husband and bairns, to come and help us."

Jenna blinked. "Actually, I don't have either," she said carefully.

Rosaline gave her a strange look. "But ye must be in yer twenties at least! And ye are unmarried?"

"Yep. And I'm not an outlier or anything. It's perfectly normal where I come from."

"Oh," Rosaline said, looking slightly scandalized. "I see. But ye must have other family ye have left behind. A mother? Father?"

Jenna shrugged. "My mom died. I never knew my dad. He left when I was a baby and my mom always said it was for the best. Apparently being with a MacFinnan spellweaver is a little too much for most men."

Was that the problem with Alex? She'd never shown him her magic and he had no idea about her abilities, but that didn't mean he might not have subconsciously picked up on it. Might that have been what drove him to cheat on her? Might it have all been her fault after all?

Don't be stupid! she told herself savagely. *How can you blame yourself for what that bastard did? Aunt Elise would kick your ass if she knew you were thinking such things!*

"I'm sorry, my dear," Rosaline said, patting her hand. "Ye must miss yer mother very much."

"I do. But I have my two aunts, Rose and Elise. They keep me on the straight and narrow."

"And they are spellweavers like yerself?"

"That's right. They taught me everything I know."

Rosaline let out a slow breath. "My. Ye must be quite the formidable trio."

Formidable? That wasn't exactly how Jenna would describe her slightly dysfunctional family. Elise was a free spirit who didn't give a damn what anyone thought of her, but she drifted from job to job, place to place, never really settling down or finding a direction in life. Rose was the opposite: house, marriage, career as a nurse. On the surface she had it sorted, but in reality her marriage was on the rocks and she and Uncle Dennis had been going to couples' therapy for months.

No, formidable was not the word Jenna would use. Add her own shit-show of a life into the mix and the phrase "barely holding it together" would be a more appropriate way to describe her family.

But she missed them all the same.

"Yeah," she said. "Something like that."

With a sigh, Jenna opened the next book in the pile, but she'd barely begun to read when heavy footsteps drummed in the corridor outside. Jenna looked up just as the door was flung open and Arran came bursting in, skidding to a stop on the flagstone floor.

Rosaline's hand flew to her chest. "Arran! What is it?"

"Where is—?" His gaze fell on Jenna and his shoulders slumped as the tension leaked out of him. "There ye are. Are ye well? Unhurt?"

"Of course I'm unhurt," Jenna replied, puzzled.

"Good," he breathed, running a hand through his tousled hair. "That's good."

He looked exhausted. There were rips and tears in his clothing and he was spattered with mud. And, as Jenna looked closer, she saw that he was spattered with something else, something rust-colored.

Blood.

Rosaline had seen it too. She rushed around the table, grabbed her son by the arms, and looked up into his weary face.

"By the Saints! What's happened, Arran?"

ARRAN TORE HIS gaze away from Jenna and concentrated on his mother. "Dinna worry," he said. "The blood isnae mine."

"Dinna worry? I worry every time ye step out of the gates of Dun Tabor! Look at ye! Dinna tell me ye are fine, Arran MacLeod, when ye clearly are not!"

Her voice was shrill and wavering and Arran forced a smile. He had to remember that his mother had already lost a husband and son to raiders and what it must be like for her to live under constant threat of losing him as well.

He took her hands from his shoulders and squeezed them. "There was an attack on Tollman's Gate. The same raiders who hit the fleet the other day, unless I miss my guess. But they didnae bank on the village's defenses, or on our warning system. We got there before they could do much damage and drove them back."

Rosaline let out a shaky breath. "Thank the Lord. And ye are unhurt?"

He shrugged. "A few scrapes and bruises but naught I canna handle." In truth, his body was aching like an old man's and he suspected his hip and thigh would be black from where he'd been dragged from his horse, but his mother didn't need to know that.

Rosaline nodded, reassured, and with another squeeze of his mother's hand, he released her and approached Jenna.

She was sitting at a table piled high with books and scrolls and was staring at him with wide eyes. Ah, those eyes. Like a forest pool on a sunny day. At the sight of her, the tension that had knotted his muscles on the ride here began to drain away. Exhaustion came in its wake, and he felt every bruise, every scratch and scrape, tenfold.

It was ridiculous how his heart lifted at the sight of her. It was beyond ridiculous how warmth spread through him when she gave him a tremulous smile, spreading through his stomach and all the way down to his groin. What was wrong with him?

He took a deep breath and moved to stand in front of her. "The raiders know about ye, lass. They know ye are here to help us. That puts ye in danger. From now on, ye are not to leave the castle without guards. Aye?"

The blood drained from Jenna's face. "You don't think they would… hurt me, do you?"

"They would do whatever it takes to keep Skye within their grasp. Ye saw the burned-out ships the other day; ye know what they are capable of. I swore to keep ye safe and I will, but that means doing as I say. Do I have yer word?"

A range of emotions passed across her face. Fear, yes, but also annoyance and a flash of irritation. It seemed that Jenna MacFinnan did not like being told what to do.

But finally, she nodded. "Fine. Whatever you say."

Her lips were parted slightly and he could see a faint pulse beating in her temple. He cleared his throat and gestured to the books and scrolls piled on the table. "So… er… how has yer search gone? Did ye find what ye need?"

Jenna rolled her eyes. "Hardly. I had no idea that I'm descended from a line of giants and shape-changers and God-knows-what-else. And here's me thinking we were just a bunch of ordinary women with some small ability to manipulate energy. If I'd known, I would have charged more."

Arran smiled. "A bargain is a bargain, lass. And ye are anything but ordinary."

He hadn't meant to say it but the words were out of his mouth before he could stop them. Jenna looked up at him and her cheeks flushed before she looked quickly away.

Why did his common sense seem to go out of the window whenever this woman was around?

"Er, where is Merrick?"

Jenna hiked a thumb over her shoulder. "Somewhere at the back, digging out another load of fairy tales for me to read."

Arran took his chance to escape and hurried through the library towards the farthest shelves. He found Brother Merrick holding a faded scroll up to the light as he tried to make out its contents. He rolled it up as he spotted Arran approaching.

"Ah! There ye are, my laird! Look at this! It's a record of the granting of the northern pastures to the Dougalls. It's over a hundred years old and signed by yer great-grandfather. What a find!"

"Fascinating," Arran said drily. "But I'm not interested in land grants. I want yer opinion on something else. Do ye have pen and parchment?"

"Of course, my laird."

Merrick fetched what Arran needed and laid it out on a nearby desk. Arran dipped the quill in the inkpot and then sketched out the swirling design he'd seen on the raiders and Ingold's neck, along with the rune that had been inked above it. When he was finished, he held it up, scouring his memory to check he'd gotten it right. It was as near as he could remember.

"Have ye ever seen this design before?" he asked, thrusting the parchment towards Merrick.

The monk took it, bringing it close to his face as he squinted at the design. "I'm not sure," he murmured, rubbing his chin. "It isnae Christian, I know that much. Something about it looks familiar, as though I might have seen it in some of our texts on the old religion."

"Then find it," Arran commanded. "I need to know what it symbolizes."

Merrick nodded, his eyes alight with the excitement only a scholar can feel at the prospect of new research. "I'll get to it right away."

Arran clapped him on the shoulder. "Good man. Send for me when ye find aught."

He turned and strode to the door of the library but paused on the threshold. Jenna and Rosaline were engrossed in their reading again, but both looked up as he paused. "I'll be back for the evening meal," he said. "Neither of ye are to leave the castle in my absence."

He turned and left, hurrying through the castle towards the stables where he would find a fresh horse. If luck was on his side, Mal and the others had managed to capture some of the raiders and Arran could start getting some answers. If luck wasn't on his side… Well, he didn't want to think about that.

Chapter Eleven

MIDDAY CAME AND went, and Jenna ate a meal of bread, cheese, and apples, which Ingrid brought to her desk in the library. She'd been invited to the great hall to eat with everyone else—as seemed to be the custom for every meal in Dun Tabor—but she was reluctant to halt her research. The answer must lie in these books somewhere and she was determined to find it.

She sighed, leaning back and rubbing at her eyes. Aunt Rose was more of a scholar than Jenna was. She'd spent years tracing their family tree and researching the magic, and no doubt *she* would have figured out a way to restore the magic almost as soon as she arrived here. But if there were clues in these semi-allegorical ramblings and exaggerated accounts, Jenna was damned if she could see them.

I mean, seriously, Jenna thought as she tossed the latest account away in disgust. *How am I supposed to call down lightning from the sky and command it to do my bidding? I'd be burned to a crisp!*

No, she was sure the answer was far simpler and less grand than any of that. The web of earth energies she'd felt at Bail Nan Cnoc needed to be restored and she suspected it had to do with the keystones she'd sensed at the cardinal points of that web. But try as she might, she could find no mention of those keystones or where they might be located.

Merrick pottered over, humming to himself, and carrying another stack of books, which he placed on the desk in front of Jenna. The stack wobbled dangerously, and Jenna put out a hand to steady it.

"What are these?"

"Records of local festivals," Merrick replied. "Yule, Midsummer, Harvest, and so on. The islanders like to cling to their superstitious ways even though the Good Lord's word was brought here from Iona long ago. I thought there might be some clues in them."

"Thanks," Jenna said, forcing a smile even though inside she was cringing. She didn't think tales of burning wicker men or dancing around maypoles was going to help her much, but at this stage she was willing to try anything. She nodded at a rolled-up scroll tucked under the monk's arm. "What's that?"

Brother Merrick blinked, looking surprised to see it there. "This? It's just a land grant from the laird's grandfather's time. I meant to reshelve it." He put it down on the desk with the rest. "I'll put it back later." He wandered off among the shelves, humming to himself again.

With a sigh, Jenna pulled over one of the records of harvest celebrations and began reading. Hours passed. Rosaline came to check on her following the midday meal, and Ingrid came to bring her a drink of ale, but Jenna barely looked up from her reading.

The news that Arran had brought back with him only made it even more imperative that she finish her task here and get home. She wasn't cut out for this time, with its dangers and uncertainty. And now she'd become a target for the raiders? She shuddered. She'd never been threatened with violence in her life unless you included fights in the school playground. But she had no illusions as to what the raiders would do if they got their hands on her, and it left her feeling unsettled and vulnerable.

I will keep ye safe, Arran had said.

Her thoughts drifted to the golden-haired laird. They did that a lot. No matter how hard she tried to concentrate on what she was doing, thoughts of him kept popping into her head with alarming regularity.

Annoyed with herself, she tossed the book aside and plonked her chin on her hand, scowling. Outside, the sun was setting, turning the sky into a sea of gold and crimson streaks and sending dazzling beams of light through the windows. They lit a patch on the desk in front of her in which the scroll that Brother Merrick had placed was sitting.

Hooking it with a finger, she dragged it over, unrolled it a little, and leaned her elbows on it to keep it flat as she read. Hmm. It was nothing important, just a dull land grant like Merrick had said. She was just about to roll it up and toss it onto the ever-growing pile of discards when something at the bottom caught her eye. Looking closer, she saw that it was an ink drawing of the four compass points—the kind that you would find at the top of a map.

Intrigued, she unrolled the scroll the rest of the way and discovered that it was much bigger than she'd originally thought. Although the top half of the scroll contained the legal jargon about granting land rights and blah blah blah, the bottom half contained a map of the whole island. Jenna rolled out its full length across the desk—using books to weigh down each corner—and then peered closely at the ink-drawn map.

Towards the top of the island, the area of land contained in the grant was clearly marked—but that was not the only thing. Dun Tabor was labeled as well, as were other settlements, most of which she'd never heard of. Then, at certain points around the coastline, she noticed that smaller compass-like symbols had been drawn, each bearing a single-word label. Clach.

She felt a shiver of excitement. "Merrick! Can you come take a look at this?"

The monk appeared from among the shelves. "Aye?"

Jenna pointed at the symbols etched around the edge of the map. "Can you read this word? I just want to check that it says what I think it says."

Merrick leaned over the map, squinting in the fading light. "Aye. It's the same word for each of those symbols dotted around the coast. Clach. It means stone."

A sudden rush of triumph went through Jenna. With a jubilant cry, she grabbed Merrick and planted a noisy kiss on his cheek. "Ha! You did it!"

The monk's cheeks flushed scarlet. "I did?"

"You bet you did! It was in that land grant all along and you found it! This might be the very thing that helps me stop those raiders!"

"Well," the old man said, a delighted grin spreading across his face. "Who says old records are dull, eh?"

ARRAN HOBBLED UP the path, doing his best to bear Rhodry's weight. The man's arm was slung across Arran's shoulder, Arran's free arm was around his waist, but even so, Arran staggered under the burden.

"Not much farther," Arran muttered. "Ye are gonna be just fine."

Rhodry groaned, his head lolling on his neck, his feet scrabbling at the dirt as he tried and failed to take his own weight.

"It… bloody… hurts," he wheezed, a line of bloody drool hanging from his lips. "But I… got the bastard… eh?"

"Aye," Arran agreed. "Ye got the bastard."

In doing so, Rhodry had taken a sword thrust to the gut. The wound had been packed and bandaged as best Arran was able for the ride home, but it had been touch and go whether Rhodry would make it back at all. Arran had seen such wounds before. If the sword thrust had missed any of Rhodry's internal organs, then he had a chance. If it hadn't and he was bleeding internally… well, there would be only one outcome of that.

Arran's stomach clenched with angry frustration. Rhodry had been one of his father's men and had been a rock of stalwart support once the leadership had fallen to Arran. Without him and his sensible advice, he would have made far more mistakes than he had and the clan would have been in even worse straits than they were. Now, it seemed, the clan was going to lose one of its most experienced and valued warriors, and all because of those thrice-cursed raiders.

Dun Tabor's three healers—Martha, Evangaline and Bethan—were waiting at the door to the infirmary, holding it open as Arran helped Rhodry inside, followed by the rest of the wounded that had made it back from Tollman's Gate. In truth, he should be pleased. Their casualties were far fewer than they had any right to expect, and they'd driven off the raiders. Arran would have liked to take some of them prisoner, but they fought so ferociously that Arran's men had been forced to kill or be killed. What kind of zeal drove a man to face death rather than be captured?

Njord sends his regards and thanks you for keeping his islands warm for him.

Who was this Njord? A Norse lord? Some Norwegian or Danish chieftain who coveted Skye for himself? If so, he would not be the first, but Arran was determined that he would bloody-well be the last.

He helped Rhodry onto one of the many beds inside the infirmary, all filled now that Arran and his warriors had returned from Tollman's Gate. He stepped back as the healers fussed around Rhodry, unwinding the bandage to get a look at the wound. Arran looked away. He had no desire to see the damage the raider's sword had done to his friend. He looked around at the beds full of his warriors, some groaning, some unconscious, some thrashing and shouting with pain as the healers tried to work on them.

Impotent rage churned in his belly like acid. These were his men, his people. They followed him with a loyalty that left him humbled. But what had he led them to so far? To pain and death and a home that seemed to be in terminal decline.

He felt a hand touch his arm and turned to see Sister Evangaline looking up at him. She was dressed in a nun's habit, as she always was, even though she'd left the convent of Saint Maria's on the mainland many years ago to return to her ancestral home on Skye. She was elderly now, but vigorous all the same, and along with Martha and Bethan, was one of the best healers in all of Alba. Arran was lucky to have them.

"Leave them to us, my laird," she said in her soft voice. "Go get some rest. There is no more than ye can do here."

Arran nodded at Rhodry who was swearing loudly enough to turn the air blue as one of the healers cleaned his wound. "Will he be all right?"

"It is in God's hands now," Sister Evangaline said. "We will do all we can for him, but whether he lives or dies is for the Lord to decide." She squeezed his arm and moved off to tend one of her patients.

Arran sighed and scrubbed a hand through his hair. Lord above, he was tired. Every one of his muscles felt like it was made of iron and it took all of his willpower to walk to the door, pull it open, and step outside. He leaned against the wall, pulling in a deep breath of the evening air.

The sun was setting, and the air was still and redolent with the scent of spring flowers. The herb garden where the healers grew medicinal plants to use in their cures was filled with the heavy drone of bumblebees as they went from flower to flower collecting nectar. It was a peaceful scene, ruined only by the sudden scream of pain from one of his men inside. His eyes slid closed. Gods, he needed sleep.

"Arran!"

His eyes snapped open, and he saw Jenna hurrying down the path towards him. At the sight of her, some of his exhaustion fell away and he walked to meet her, hoping to shield her from the sights inside the infirmary.

"Jenna. What are ye doing here?"

"Looking for you. Mal said you'd returned." She looked him up and down and her bright green eyes, he noticed, held an odd shimmering cast like sunlight through new leaves. "Are you all right?"

"Fine."

A strange tingle went along his skin as she studied him, and that odd shimmer in her eyes intensified. "You are *not* all right," she said. "You have a cracked rib and lots of bruising."

Arran started as he realized she'd been using her magic on him. He shifted uncomfortably. He wasn't entirely sure he liked it.

"Come, lass," he said. "Let's get back to the keep."

"Mal said your injured were being brought here."

"That's right. This is the infirmary. The healers are working on the wounded as we speak."

"Good. Take me to them."

"What?"

She frowned. "I didn't detect anything wrong with your hearing when I scanned you just now. Take me to the injured men. I'll do what I can for them."

Her words seemed to take an age to work their way through his muddy thoughts. "Ye are a healer?"

She rolled her eyes, then barged past him towards the infirmary door. "I'm a MacFinnan spellweaver, in case you've forgotten!"

Before he could stop her, she pushed the heavy door open and entered. He caught up with her just as she juddered to a halt a few steps beyond the threshold and stared around her. Her eyes widened, the blood draining from her face. Arran could hardly blame her. The place stank of blood and misery.

Squaring her shoulders, she asked, "Who is the most seriously injured?"

"That would be Rhodry," said Sister Evangaline, wiping bloodied hands on a cloth as she walked towards them.

The nun looked Jenna up and down, her lips pursed slightly in disapproval. She was a Christian and as such, many of the old ways that the islanders adhered to were difficult for her to accept. Yet she was an islander herself and so had a foot a little in both camps.

"Ye must be the spellweaver I've heard so much about."

"I am," Jenna said, lifting her chin. "I'm here to help."

Sister Evangaline sighed, her shoulders sagging. "And we would be grateful for any help ye could give, my dear. Come."

Arran followed as the sister led Jenna over to Rhodry's bed. The big man was no longer swearing. In fact, he was no longer doing much of anything. Barely conscious, his eyelids flickered as though he was dreaming and a thick sheen of sweat stood out on his brow. A fresh bandage had been wound around his middle, but Arran could see ruby stains beginning to seep through it.

Jenna pulled over a wooden stool and sat by Rhodry's side. "Shit," she said. "It's been a long time since I've done this, and I always had my mother and aunts to help. I hope I can remember what to do."

She reached out to hover her hand over Rhodry's bandage and closed her eyes. Her lips began moving although Arran could hear no words. A faint tingle walked across his skin, which he now recognized as the touch of Jenna's magic. He shared a look with Sister Evangaline, but neither spoke as Jenna worked. Her brow furrowed and something like pain flashed across her features. Beads of perspiration appeared on her forehead, which she dashed away irritably with her free hand.

Rhodry suddenly began tossing and turning, limbs flailing to and fro, although he didn't wake.

"Hold him down!" Jenna hissed through clenched teeth. "I don't much fancy a whack in the mouth!"

Arran hurried to grab Rhodry's arms while Sister Evangaline leaned her weight on his ankles, pinning them to the bed. Rhodry was a strong bastard, and it took all of Arran's strength to hold him still while Jenna worked.

"Ye better hurry, lass," he murmured as the unconscious Rhodry fought his grip. "Or I think the lot of us are going to get a whack in the mouth."

A long sigh escaped Jenna's lips, and she suddenly slumped forward, her hand dropping to her side. At the same time, Rhodry went as limp as a boned fish and his breathing turned deep and steady. His eyelids no longer flickered and to Arran's untrained eye there seemed to be more color in his cheeks. He released his grip on Rhodry and knelt by Jenna's side.

"Are ye all right, lass?"

She pushed back her hair and gave a weak nod. "He had a laceration to his spleen. I've repaired it, but he'll have to do the rest himself. As long as he doesn't get an infection, he should be fine now. Use honey to keep his wound clean."

Arran stared at her, lost for words. All the stories he'd heard of the MacFinnan spellweavers suddenly paled in comparison to the woman seated in front of him. She was sweaty, pale, and looked utterly exhausted, not at all like the all-powerful images the stories had painted of the spellweavers. Yet she was so much more than any of those figures in the stories.

Jenna looked up at Sister Evangaline. "Who's next?"

The nun seemed to be struggling to form words as much as Arran was. "Thomas has arrow wounds to his back. This way."

Jenna climbed wearily to her feet and followed the sister to the next bed. Arran rose and looked down at Rhodry. Was it only moments ago that he'd been on the verge of mourning his old friend? Was it only hours ago that he'd been riding home from the skirmish with a trail of wounded and despair in his heart? Now he felt a different sensation, one lighter and warmer. It took a moment for him to recognize what it was.

Hope.

His eyes tracked Jenna as she knelt next to Thomas's bed. The young lad, no more than sixteen, was lying on his stomach with several raw puncture wounds in his back. One of them was leaking a clear fluid and seemed to have punctured his lung. The lad's breathing rattled and rasped like that of an old man, but he was aware enough to respond to Jenna's questions as she quietly spoke to him. She closed her eyes and went to work just as she had with Rhodry.

After several moments, the clear liquid stopped oozing from the wound and Thomas's breathing lost its death-rattle. The lad burst into tears and grasped Jenna's hand, whispering words of thanks in a sob-choked voice. Arran's heart clenched at the sight. Thomas had been so brave in the face of the raiders and his own death, but now, having been given a second chance at living, all that terror and relief came pouring out of him.

Arran squeezed his shoulder. "It's all right, lad. It's all right."

For the next three hours, Arran helped Jenna as she tended to the wounded warriors. She burned away infections, stopped internal bleeding, dampened pain while the healers set broken bones. Arran helped where he could, holding people down, passing clean bandages, washing out wounds. By the time the last casualty had been tended, they had both missed the evening meal and Arran was about ready to drop from exhaustion.

Jenna was even worse. Using her magic clearly took a toll on her and as she rose from the final patient's bedside, she looked haggard. Her legs shook as she tried to stand and she would have fallen had Arran not supported her.

"Come, lass," he muttered. "Time for sleep."

He took her weight as they made their way from the infirmary and back into the main keep. One of the healers had wrapped his chest in tight bandages, but the pain from his cracked rib was still enough to make him gasp with each step. Rosaline and Ingrid came to meet them at the doors, enquiring after Jenna's welfare and the rumors they'd heard of what was happening at the infirmary. Arran waved away their questions and helped Jenna up the stairs to her chamber.

She sank down onto the bed with a grateful sigh. "I don't know about you, but I'm knackered," she said with a wry smile. "I haven't done that much healing in years. Wasn't sure I still had it in me to be honest."

Arran shook his head. "I've never seen aught like it. Ye do realize that when word of this gets out, ye will have a line of patients a mile long?"

Jenna groaned. "Don't joke about it. I'd forgotten how exhausting it is. I think I might sleep for a fortnight."

"And ye would be within yer rights to do so, lass. I didnae know the MacFinnan magic could heal like that."

Jenna shrugged. "It's what I was trained for. I used to help my mother when I was younger. But it's not infallible. It can't heal everything." Her expression clouded, an old pain flashing in her eyes. "I haven't used it in a long time."

"Why not?" he asked softly.

Jenna's gaze met his eyes and that old pain shone clear and bright within hers. "In my time, we have medicine that can heal better than the magic can. And besides, it failed me when I needed it the most."

She looked down, fiddling with her hands in her lap. Arran wanted to ask her what she meant, but sensed she did not want to talk about it.

"I'll leave ye to sleep and I'll ask Ingrid not to wake ye till late tomorrow. I think it safe to say ye've earned a bit of rest."

"Wait!" She caught his wrist. "I need to show you something. That's why I came to look for you earlier." She stuck her arm up her sleeve and pulled out a parchment.

He unrolled it and held it close to his face to make out the words in the candlelight. "It's just a land grant."

"That's what I thought at first, but look at the bottom."

"It's a map of the island showing the area of land bestowed in the grant. What of it?"

"Look more closely!" Jenna said, her exhaustion seeming to fall away as she broke into an excited grin. "You see those symbols marked around the coast? Those are the anchor stones; I'm sure of it!"

Now that he examined it more closely, he saw that Jenna was

right. Each of those symbols was marked by the word clach, which meant stone. Could she be right? Could this have been what they had been searching for? He traced his finger from Dun Tabor to the nearest stone.

"That's only a few miles south of here," he said, looking at Jenna.

"I know," she said, practically bouncing on the edge of the bed. "We need to go there as soon as possible."

"And we will. Tomorrow. I dinna think I'm the only one who is likely to collapse if he doesnae get some sleep soon. Rest, lass. We'll go in the morning."

Jenna nodded, then flopped back onto the bed, limbs spread-eagled and hair spread around her head like a halo. "First thing though, right? I don't want to waste any time. I guess I'm not gonna get that fortnight of sleep after all. No rest for the wicked, eh?"

"Nay, lass," he agreed with a smile. "No rest for the wicked. Sleep well, lass. I'll see ye in the morning."

She raised her head and looked at him. "Good night, Arran."

The sight of her like that on the bed, with her tousled hair spread across the pillow, sent an ache of desire through him. Before he could do or say something stupid, he walked to the door and yanked it open.

"Good night, Jenna."

With that, he hurried down the corridor towards his own rooms, deciding that it would probably be a good idea to dunk his head in cold water before he went to bed.

Chapter Twelve

J ENNA YAWNED WIDE enough to crack her jaw and loud enough to send a flock of crows winging into the air in fright. Some of Arran's men, riding around them in a tight formation, glanced at her in alarm.

"Sorry," she said with a sheepish smile.

She had slept like a stone after Arran had left her last night, not waking until Ingrid came in this morning with her breakfast. Yet she was still exhausted. Her eyes felt grainy, her thoughts thick and sludgy, and her limbs ached as though she'd gone ten rounds with a heavyweight.

"My," Arran said from where he sat in the saddle behind her. "Anyone would think we've dragged ye out of bed in the middle of the night."

Jenna looked around at the landscape that was slowly rolling past. The sea lay straight ahead, a smooth, dark sheet that stretched to the horizon, with the just the faintest blush of dawn turning its edges pink.

"Arran," she said drily, twisting in the saddle to look at him. "This *is* the middle of the night. Humans are not supposed to be up before dawn, and you'll never convince me otherwise."

He laughed softly and the sound lit a little warm glow in her belly. She liked it when he laughed. "Then I willnae try. But if ye remember, *ye* were the one who wanted to set out at first light.

Ye were quite insistent about it, as I recall."

Jenna harrumphed. "Yeah, seemed a good idea at the time. Now? Not so much. How long until we get there?"

Arran dropped the reins, leaving Bran to plod along docilely with the other horses, and unrolled the map Jenna and Merrick had found yesterday. "It's just a few more miles along the coast. We should be there within the hour."

Within the hour. A tremor ran through her, and Jenna couldn't decide whether it was excitement or trepidation or a bit of both. In under an hour, they would reach the first of the anchor stones used to place Skye's magic. When they did, Jenna would repair it, restore the magical barrier that protected Skye and its people from raiders, and Arran would pay her the agreed fee.

She could be home by lunchtime. She could have paid off her debts by this afternoon. She could be curled up on her sofa watching a trashy movie and demolishing a family-sized tub of ice cream by this evening! Hallelujah!

And yet, she didn't feel *quite* as relieved by this as she expected. Sure, she would be going home to her normal life, but that meant returning to that sinking feeling in her stomach when she woke every morning and that horrible hollow feeling when she returned home to an empty house each evening. She hadn't felt like that since she'd come here to Skye. It was, she had to admit, in large part because she was kept so busy and was so bewildered half the time that she didn't have time to think about anything else.

But, she also had to admit, it was also in large part due to the man seated behind her right now.

She could feel the warmth of him against her back, even though she did her best to keep space between them. Every now and then, if Bran stumbled on a rock or picked up speed, she would find herself pushed back against Arran and she found she liked it. A lot. Why was that? Why was she having confusing feelings about a man she barely knew, and who was from another time?

You're just confused, she told herself. *You're just on the rebound after Alex. That's all this is. There's nothing more to it.*

Jenna spotted Mal up ahead, riding back towards them. Arran pulled Bran to a halt and waited for his cousin.

"It's just over the rise," Mal reported. "Right on the shore. It's lucky we came now, as it will be submerged at high tide."

"Any sign of enemies?"

Mal shook his head, his blond braids whipping. "I've sent scouts north and south along the coast and a couple are posted up on Carrick's Rise behind us to keep an eye on the sea. If anyone tries to take us by surprise, we'll know about it long before they get here."

Since the attack yesterday, and discovering that the raiders knew about her, Arran had been taking Jenna's safety *very* seriously. A little *too* seriously, in Jenna's opinion. He'd given four of his men the sole duty of guarding her. They followed her everywhere she went, even inside Dun Tabor itself, and she was pretty sure they would even have come into the privy with her had she not slammed the door in their faces and told them to wait outside.

Arran had brought thirty of his men this morning and they surrounded her and Arran like an iron fist, each one of them grim, with hands never far from their weapons. It was overkill, surely? As far as they knew, the raiders didn't know what she looked like, but if Arran wanted to advertise to all and sundry who she was, having her surrounded by thirty of the laird's best warriors was a sure way to do it! Not that Arran would listen to this argument, mind you. The man was as stubborn as a mule.

They carried on riding and the rocky trail they had been following reached the brow of a rise and then began to angle sharply down towards the sea. The sun was fully up now, hanging just above the horizon, a blazing yellow ball that turned the sea to polished amber and promised a sultry day ahead. There was hardly any wind and so the sea was still and calm, with only the soft sound of breakers on the shore to interrupt the silence.

It was a beautiful morning and at any other time Jenna might have stopped to appreciate it. But now she felt her stomach squirming with nerves. The moment they had topped the rise, she had felt the presence of the anchor stone. It pulled on her senses like a magnet, sending a faint tingle across her skin. It might be weak and fading now, but she sensed that the magic the anchor stone had once held had been immense.

"Wait here," Arran commanded his men. "Keep a watch on the approaches from all directions and sound the alarm if ye see anything untoward."

"Aye," Mal replied. "Dinna worry, cousin. We willnae be caught unawares."

While the men spread out in a cordon fifty feet back from the shore, Arran guided Bran farther down the trail and pulled him to a halt right on the edge of the water. There was only a thin beach to speak of, full of sea-rounded pebbles and driftwood brought in by the tide, and the rest of the shoreline was made up of shelves of rock and boulders, pitted with hollows and depressions that formed rock pools at low tide.

Arran swung from the saddle and then helped Jenna down. She suppressed a wince as she landed on her aching feet. First thing she was going to do when she got home was book herself a massage. In fact, she might go the whole hog and treat herself to a spa day. Manicure. Pedicure. Perhaps even a new hairdo. Heaven.

"The stone is just there, lass," Arran said, raising his finger and pointing at a single standing stone that rose out of the shingle and driftwood on the beach.

"I know," she replied. "I can feel it. Stay here. I'll go alone."

Arran nodded tightly. "As ye wish. Call me if ye need aught."

Jenna took a deep breath, gave Arran a shaky smile, and began picking her way through the boulders and rock pools. The standing stone dominated her vision. Its sides, submerged during high tide, glistened darkly. She didn't know what stone it was made from, but it was so dark as to be almost black and seemed to suck all the light into itself.

As she reached it, she saw markings were carved into its weathered face, words in a language she couldn't read, and swirling symbols that she didn't recognize.

"There you are," she said to it. "Let's have a look at you."

Folding onto her knees on the damp pebbles, she examined the stone. With its regular submerging in the salty water with the incoming tide, it ought to be more weathered than it was. Its sides, though, were smooth and shiny, marked only by the carvings that had been cut into it.

"So my ancestors made you, eh?" she said. "How did they do it, I wonder?"

Jenna closed her eyes and took slow, steady breaths. This close, she could feel the energy of the stone pulsing through her like a second heartbeat, slow and ancient. She had felt things like this before in the twenty-first century, in stone circles or fairy glades—fading remnants of a once-powerful magic that clung on stubbornly despite being long forgotten by those whose ancestors had once lived by it.

Hesitantly, she reached out a hand and placed her palm flat against the stone. To her surprise, it felt slightly warm and her skin tingled slightly. The energies in the stone shifted, seeming to concentrate on her hand, as though they were aware of her presence.

Do you recognize me? she thought. *I'm a MacFinnan, just like those who made you. What do I need to do to fix you? Tell me.*

Opening herself up to her own magic, she sent her awareness spiraling into the stone. At once, she became aware of the web of magic she'd first encountered at Bail Nan Cnoc. It appeared in her mind's eye like a golden net spreading out across Skye, shimmering like ropes of flame. She saw the dark spots too where the net was broken, but here, anchored as she was by the stone, she was in no danger of losing herself as she had before.

Three lines of power converged on the anchor stone, two that stretched out along the coast in both directions, and one that went inland, towards the nexus at Bail Nan Cnoc. All three lines of power were weak, but not broken, and Jenna was pretty sure that if she first strengthened the magic that emanated from the stone to the level it should be, she could work her way out from there, repairing the whole web.

Not for the first time, she wished that her aunts were here. She guessed that in the distant past the MacFinnan spellweavers had not worked alone. In fact, there had probably been a whole group of them, aided and supported by others who lent their strength.

But Jenna was alone. She was all this place had. She had better be up to the job.

"Right," she said aloud, shaking herself down and trying to loosen any tension in her body. "Here goes nothing."

Slowly, she began feeding magic into the anchor stone. To her delight, it responded immediately, like a man dying of thirst suddenly offered water. It drank the magic; the symbols etched into its surface began to glow, and in her mind's eye, the three lines of power anchored to it began to shine white-hot.

Bit by bit, Jenna began to push the magic farther out, towards the other anchor stones in the net, strengthening and brightening the lines of power that radiated from them one by one. Finally, she reached one of the dark spots in the net and paused. Here there was no magic left to work with, only the dark void in which she'd nearly lost herself the other day, so merely trying to strengthen it wouldn't work. She would have to build a bridge across it somehow.

Teasing at the magic at the edges of the void, where it was shorn away as if sliced by a knife, Jenna began gently coaxing it out, like pulling out the threads of some garment. When the threads of magic came free, she channeled her energy into them, and slowly, slowly, they began to grow. It was slow going. Jenna could feel her strength beginning to ebb as the tendrils of golden magic began to slowly inch their way across the gap, like the roots of some thirsty plant reaching down through the soil looking for water.

She began to feel lightheaded, and the back of her throat was raw and parched. Wiping her forehead with the back of her hand, she gritted her teeth and pushed on. Had she called Arran MacLeod stubborn? Well, that was nothing compared to the stubbornness of a MacFinnan. She would *not* be beaten. She *would* complete the patch, damn it!

Inch by inch, the tendrils of magic grew across the gap. Jenna's arm began to shake, and her lungs burned as though she'd run a 5K. Still, she didn't let up. The tendrils had almost reached the far side now. Just a little more. Just one final push...

With a cry, she poured the last of her strength into the magic and the tendrils finally reached the far side of the hole, where they meshed with those already there, forming a patch over the gap in the net.

Triumph washed through Jenna. Yes! She'd done it! Who said she needed her aunts' help? Who said she wasn't strong enough for this? Ha! She was a MacFinnan spellweaver and she could do anything! She could—

With a silent concussion that sent a shockwave right through the island's bones, Jenna's repair suddenly snapped. Like an elastic band pulled too tight, it rebounded back towards its maker. Power struck Jenna in the chest with the force of a mule-kick, and she was suddenly flying through the air. She didn't even have time to scream before she slammed into a pile of driftwood and lay there stunned, staring up at the cloudless blue sky.

"Jenna!"

She heard her name shouted but it sounded far away, faint and distant. Blackness filled her vision and suddenly she was falling, falling, falling—until something caught her. Strong arms grabbed her shoulders, tilted her up, and her vision cleared. She blinked and saw a figure above her, blocking out the sky. It took a moment for her to recognize Arran's concerned face. He was kneeling beside her, one of his warm hands around her upper arm, while the other cupped her face.

"Jenna?" he said hoarsely. "Are ye all right?"

Gingerly, Jenna scanned her body, testing for injuries. She found nothing worse than a few bruises although she'd whacked her head when she landed and she suspected she'd have a lump the size of a duck egg come the morning. But it could have been worse. The driftwood she'd landed on had been half rotten and had crumpled under her weight, taking the sting out of her landing. She supposed she should be grateful, but all Jenna felt was annoyance.

Damn it! What had gone wrong? She didn't have to be touching the anchor stone to know that the lattice of magic that covered Skye had once again reverted to its shriveled state. She could feel it with every fiber of her being.

"Lass?" Arran said. "Did ye hear me? Are ye well?" His blue eyes were intense as he stared at her, his brow furrowed with concern.

"I'm fine," she croaked, struggling into a sitting position. A wave of dizziness swamped her, and she grabbed Arran's arm to steady herself. It felt as strong and reassuring as an oak tree.

"Ye dinna look fine. What happened? When ye were thrown across the beach like that I thought—" He swallowed before continuing. "Well, I feared the worst."

"Don't worry about me," Jenna said, waving a dismissive hand. "We MacFinnans are made of strong stuff. It will take more than a little tumble to do me any harm. But the magic?" She snorted, shaking her head. "That's another story."

"Yer plan didnae work?"

Jenna turned to glare at the anchor stone. The tide had turned and already the bottom part of the stone was submerged beneath frothing waves.

What happened? she asked it. *What did I do wrong?* The stone stared at her, impervious to her questions.

She sighed and looked at Arran. "No, it didn't work. *This* time. But I *will* figure it out."

"I've no doubt ye will," Arran said gently. "But not today.

The tide is coming in and I willnae have ye risk further injury."

"But—"

"No buts, Jenna. Ye have a lump on yer head the size of a plum, did ye know that? I want Martha to take a look at ye. I willnae have my spellweaver take unnecessary risks just because she's stubborn and doesnae know when to call it a day."

"I am not stubborn!" Jenna said, crossing her arms and frowning at him. But, she had to admit, she was starting to get a headache and her bruises were also starting to make themselves known. Arran said nothing, merely watched her with one eyebrow raised. "Fine!" she cried, throwing up her hands.

"Good." Arran rose smoothly to his feet then held out a hand to help her up. Jenna took it, stumbling a little as she rose. Arran steadied her and the two of them began walking back up the beach to where they'd left the horses.

As she passed, Jenna shot an annoyed glare at the anchor stone, as though it was the cause of all her woes. So much for being home by lunchtime! So much for the trashy movie and the tub of ice cream! She was going to have to spend another night in this century, with all the danger of craziness that brought.

But, she thought, as she leaned heavily on Arran, feeling the reassuring solidity of him, perhaps that wouldn't be so bad after all.

Jenna didn't know what had gone wrong with the magic of the anchor stone. But one thing she *did* know.

She would figure it out if it was the last thing she did.

Chapter Thirteen

THE NIGHT WAS unseasonably warm as Arran paced. The air was still and the heat of the day lingered, even though the sun had long since disappeared and night had enveloped Skye. Up here on the battlements of Dun Tabor there was normally a breeze—and in the winter a howling gale that froze your stones if you weren't careful—but tonight even here he could not escape the heat. It was barely May and yet it felt like midsummer. Just another indication that all was not well with his homeland.

Glancing at the position of the stars, he guessed it was somewhere in the small hours of the night. Around him, Dun Tabor was sleeping, with only the guards who kept constant watch over the castle still awake and vigilant. Unable to sleep himself, Arran had risen from his bed and joined them. It had become his habit of late, and these days he was pretty sure he spent as much time walking the battlements as his guards did.

He paused and rested his hands on the rough stone of the wall, gazing out into the darkness. There was little to see except a few candles burning in the village windows and the quick outline of a fox as it darted through the shadows.

He sighed, thumping his fist against the hard stone, thinking over the events of the day. He had hoped Jenna would fix the magic today. She had seemed so confident that he'd gone along with her, allowing himself to hope, even though he suspected in his heart that it wouldn't be as simple as she seemed to think.

He had seen what Jenna was capable of when she'd healed all those people in the infirmary, but he could not deny the sinking sense of disappointment he felt when things hadn't gone to plan. And yet, that sense of disappointment paled in comparison to the fear that had washed through him when she'd been tossed across the beach like a piece of flotsam.

After her faint at Bail Nan Cnoc and then learning that the raiders knew of her existence, Arran had been very careful in ensuring her safety. Jenna herself, though, didn't seem to share his concern, and she was more than cavalier with her own wellbeing, taking risks and pushing herself beyond what was reasonable.

He wished she would be more careful. The last thing he wanted to do was lose his spellweaver. No, not his spellweaver. Jenna. He didn't want to lose Jenna.

It made no sense to him, the way this strange woman from the future stirred such feelings in him. She was here to do a job and when that job was done, she would be gone. Their arrangement was a simple business transaction, so why did he find himself looking for her whenever he entered a room and longing to hear her voice when she wasn't around?

He scrubbed a hand through his hair, his thoughts and feelings tangling into a knot he struggled to unpick. No wonder he couldn't sleep. How could any man be expected to sleep when they were ensnared in the knot of conflicting emotions in which he found himself?

It would be best if he stayed away from the lass. Mal could easily deputize for him. Aye. That's what he would do. Come the morning he would ride out on patrol and put some distance between himself and Jenna MacFinnan. Maybe that would help to calm the turmoil she caused whenever she was near.

He turned to head down the steps but paused as movement by the gate caught his eye. Squinting, he leaned on the wall to get a better view. A figure was walking along the edge of the courtyard towards the gates, keeping to the shadows.

The hairs on the back of Arran's neck rose. An intruder! He opened his mouth to bellow a warning, but as the figure darted through a patch of torchlight, the words died in his throat.

It was Jenna.

She paused, glanced around, and then hurried towards the two guards standing on duty in front of the gate. Arran watched, perplexed. What was she doing? Why was she sneaking around the castle at this time of night?

Fully expecting the guards on the gate to stop her, Arran's mouth dropped open when she walked between them without them so much as glancing in her direction. What the—? He watched in dumbfounded disbelief as she opened the small postern gate set into the larger gate and let herself out, closing it quietly behind her.

The guards never even so much as moved.

With a snarl, Arran tore down the steps, taking them two at a time, and sprinted across the courtyard. Spotting him barreling towards them, the guards snapped to attention.

"My laird!"

"What the hell was that?" Arran snapped. "Why didnae ye stop her?"

The men glanced at each other. "Stop who, my laird?"

"The spellweaver! She just walked right past ye!"

The guards' faces paled. "But… we didnae see anyone, my laird."

Arran let out a string of curses. Damn the woman! Was she trying to get herself killed? Clearly she'd used her magic on the guards. What was she up to now? He'd wring her neck when he got his hands on her!

"Stand aside!" he snapped, pushing past the guards. He grabbed the handle of the postern gate and yanked it open.

"My laird!" one the guards cried. "Wait and we'll form a company to accompany ye!"

"No," he replied. "Go back to yer posts. I willnae be long."

Before they could reply, he pulled the gate shut behind him and stepped out onto the road. There was no moon and the darkness was almost absolute, with only the faint starlight to light the night. He paused, letting his eyes adjust, and the outline of the village and landscape beyond slowly came into view.

There was no sign of Jenna.

Biting back a curse, he knelt and examined the mud. It did not take long to find her footprints, but to his surprise they did not lead down the road but rather cut around the outside of the keep and turned across country—in the same direction in which the anchor stone lay.

She'd been withdrawn when they'd returned to Dun Tabor, and had spent the rest of the day sequestered in the library, studying the texts Merrick had dug out for her. She'd retired early from the evening meal, taking one of the books up to her room, saying she'd wanted to study it some more.

Had she really been hatching a plan to sneak out and return to the stone alone? What was she thinking? Had she not listened to a word he'd said to her? Did she not realize how dangerous it was to go wandering the wilds alone? Reckless, headstrong, stubborn woman!

He broke into a jog in the direction she'd taken, stopping every now and then to check he was still following her footprints. She couldn't have gotten far so that it wouldn't take long to catch up and when he did, he'd be giving her a piece of his mind she wouldn't forget in a hurry.

But Arran didn't catch her as quickly as he'd imagined. Even though she was traveling in the dark, through a landscape she was unused to, she seemed to be moving far more quickly than Arran would have expected, as though she knew exactly where she was headed and was sprinting for all she was worth. Was she using magic to aid her flight?

Arran didn't know but he *did* know that he had to find her and bring her back before some calamity befell her.

Yet try as he might, Arran was unable to gain on her. He ran as fast as he dared through the darkness, moving more quickly now that he was sure of her destination, but he caught no sign of her on the trail ahead. By the time he reached the rise that they'd climbed earlier, his lungs were on fire and sweat was pouring down his forehead, plastering his hair to the sides of his face. He staggered to the top of the rise above the beach and leaned on his knees, trying to catch his breath.

The tide was out and the anchor stone rose up from its spot on the beach like an accusing finger. Jenna was on her knees in front of it and her voice floated to him through the darkness. She seemed to be arguing with it.

"Look, if this is gonna work, I'm going to need your help. And it's no good staring at me like that, all moody and brooding, because I'm not going to fall for it. We both know you want me to fix you, so how about you give me a break, huh?"

Arran stepped forward and a piece of driftwood snapped beneath his boot.

Jenna spun around. "Who's there? Come out right now! I've got a gun and I'm not afraid to use it!"

She did *not* have a gun—muskets and wheellocks were a rarity in the Isles—but Arran had to admire her spirit. He walked towards her, holding his hands out to either side.

"It's me, lass."

Her eyes widened and damn him if he didn't feel an involuntary little clench in his gut. Relief flashed across her lovely features and for a fleeting instant she looked as pleased to see him as he was to see her.

"Arran! What are you doing here?"

"What am *I* doing here? What are *ye* doing here, woman? What in God's name possessed ye to come out here alone in the middle of the night? Have ye lost yer senses?"

"I haven't lost anything," she snapped back, that familiar look of defiance flashing across her features. "And I think it's pretty obvious why I've come out here, isn't it?" She gestured at the stone rising behind her as though he might have missed it.

Arran scowled, crossing his arms. "I seem to recall us having a conversation about the dangers of this place and I also seem to recall ye agreeing to not go anywhere without an escort. Or did I dream that?"

She flushed. "A conversation was it? It was more of a lecture from where I was standing! I remember you laying down the law and expecting me to go along with it!"

"Aye, I expect ye to go along with my orders when they are designed to keep ye safe!" What was wrong with her? Did she not realize what could have gone wrong? Anger flashed through him. "Dear God, woman! Do ye have any idea the danger ye have put yerself in?"

Her eyes flashed in the gloom. "I can take care of myself!"

Aye, maybe she could at that, but that didn't mean her safety was any less Arran's responsibility. That she would disregard it so readily made fury and fear course through his veins in equal measure.

He stepped closer until they were less than an arm's length apart. Jenna glared up at him, chin lifted, fists clenched, eyes flashing with defiance.

"While ye are a guest in my home," Arran said in a deathly quiet voice. "Ye will abide my rules. Is that clear?"

"And if I don't? What will you do, oh mighty caveman? Thow me over your shoulder and carry me away?"

God give him strength! He would like nothing more than to do that very thing.

"Dinna tempt me, woman," he growled. "I dinna know what ye mean by 'caveman' but throwing ye over my shoulder seems very appealing right now."

"Ha! I'd like to see you try!"

She pushed past him, but as she did so, Arran grabbed her arm, yanked her back towards him, and kissed her fiercely.

He didn't know how it happened. He hadn't meant to do it. He only knew that his blood was suddenly roaring, his skin was suddenly tingling, and he was powerless to do anything but kiss her, kiss her like his life depended on it.

For an instant, she went rigid, and he expected her to push him away, or slap him, or both. She did neither. After her initial moment of shock, she leaned against him, her arms went around his neck, and she kissed him back, just as passionately as he was kissing her.

Everything around Arran evaporated. He was no longer aware of the sea lapping at the shore just a few feet away, or the driftwood beneath his feet. He could no longer feel the breeze or hear the call of night birds. The only thing that existed was her.

He pressed his hands into the small of her back, pushing her against him. Heat raged through him, desire and longing, and a hundred other different emotions that he couldn't identify. Jenna filled his senses. All he could feel were her warm lips. All he could taste was her tongue as it danced with his own. All he could smell was the soft scent of her hair as it swirled around him.

But then a branch suddenly snapped behind them and they sprang apart as if stung. Arran whirled, drawing his claymore from across his back and gripping it two-handed as he crouched in front of Jenna, eyes scanning the darkness.

Two bright pinpoints of light regarded him from the shadows and it took a moment for him to realize they were eyes. The eyes blinked and then disappeared and he caught sight of a fox's bushy tail as it disappeared back into the night.

Arran let out a long breath and straightened, wiping his fore-head with the back of his hand.

"Naught to worry about. Just a fox."

Jenna swallowed thickly. "Right. Just a fox. Great."

She glanced up at him, biting her lip in a way that made him want to kiss her again. Hell, just the *sight* of her made him want to kiss her again and do much more besides. He wanted to lay her down in the sand and make her his. He wanted to hear her moaning his name.

But the moment had passed. Jenna wrapped her arms around herself and took a step back. Away from him. Her lips were swollen from their kiss and there was a faint blush to her cheeks, but she looked uncertain now, as if she couldn't believe what had just happened between them.

God help him, *he* couldn't believe what had just happened between them. Had he completely lost his mind? What had possessed him to kiss her? She was a MacFinnan spellweaver for pity's sake!

And yet… he couldn't bring himself to regret it. He would do it again if he could.

"I… um…" he stammered.

"We should be getting back," she said, cutting him off.

"Um. Aye. We should."

They climbed the trail up from the beach and began the trek back to Dun Tabor. Neither of them spoke. They walked for perhaps twenty minutes until the silence became too much for Arran to bear.

"Ye still havenae explained why ye came out here alone."

She opened her mouth for a retort but then her shoulders slumped and she let out a long sigh. "Isn't it obvious?"

"Nay, lass. It isnae."

She stared out into the darkness for a while. "Because I didn't want everyone to see me fail again," she replied at last. She looked over at him. "I didn't want *you* to see me fail again."

His breath hitched. He stopped, forcing her to do the same, and looked down at her. "Is that what this is about? Ye think ye have somehow failed?"

"Of course, I have! You were there; you saw what happened. I'm supposed to be this all-powerful spellweaver, aren't I? I'm supposed to know what to do. Half your people are terrified of me and the other half seem to think I'm some kind of messiah!" She wrung her hands. "I promised I would save Skye and so many people are depending on me. If I can't figure it out, what will happen to them? And if I can't fix it, I won't get paid, then I'll lose my house, and *he* will have won, and I'll have nothing!"

It was the most vulnerable he'd ever seen her. Gone was the

confident, headstrong spellweaver and in her place was just Jenna MacFinnan, a young woman tossed into a world not her own who was trying her best to make sense of it. She looked scared and lost and riddled with self-doubt. Arran's heart clenched at the sight. In that moment he ached to take her into his arms and tell her that everything was going to be all right.

But he didn't. Instead, he put his finger under her chin and lifted it until she was forced to meet his gaze.

"Listen to me. I dinna know what troubles ye face in yer own time but I know this: Jenna MacFinnan, ye are the most remarkable woman I have ever met. Ye are strong and brave and like a firebrand that's been tossed into our lives. I dinna think anyone on Skye has ever seen yer like nor will again. Ye shouldnae be surprised that half my people fear ye and the other half are in awe of ye. I often feel that way myself."

A faint smile curled her lips. "Ah, so you're not as stupid as you look then?"

"Aye, I'm every bit as stupid as I look, lass. I think I must be if I ever thought I could order a MacFinnan spellweaver around. I shouldnae have shouted, but I was afeared for ye. Regardless of what ye may think, yer safety is my responsibility now, and I swore I would let no harm come to ye. I will keep that promise, Jenna, if it's the last thing I do."

She gazed up at him and he could see starlight reflected in her emerald eyes. "And I didn't make that exactly easy for you by sneaking out, did I?"

"Nay, lass. Ye didnae. And there was no need to take such a risk in the first place because there isnae a single person on this island, me included, who thinks ye are a failure. The magic has been broken for many years. It's unreasonable to think it could be mended in a day." He placed his hands on her shoulders. "I've no doubt ye will succeed, lass. Lir wouldnae have sent me to ye otherwise. I trust her judgment, and I trust ye."

Tears gathered in the corners of Jenna's eyes, sparkling like diamonds. She dashed them away angrily. "I think I preferred it when you were shouting at me. Now I feel doubly bad for sneaking out. How about we forget tonight ever happened and go on as before, eh?"

There was one part of tonight that Arran most definitely did *not* want to forget. In fact, if he had his way, they would reenact that part many times over. But it seemed Jenna did not feel the same.

He had to force out words. "Aye. We'll forget it ever happened."

They set off once more, and neither spoke as they walked back to Dun Tabor, Jenna seemingly lost in thought, Arran spending his time scanning the darkness for danger.

Finally, the gates of Dun Tabor came into view and Arran found the walls ablaze with torches and guards on high alert along the battlements.

"Stand down," he shouted as he and Jenna reached the gates. "All is well."

His men were obviously full of questions, but were wise enough not to voice them.

Arran led the way back into the keep and escorted Jenna up to her room. She paused at the threshold and turned to face him. "I... I... thank you for coming to look for me. I can't remember the last time anyone was so concerned for my wellbeing—other than my aunts."

Arran forced himself to keep his arms by his sides, resisting the urge to run a thumb down her cheek. She was so close that all it would take would be the slightest movement, just a tiny step forward, and she could be in his arms. It took all of his willpower to remain where he was.

"Ye are welcome. Well, good night, lass."

"Good night, Arran."

He stared at her a moment longer, then turned and strode away.

Chapter Fourteen

Jenna awoke with a groan as sudden light flooded her room. She cracked her eyes open to see Ingrid yanking back the heavy drapes.

"Aargh!" Jenna cried, putting a pillow over her head. "Are you trying to kill me?"

Ingrid came to stand by her bed. "I'm ensuring ye get up at a decent hour," she replied, an amused tone to her voice. "Which is what ye asked me to do, if ye remember?"

Jenna pulled away the pillow and squinted up at the maid. "I did? Well please ignore me the next time I say something so idiotic."

"Oh dear," Ingrid said. "Ye sound a little grumpy this morning."

"Grumpy? I am *not* grumpy. Just… tired."

Ingrid busied herself tidying. "That's hardly surprising considering ye and the laird's… nocturnal activities."

Jenna bolted upright. "What do you mean by that?"

Ingrid shrugged nonchalantly but Jenna could tell the young woman was burning with curiosity. She could barely conceal the grin that kept trying to creep across her face.

Jenna scowled and crossed her arms. "Come on. Out with it."

Ingrid giggled. "Oh, all right. It's all over the castle anyway."

"What is?"

"Stories about how ye and laird Arran went out together in the middle of the night."

Jenna stifled a groan. Great. This was all she needed. It wasn't hard to figure out what conclusion the gossips had reached when the guards had seen her and Arran returning together in the small hours.

"It's not like that," Jenna protested. "We were just... working."

Her protests sounded feeble even to her own ears. Sure, the night had started with Jenna merely wanting to see the anchor stone and see if she could get the magic working. But the night had most definitely *not* ended that way.

Thoughts of the kiss she'd shared with Arran flashed through her mind and the heat in her cheeks only intensified. Oh, my. That kiss...

Even now, as she thought about it, as she thought about *him*, she felt her heartbeat quicken and her skin tingle. She'd never felt anything like it. In that instant on the beach she'd wanted him so badly that nothing, *nothing* else in the world had mattered.

And that terrified her.

She was here to do a job, get paid, and go home. Getting involved with the man who'd employed her was a bad idea. She couldn't afford to get distracted. And besides, hadn't she sworn off men? That she would never, ever, risk her heart again?

Risk your heart? she asked herself. *Don't be ridiculous. Your heart is the last thing that's involved in this. It's just lust. Nothing more. So forget it and get on with what you're being paid for.*

She swallowed, then looked at Ingrid. "Well, I'd be grateful if you could set the gossips straight. There is definitely nothing going on between me and Arran MacLeod."

Ingrid dipped her head. "As ye wish."

Jenna scowled. Why did she get the impression that Ingrid hadn't believed a word she'd said and that denying it would only incite the gossips even more? She threw back the covers and swung her legs out of bed in annoyance. "Have I missed breakfast?"

"No, my lady. It's being served in the great hall."

"Good. I'm starving."

She climbed out of bed, had a quick wash, and then allowed Ingrid to help her dress in a long yellow gown that matched the primroses that grew outside the castle walls. This done, Jenna made her way through the corridors to the great hall.

She thought through the events of last night. She had gone to the anchor stone alone in the hope of being able to connect with it somehow, to find a clue as to what she'd done wrong the first time. But as she'd examined the stone—and had a blazing row with it, truth be told—she'd discovered no hints as to what she needed to do to make the magic work.

But that didn't mean she was about to give up. She felt a renewed sense of purpose this morning.

I've no doubt ye will succeed, lass. Lir wouldnae have sent me to ye otherwise. I trust her judgment, and I trust ye.

A warm sensation lit in her stomach as she remembered the earnest look in Arran's eyes as he'd spoken those words to her. Arran was not a man to say things lightly and his belief in her was like a warm breeze that lifted her up, made her feel a little lighter. She couldn't remember when anyone other than her aunts had said anything like that to her. Certainly not Alex.

She would try again today. She would *succeed* today. Pulling the folded map from the pocket of her dress, she unfolded it and studied it as she walked down the stairs. Running her fingers along the ink that marked the coastline, she saw that there was another anchor stone slightly south of Dun Tabor. She bit her lip. Maybe that one would work...

"Good morning, Jenna."

She looked up to see Rosaline waiting for her by the door to the great hall. "Oh, morning! Sorry, I was miles away."

Rosaline glanced at the map. "So I see. Are ye joining us for breakfast?"

Jenna nodded and the two women opened the door only to

be met by a group of men coming the other way, Arran in the lead.

He froze as he spotted Jenna. "Er… Mother," he said, giving Rosaline a slight bow. "Jenna. Good morning."

Jenna's insides fluttered as his gaze landed on her. Unbidden, memories of last night's kiss flooded through her, and she had to swallow a few times before she could speak.

"Um. Good morning." She brandished the map at him. "Actually, I'm glad I caught you. I'd like to go to the second anchor stone today." She pointed at the mark on the map. "It's not far and with any luck, it might have more residual magic than the first one. What do you think?"

Arran glanced at the map then back at Jenna. Was she imagining it, or was there a slight blush to his cheeks?

"Aye, fine. Whatever ye wish. Mal will attend ye after ye have finished breakfast. He will escort ye wherever ye wish to go."

Mal? Eh? "But I thought we would—"

"Ye must excuse me," Arran cut in. "There are matters I have to attend to."

He gave Jenna and Rosaline another small bow and then hurried off with his men. Jenna watched him go with a sinking feeling in her stomach. They had agreed to pretend that last night never happened, and it seemed that Arran was determined to stick to that agreement. She knew it was for the best, but that didn't stop her feeling like she had a bowling ball sitting in her stomach.

"Jenna? Is everything all right?"

She blinked and, realizing she'd been staring after Arran, forced a smile as she looked at Rosaline. "Never better. Let's go get some breakfast, shall we?"

Yet even though she was hungry, Jenna found herself hardly eating a thing. Throughout breakfast she felt restless and out of sorts and kept catching herself glancing at the door, hoping that Arran would walk through it. He didn't.

Annoyed with herself for feeling this way, she was glad when

Mal strode in and came over to where she was sitting with Rosaline at the head table. He gave a slight nod in greeting, brushing back a blond braid. Even though they were cousins, Jenna could see little family resemblance between him and Arran. Their coloring was similar but Mal was bigger and blockier than his cousin, and seemed more inclined to smile than the laird.

He bestowed that smile on Jenna now. "Arran tells me ye wish to ride out today? Well, I've organized the men so if ye are ready, we can be on our way."

Jenna pushed away her half-finished bowl of porridge and stood. "I thought you'd never ask."

Outside, she found a guard of at least thirty men waiting in the courtyard with their horses. Jenna tried not to scowl as she looked them over. Thirty men? Really?

Mal led her over to a docile gray horse whose head was hanging down, half-asleep. "This is Misty. She's a gentle beast who we use for teaching youngsters to ride. Ye should be able to handle her."

A child's horse? Did they really think she was *that* useless?

At her stony silence, Mal cleared his throat. "Or, if ye prefer, ye can ride with me—"

"No, Misty will do just fine. Thanks." She most certainly did *not* want to share a saddle with Mal. He wasn't Arran, after all.

She thrust the map at Mal and pointed to the spot on the coast where the second anchor stone was marked. "That's where I'd like to go, please."

Mal took the map and nodded. "Aye. I know it."

"Right." She approached Misty cautiously, as though she was some wild stallion who might stomp her into mush. Misty raised her head and watched Jenna dolefully.

"Hello, girl," she muttered. "I don't like this any more than you do, but I'm sure we can be friends, huh?" As she'd seen Arran and the others do, she got her foot in the stirrup and then bounced a few times on her other foot to work up momentum before boosting herself into the saddle. It only partially worked and she ended up with her belly over the saddle and had to wriggle her way around to the proper position before pulling herself upright and taking the reins.

Mal and his men studiously looked away.

"Well?" she demanded. "What are we waiting for?"

It was a bright, still morning, with a warm sun beating down on the countryside and the sparkling blue ocean spreading out to the horizon. Jenna guessed it was the kind of day that horsey people the world over would love to spend out on a hack, enjoying the great outdoors, but to Jenna, the two-hour journey was nothing short of torture.

By the time Mal announced that they were nearing their destination, Jenna's backside was numb, her fingers hurt from clenching the reins in a death grip, and she felt like she was slowly being sawn in half. As Mal called a halt and Misty followed the lead of the other horses by plodding to a stop, Jenna swung her leg over the saddle and slid ungracefully to the ground where she landed in a heap among a pile of prickly heather.

Groaning, she sat up. People rode these things for *fun*? Were they out of their minds?

Rubbing her backside, she climbed gingerly to her feet and looked around. The thirty men that had accompanied her had spread out in a broad circle around her and Mal, and none of them had dismounted. They watched the landscape in every direction, their expressions hard, their gazes intense. She had no doubt that Arran had given them strict instructions to ensure her safety, and they were taking that duty *very* seriously.

Jenna pushed thoughts of Arran out of her mind and took a deep breath. She closed her eyes. Almost immediately, she felt the presence of the anchor stone somewhere nearby. Like the first one, it brushed against her senses like an electric current, pulling her towards the shoreline.

She opened her eyes and began walking. Mal strode by her side although he didn't speak. On this part of the island the coast was comprised not of pebbles or driftwood or even rock pools.

Instead, a craggy, pockmarked cliff descended almost straight down into the booming waves below. Hesitantly, Jenna edged her way to the cliff edge and looked down. A dizzying distance below her, waves pounded against a thin strip of blackened rocks that looked as if they had fallen from the cliff some time in the distant past. Froth and spray went shooting into the air every time the waves broke over the rocks, and the air was filled with the boom and thump of their impact.

It was not an inviting place.

"Is there any way down there?" she asked Mal.

The big man rubbed his chin as he peered over the cliff. "Aye, there's a trail of sorts that leads down to the cove. This area was used by smugglers back in the day. But it's steep and treacherous and I wouldnae recommend—"

"Let's go."

"It's not a climb for the faint-hearted, lass. Perhaps—"

"The second anchor stone is down there, and I need to find it. If smugglers can get down there, I'm sure I can."

Mal studied her dubiously. She could tell he wanted to refuse but had sense enough not to voice his doubts aloud. He sighed. "Fine. But I must insist ye are roped. Arran would flay me alive if aught should happen to ye."

"That makes two of us. I'll be careful, I promise."

In short order she had a rope tied around her middle which was anchored to a rock at the top of the cliff. Mal insisted on going down first, and she was to follow closely behind. This didn't seem like a good idea to Jenna seeing as if she fell, she'd likely take Mal with her, and he wasn't wearing a rope. Still, she didn't argue. She'd learned that these fifteenth century Highlanders would put bravery before common sense any day of the week.

To her immense relief, the trail didn't turn out to be as steep as she expected. Once she and Mal began their descent, she found that although it had been out of sight from the top, the trail that zigzagged down the face of the cliff was wider than her outstretched arms. The footing was sometimes treacherous, but there were thorny bushes she could grab to steady herself if needed.

Even so, she was mightily glad when they reached the rocky shore at the bottom and Mal untied the rope around her waist. Looking up, she felt a little giddy to realize how far they'd descended, and the cliff above seemed to blot out the sky. Down here, the roar of the surf was so loud she would have to shout if she wanted Mal to hear and they would be lucky if they didn't return to Dun Tabor spray-drenched and freezing.

She took a deep breath and tried to steady her breathing. The pull of the anchor stone was so strong she could feel it in her chest like a second heartbeat. It lay straight ahead somewhere, along the base of the cliff.

Signaling for Mal to follow, she began picking her way along the base of the cliff, over and around the huge boulders that littered the shoreline. She heard Mal curse in Gaelic as he followed.

More than once she cursed the ridiculous dress she was wearing. It kept snagging on sharp rocks and billowing out in the wind, threatening to tear her from her precarious perch. Give her a good old pair of jeans and some stout boots any day.

As she battled her way along the treacherous path, the pull of the anchor stone grew stronger and stronger. Yet, when she looked ahead, she could see no sign of it, just the rocky shore and the cliffs looming up on her right. But as she rounded a corner, she stopped dead, so quickly in fact, that Mal walked into the back of her.

To her right, the cliff rose up even higher than before, a craggy black monolith that seemed to suck in all the light. But in the base of that soaring monster, Jenna spotted a cave. It was no wonder smugglers had once used this place. The cave was completely invisible from above.

"What is it, lass?" Mal rumbled from behind her. "Why have ye stopped?"

"There," she said, lifting a finger and pointing at the cave.

"That's where we need to go."

Mal frowned at the dark maw of the cave. Jenna had to admit, it did not look very inviting. Mal drew his claymore with a rasp of steel loud enough to be heard over the crash of the waves.

"Then I'll go first. Stay behind me."

Jenna didn't argue and stood back to allow Mal to stride past. A trail of sorts led up to the mouth of the cave, a path where the rocks had been worn down by the tramp of many feet.

"Hello?" Mal called as they reached the cave mouth. "Anyone here?"

There was no answer but the crashing of the waves and the call of gulls. Slowly, Mal stepped over the lip of the cave and went inside. Jenna followed him cautiously. Inside, the cave was large and surprisingly dry, with a floor of pulverized rock dust and walls of smooth granite. The shape of the cave amplified sound and the roar of the waves was so loud it seemed as if they had somehow fallen into the sea, even though it was a good way behind and below them.

Mal sheathed his claymore in the scabbard across his back. "Are ye sure the stone ye are looking for is here? I dinna see aught."

"It's here," Jenna said. "I can feel it."

She walked past him, towards the back of the cave, where the light barely reached. And there she found it. The second anchor stone rose from the cave floor like an accusing finger. It was different from the first. This wasn't a stone that had been raised by human hands but rather was a stalagmite of yellow calcium deposits that had grown up over countless millennia. A stalactite grew from the ceiling right above it, so long that the two almost touched. Almost, but not quite. What would happen when they did?

The stalagmite was easily as tall as she was and carved with the same glyphs and runes as the first anchor stone. She could feel its power pulsing against her senses like a summer storm.

"Could you wait outside?" she asked Mal. "I need some space."

Mal looked about to argue, but then thought better of it. "Aye. Yell if ye need aught."

As he left, Jenna approached the stalagmite and placed her hands on its surface. It was smooth and strangely warm to the touch, as though it was alive.

"I hope you're more helpful than your brethren," she muttered as if the rock could hear her.

She sat cross-legged in front of it and closed her eyes. As she sent her magic into the rock, the golden net of Skye's magic immediately sprang into focus in her mind's eye. Just as before, she saw the twisted lines of golden power that stretched from this anchor stone across the land. And, just as before, she saw the dark holes where that golden power had failed.

Centering herself and slowing her breathing, Jenna exerted her will. The glowing ball of energy that swirled inside her expanded, sending out tendrils that fused with the magic of the anchor stone, strengthening it and making it glow in her mind's eye like a fallen star. Slowly, oh so slowly, she pushed her magic out along the net, towards a dark hole that lay nearby.

She wove a patch from her own energy and placed it over the gap, weaving it in place with tendrils of magic. The repair grew bright, brighter than the rest of the web, and Jenna felt a rush of exhilaration rush through her. She'd done it!

But the exhilaration lasted only an instant. The next moment, the tendrils of magic snapped with a silent concussion and the hole once again went dark. With a yelp, Jenna withdrew her consciousness before the magic could recoil and blast her across the cave like it had done the day before.

She opened her eyes. The stone and the cave looked exactly as it had before, with only Jenna's rapid breathing and racing pulse to indicate that anything had happened.

Jenna pounded her fist into the ground. "Damn it!" she yelled. "Why won't it work? Why can't I do this?"

She felt tears of frustration gathering in her eyes and wiped them away with her sleeve. That horrible sense of despair was creeping up on her again, that feeling like she was falling into an oubliette she couldn't escape from. It had been kept at bay by Arran's confidence in her, but now it came rising up to the surface. She couldn't do this. She wasn't strong enough or skilled enough. Arran had chosen the wrong MacFinnan spellweaver. She was going to let all these people down. She was going to let Arran down. The thought was unbearable.

"What am I doing wrong?" she whispered to the impassive face of the stalagmite. "What am I missing?"

"Ah! Now ye ask the right questions," said a voice.

Jenna spun with a yelp to find a woman standing behind her. Jenna scrambled to her feet in sudden fright.

"Who... who are you?"

The woman was willowy, with long hair that seemed to move of its own accord. But it was her eyes that caught Jenna's attention. They were completely silver. The woman smiled. "My name is Lir. And ye are Jenna MacFinnan."

Lir? Wasn't she the one who'd sent Arran through time to find her? But that meant...

"You're a goddess!" Jenna gasped.

Lir cocked her head, her silver eyes alight with warmth and amusement. "Aye, I suppose I am, although right now I'm just a concerned friend. I can feel yer sorrow and frustration, lass. It reverberates across the land. What is it that ails ye?"

Jenna opened her mouth and closed it again. She could feel the power that emanated from Lir even more strongly than what came from the anchor stone. It was like standing too close to a bonfire.

"I... I... can't fix the magic," Jenna blurted. "You brought me all the way here, and I can't do it. It won't work."

Lir studied her. Her face was ageless but her eyes were ancient, full of knowledge and wisdom. "That's because ye are missing a key ingredient."

"What?" Jenna stepping forward eagerly. "What key ingredient? Tell me so I can find it!"

Lir smiled. "Love, lass. That is the ingredient ye are missing."

Jenna blinked. "Love? What has that got to do with magic?"

"Everything, that's what." Lir raised her hands to indicate the cave around them. "The original spellweavers who wove the magic that protects Skye loved this land. They loved the mountains, the valleys, the streams, and the lochs. They loved the people. Skye was a part of them and they were a part of it, and it was from this love that the magic was born. Without it, there is nothing."

Jenna stared at the goddess. Love? She needed to weave the magic with *love*? Then no wonder she had failed. There was nothing here she loved. Her presence here was a simple business transaction, cold and clinical. With a sinking sense of despair, she realized there was no way she would be able to restore Skye's magic.

"Can't *you* do it?" she asked Lir in desperation. "Can't *you* fix the magic? You're a goddess! You could do it with a wave of your hand!"

Lir shook her head. "I am of the sea. Skye's magic is of the land. I cannae touch it."

"But… but what am I supposed to do? I'm going to let all these people down!"

A soft smile curled Lir's lips. "Do ye think I would have brought ye through time if ye couldnae do this? What ye need is already inside ye. Ye just have to find the courage to recognize it." She took a step forward and placed a hand on Jenna's shoulder. Her touch sent prickles of electricity across Jenna's skin. "Ye hurt, child. Ye are full of pain and loss and confusion. But that is yer past. It need not be yer future. Look inside. Find yer truth, and ye will find yer strength as well." Her fingers squeezed Jenna's shoulder until it was almost painful. "Trust yerself, Jenna."

Jenna's eyelids suddenly felt heavy. Her eyes closed for an instant and when they opened again, Lir was gone.

Jenna sat down heavily on a rock, despair washing through her. She could think of no way to do what Lir suggested. No matter what angle she thought about it from, she came to the same conclusion.

She was going to fail.

Chapter Fifteen

ARRAN REALIZED HE was drumming his fingers on the table and forced himself to stop. Straightening in his chair, he plastered an attentive look on his face as Maurice, his castellan, droned on about the rising price of wheat.

The truth was, Arran had missed most of what Maurice had been saying. No matter how hard he tried to concentrate, the price of wheat just couldn't hold his attention. His thoughts kept drifting back to Jenna. Where was she now? Had she and Mal reached the second anchor stone? Was she safe? Had they met any hazards on the way?

His thoughts had been going around and around like this ever since he'd sent Mal with Jenna this morning instead of accompanying her himself. It was the right decision; after all, hadn't they agreed to pretend last night's kiss never happened? If he was to do that he needed to keep his distance. But it didn't mean he had to like it.

Somebody cleared their throat. Arran blinked, realizing he'd been staring at the table, and looked up.

Maurice was watching expectantly. The other two people at the table—his mother Rosaline and David, Arran's steward, were also watching him.

Arran straightened in his chair. "Er... sorry... what?"

To his credit, Maurice didn't let his annoyance show on his

face, but Arran knew the old man well enough to recognize the slight tightening around his eyes that betrayed his frustration. This was not the first time this morning he'd had to repeat himself.

"I said, do I have yer permission to call a meeting with the grain merchants? If we look at increasing our exports of barley, and reducing our reliance on imported wheat, it should start driving the price down again."

Arran waved his hand. "Aye, whatever ye think best."

Maurice inclined his head. "My thanks, my laird. Now onto item three. It's been brought to my attention that the repair to the wall in the eastern stable block is going to be more expensive than we thought due to the instability of the foundations. As it's a later addition, the stone used was of a lower quality—"

Arran stopped listening. His gaze drifted to the window, beyond which a brilliant blue sky could be seen. Where were Jenna and Mal now? He began mentally measuring the distance and time their journey would take. If they'd met with no mishaps, they should be somewhere near—

"Arran!"

He looked around to find his mother glaring at him. "Have you listened to a single word Maurice just said?"

"What? Aye, of course! I—"

He was saved from further explanation by the door suddenly bursting open and banging loudly into the wall. Brother Merrick came hurrying in, his sandals slapping on the stone. He stopped abruptly when he realized Arran wasn't alone.

"Oh! My apologies, my laird. I didnae realize ye were in a meeting, but ye said that I was to come to ye as soon as I found anything." He waved a rolled scroll in Arran's direction before his eyes slid to Rosaline, Maurice, and David who were all looking annoyed at the interruption. "I... um... I'll come back later."

"It's all right, Brother," Arran said, leaping on any excuse to get out of listening to more tedium about market prices or building repairs. "What is it?"

Merrick licked his lips and glanced at the others again. "Um… that thing ye told me to look into? Well, I think I might have found something."

Arran's breath quickened. He pushed himself up from his seat. "Ye must excuse me," he said to Maurice, David, and his mother. "I must see to this. Please, carry on."

Rosaline frowned and opened her mouth to speak but before she could, Arran took Merrick by the shoulder and bundled him through the door, pulling it shut behind them. He took a deep breath. Already he could hear Maurice's voice droning again from within.

"Yer timing is impeccable," Arran said to Merrick with a wry smile. "Perhaps we should set up some kind of code system so ye can rescue me from such meetings in the future."

Merrick looked puzzled. "My laird?"

Arran waved a hand. "Never mind. What have ye found?"

A flash of excitement passed over Merrick's face. Stepping close, he unrolled the scroll and held it up for Arran to see. Densely packed script filled the page in a flourishing style that made it difficult to read.

Arran squinted. "Is that French?"

"Aye. It's an ancient text that describes the siege of Chartres when Scandinavian invaders attacked the city. It describes how the attackers were fearless because they believed they were protected by one of their heathen gods. And it says they all wore the same ink design. Look, they've even drawn it."

Arran took the scroll from Merrick and peered at it. Sure enough, towards the bottom of the scroll a crude symbol had been drawn: three interlocking spirals with a spiky rune above. The same symbol that had been inked into Ingold's neck.

Arran looked at Merrick. "Does it say what the symbol means?"

The monk nodded triumphantly. "It does. It's the symbol of the god Njord and anyone that bears the mark is one of his followers. Of course, it's all heathen nonsense, but what can we expect from barbarians who have yet to embrace the one true God?"

Njord thanks you for keeping his isles warm for him. The words Ingold had spoken to him at Tollman's Gate.

Njord. A god. Despite Merrick's assertion that such beliefs were heathen rubbish, Arran knew better. He knew that gods and goddesses still walked the earth and that if one had taken an interest in Skye, things were worse than he'd feared. He'd believed that the raiders were opportunists with little coordination or plan beyond taking whatever they could get their hands on. But he'd been wrong.

They served a god. And that god wanted his island.

A low growl sounded in his throat and the scroll suddenly crumpled in his clenched fist. He forced his fingers to uncurl and then straightened out the parchment.

"My laird?" Merrick asked.

Arran fixed his gaze on the monk. "Speak of this to nobody. Go back to the library and find every scrap of information, no matter insignificant it may seem, about this Njord. Bring anything ye find straight to me."

Merrick bobbed his head. "Aye, my laird."

Arran strode quickly away. Merrick called after him, "But where are ye going?"

Arran glanced over his shoulder at the monk. "To find our errant spellweaver."

JENNA CLUNG GRIMLY to the saddle horn and forced herself to concentrate on keeping her seat as the men around her bantered among themselves. They'd seen no sign of danger either on the way to the anchor stone or on their way back, the day was warm and drowsy, and her guards had finally begun to relax.

Normally, their bawdy jokes and ribbing would have amused

her—she might even have joined in—but she was in no mood for banter. The sense of hopelessness that had come upon her in the cave hadn't dissipated, and she could not get Lir's words out of her head. *The original spellweavers who wove the magic that protects Skye loved this land. They loved the mountains, the valleys, the streams, and the lochs. They loved the people. Skye was a part of them and they were a part of it, and it was from this love that the magic was born. Without it, there is nothing.*

Had her quest been doomed before it began? But why would Lir send Arran to fetch her if she had no chance of succeeding?

Despair filled her stomach like bile. What was she going to tell Arran? What was she going to tell the people of Skye?

Nothing, she thought. *I'll tell them nothing. Because this isn't over. I'm not giving up. I will figure this out. I will.*

"Is everything all right?" Mal asked suddenly.

Jenna glanced at him. "Fine. Why do you ask?"

"Because ye have been scowling fit to curdle milk ever since we left that cave."

Jenna realized Mal was right. Her forehead was furrowed, and her jaw had begun to ache from where she'd been clenching her teeth. She forced her face to relax and gave Mal the sweetest smile she could muster.

"There. Is that better?"

"Better? Lass, that is absolutely terrifying."

Around them, the men laughed, and Jenna found her lips quirking into a smile. "Behave yourselves," she said, glaring around at them. "Or I'll turn you all into toads."

The laughter died out and they looked at each other uncertainly, unsure if she was joking. Jenna grinned. Perhaps being a spellweaver had some advantages after all.

The day had grown warm, and Jenna felt sweat beading on her brow, despite the cooling breeze that blew in off the sea. The sparkling waves spread out to the horizon on her right while to her left, inland, the landscape was a patchwork of forested hills interspersed with little farms and homesteads. Fluffy sheep dotted the hills like land-bound clouds while the shaggy-haired Highland cattle grazed in the fields lower down. It was beautiful.

And all under threat because she wasn't good enough.

"Damn!" Mal swore suddenly, pulling up his horse.

Misty, who followed Mal's horse like a shadow, came to a halt as well.

"What's wrong?" Jenna asked.

"Sarrach has gone lame. I think there's a stone in his shoe. Men! Take yer positions while I check this!"

He dismounted and knelt by his horse's front leg. Jenna took the opportunity to slither from the saddle and walk around a bit, rubbing her aching backside and trying to work the stiffness from her muscles.

While the men inspected Sarrach's hoof, Jenna found herself wandering among the tussocky sand dunes that led down to the shore. A horse-shoe bay lay beyond, with a golden sandy beach that would probably be a tourist hot-spot in the twenty-first century. But now she had it all to herself.

On impulse, she kicked off her boots and dug her feet into the sand, enjoying the soft, warm sensation of it between her toes. The breeze blew her hair out behind her and she spread her arms wide, allowing the fresh air to blow away a little of the anxiety and doubt she'd been feeling since her encounter with Lir.

Ahead of her, the water spread out in a shimmering blanket, so clear she could see fish of many colors darting about below the surface. It looked very peaceful. Serene. The kind of spot that would help her forget her worries—if only for a little while.

Glancing back, she saw that Mal was still busy with Sarrach's hoof and the rest of the men had spread out along the sand dunes, keeping watch for danger. It looked like the party wouldn't be going anywhere for a little while. Perfect. Just enough time.

She waved her hand. "I'm going for a dip! I won't be long!"

Mal shouted something back, but his words were lost in the moan of the breeze and the slither of the waves. And, to be honest, she would have ignored him even if she had heard him.

No doubt he was telling her that she wasn't allowed to swim because it was too dangerous. Well, tough. She'd had a shitty morning, and she wasn't about to pass up this opportunity to de-stress.

Reaching behind her back, she untied her dress and stepped out of it, leaving her in only her shift. She waded into the water, gasping in shock at the temperature. It was colder than she'd expected. But not to be deterred, she swam out a little way, getting used to the temperature and then flipped onto her back, floating and gazing up at the sparkling blue sky.

Slowly, oh so slowly, she felt the tension leak out of her. As she floated in the water, cradled by the gentle swell, listening to nothing but the call of birds and the gentle lapping of the water, that little pool of despair that had gathered in her stomach began to dissipate.

But the question remained: how could she fix the magic?

Chapter Sixteen

ARRAN SPOTTED MAL and the rest of the men he'd sent with Jenna up ahead and breathed out in relief. They were exactly where he'd expected them to be and from their relaxed demeanor he guessed they'd not run into any trouble.

Right now they were spread out along the dunes while Mal knelt by his horse's right front leg. Arran frowned. Where was Jenna?

He scanned the group but could see no sign of her. His stomach tightened. Misty, the horse he'd lent her, was there, drowsing next to Sarrach, but he could see no sign of Misty's rider.

Arran's pulse ratcheted up a notch. He kicked Bran into a gallop, skidding to a halt in front of Mal and jumping out of the saddle before the horse had even come to a full stop.

"What's going on?" he demanded. "Where's Jenna?"

"Sarrach's pulled up lame," Mal replied, pointing at the stone he'd dug out of the horse's hoof. "And dinna look so worried; Jenna is fine." He nodded in the direction of the bay. "Sounds like she's enjoying herself."

Arran turned and saw a speck floating in the water of the bay. Delighted laughter floated across the waves, followed by the sound of splashing.

Arran ground his teeth, then glared at his cousin. "Ye let her go *swimming?*"

Mal's eyebrows rose. "Let her? I dinna think ye *let* a MacFinnan spellweaver do anything. Nor do ye stop her when she has a mind to do something."

Arran growled low in his throat. He had first-hand experience of what happened when ye tried to tell a MacFinnan what to do. Turning, he strode down the dunes onto the beach and walked up to the water's edge.

Cupping his hands, he bellowed, "Jenna!"

She turned and spotted him. "Arran!" she called. "Come on in! The water is lovely!"

Lovely? He'd call it dangerous and bloody foolish. Besides the threat of the raiders, didn't she realize there were treacherous currents around Skye that could grab an unwary swimmer and sweep them out to sea? Why else did she think she was the only person in the water on such a fine day? The locals had more sense.

"Jenna!" he yelled. "Come back! It isnae safe!"

"Stop worrying!" she yelled back. "It's amazing!"

She turned onto her back and began gently scooting herself farther out into the bay.

Arran let forth a string of expletives. Why did Lir not warn him about how bloody stubborn and annoying MacFinnan spellweavers were? If he'd known how difficult they could be, he'd have turned down Lir's offer and found another way to defeat the raiders. Lord above, facing down an army of raiders was easier than dealing with one headstrong twenty-first century woman who seemed to take perverse pleasure in doing the opposite of what he told her!

With a growl, he unbelted his claymore and dropped the sword onto the beach. Then he kicked off his boots, waded into the water, and began swimming out towards her with strong, steady strokes. He'd vowed to keep the fool woman safe and if that meant dragging her bodily out of the water, then that's what he'd do. She could rail and shout at him all she liked just as soon as she was on dry land and he could keep an eye on her.

Arran was an excellent swimmer—as was almost everyone on Skye—and it didn't take him long to reach her. She laughed delightedly as he trod water next to where she was floating and gave him a smile that almost stopped his heart.

"See?" she cried. "I knew you'd come to your senses!"

"I wish *ye* would," he snapped. "Come on. We must get back to shore."

"Why?" she challenged. "What's so urgent?"

He glanced around. They were alone but for a couple of curious seals who bobbed in the water not far away, watching them with large, liquid eyes. The waters were as smooth as glass, shimmering like diamonds in the warm sunlight. Aye, it was a beautiful spot all right, and when he was younger and more carefree, no doubt he would have done exactly as Jenna was doing now. But that had been a long time ago and he'd learned the hard way that being carefree was a good way to get yourself killed.

"Dinna ye listen to a word I say? It isnae safe. How am I supposed to keep ye from harm when ye insist on putting yerself right in its path?"

She sighed. Her hair was plastered to the sides of her face and she was wearing only her shift. Through the clear water, he could see how it clung to her body, revealing way too much of her feminine curves. Arran forced himself to look only at her face.

"Look around you, Arran," she said, slapping the water and then gesturing with one hand. "There is no danger here. Do you see any raiders? Any threats? All I see is a lovely sunny day and a chance to have a bit of relaxation. Where's the harm in that?"

She was very persuasive; he had to give her that. He would like nothing more than to spend some time enjoying her company. It was hardly decent for the two of them to be swimming together like this, of course, and it would only set the gossips' tongues wagging all the more, but right now he didn't care about that.

Before he could form a suitable reply, she laughed, splashed water in his face, then began swimming away from him.

Arran spluttered as he swallowed a mouthful of seawater. With a growled curse, he set off after her, catching her in only a few strokes.

"Curse it, Jenna. Will ye listen—"

As he caught her, Jenna turned, put her arms around his neck, and kissed him.

Arran was so shocked that for an instant his arms and legs went limp and he sank beneath the water, coming up coughing and spluttering. By the time he could see again, Jenna was already swimming away from him, laughing with a joy as unrestrained as the summer breeze.

"Ha!" she called. "I've finally found a way to shut you up!"

His lips tingled where she'd kissed him. Why had she done that? Hadn't they agreed to pretend their kiss last night never happened?

She turned, perhaps around fifty feet away now, and grinned at him. She seemed inordinately pleased with herself. No doubt she enjoyed being able to unsettle him. Well, he would show her!

With a growl that turned into more of a laugh, he launched himself after her. Jenna shrieked and began paddling away as fast as she could, water splashing everywhere in her haste. A giggle of child-like delight escaped her, and Arran felt a fierce joy rising in him as he chased her.

She glanced over her shoulder, opened her mouth to say something, but then her expression changed. Her smile faltered and a look of alarm spread over her face. She suddenly began moving away from him at unnatural speed.

"Arran!" she cried, her voice now filled with fear. She flailed and kicked, trying to get back to him, but made no progress. Instead, she continued to move farther away.

In an instant, Arran understood what had happened and cold fear gripped him.

"Jenna!" he bellowed, desperately trying to reach her.

He felt something take hold of him and shove him with the

strength of a mule-kick. Suddenly, he was speeding through the water. It carried him closer to Jenna, and as he reached her, he grabbed her around the waist and pulled her against him. She threw her arms around his neck and together they trod water, trying to keep their heads above the surface as they picked up pace, moving with terrifying speed out of the bay and towards the open sea.

"What's happening?" Jenna gasped, her voice shrill with fear.

"We're caught in a rip," Arran replied. "Dinna fight it. Relax and let it take us. It will spit us out eventually, and then we can swim back to shore."

"Relax?" Jenna spluttered. "Are you insane! We're being washed out to sea!"

Arran had been caught in rips before, both as a child and an adult, and his father had taught him and his brother at an early age what to do if caught in one. Jenna, though, was doing the exact thing that you should not do: panic and try to swim against the current.

He tightened one arm around her waist while he used the other to help him tread water. "Look at me," he said. Jenna swallowed, then fixed wide, fearful eyes on him. "It's all right. I've got ye. I willnae let anything happen to ye. Do ye trust me?"

Jenna swallowed again, her face pale and frightened. Then she nodded. "I... I trust you."

An unaccountable warmth spread through him as she said those words. "Good. Then do as I tell ye for once and try to relax. Tread water but dinna fight against the current. Aye?"

Jenna nodded, and he felt some of the tension go out of her body although she kept her arms firmly wrapped around his neck. They were very close, their faces only inches apart and Arran couldn't help thinking how easy it would be to kiss her again and how much he wanted to. It was a ridiculous notion considering their predicament, and he cursed himself for a fool, annoyed at how easily he seemed to lose his head around this woman.

The shore was rapidly receding into the distance and, glancing over his shoulder, he could see his men gathered along the shoreline, waving frantically. He raised his free arm and waved back, indicating that he and Jenna were all right. Like him, his men were well versed in the capricious currents that swirled around their island home and would know what to do.

The current swept him and Jenna through a narrow channel between two rocky islets where finally, it dispersed. Their rapid movement slowed and then stopped entirely, leaving them bobbing in water that was far choppier than in the sheltered enclave of the bay.

Arran's arms and legs were beginning to ache from the strain of holding both himself and Jenna up and he knew it would be foolish to strike out for the shore now, when they were both tired. He glanced around, his eyes alighting on the nearest of the rocky islets.

"Can ye swim over there, lass?" he said to Jenna. "It isnae far, and we can take shelter and get our breath back."

Jenna glanced at the islet and nodded.

"Good. Then let's go."

They set off, Arran letting Jenna take the lead and staying close behind her in case she got into difficulty. She didn't, and it took only a few minutes before Arran felt the seabed under his questing feet. He took Jenna's arm and together they staggered through the shallows and collapsed onto the sandy beach that ringed the islet.

Arran lay flat on his back and allowed himself a moment to close his eyes and listen to the thundering of his heart. Slowly, his breathing began to slow. He opened his eyes and turned his head. Jenna lay on her back next to him, staring up at the blue sky, her chest heaving as she tried to catch her breath. Her dark hair lay spread out around her head like a halo.

"Are you a gloater?" she said suddenly.

Arran blinked. "A… what?"

"A gloater. Someone who acts all smug when they're proven right."

"Nay, lass. I'm not a… gloater."

"All right then, I admit it. You were right. I was wrong. I should have listened to you." She spoke in a rush, as though eager to get it off her chest. "There. I've said it. Remember, you promised not to gloat."

Despite himself, his lips quirked in a smile. "Wouldnae dream of it."

With a groan, he sat up. The beach they were on was not large and hemmed in on all sides by rugged black cliffs too tall to climb. Colonies of guillemots and razorbills filled the cliffs and at this time of year the clifftops would be full of puffins in their burrows.

Arran wondered what they thought of these two strange interlopers to their land. "Dinna worry," he muttered at the birds. "We'll be gone soon."

He climbed to his feet, water dripping from his hair and plaid, and strode down to where the breakers were landing on the shore. The mainland of Skye spread out across the waters, bathed in afternoon sunlight. Arran put his hands on his hips and gazed at it. It wasn't often that he saw his home from this angle and as always when he did, he was struck by its beauty. A rocky coastline, wooded hills, heath-covered uplands, all rising to the craggy heights of the mountains that formed the island's spine.

It was his. His home. He would not let Njord take it.

"Should we swim?" Jenna said, coming to stand next to him.

Arran shook his head. "Nay, lass. It's too far to swim in our present condition."

"You mean *my* present condition. I'm the coddled, unfit twenty-first century woman. You're the lean, mean, fifteenth-century Highlander, remember? I suspect you could swim there and back a dozen times if you wanted to."

"Yer faith in my abilities humbles me," he replied with a lopsided smile. "Even if it is a little misplaced."

She turned to gaze over the water. "But if we don't swim, how are we going to get back?"

"Mal and the others will come looking soon enough. We just have to wait."

"For how long?"

He shrugged. "Until they find us. Be thankful it's a sunny day. If it was howling a gale and throwing down with rain, this would *not* be fun."

She kicked at a sea-rounded pebble at her feet. "I really am sorry," she said, her voice sounding more contrite than he'd ever heard. "I just wanted a swim. I didn't know about rips and things like that."

Arran bit his tongue. She *might* know about rip currents and the other dangers that Skye posed if she stopped to listen to him once in a while. But he didn't say this out loud as he didn't fancy another argument.

Her soaked shift was clinging to her body in a way that was wholly indecent, and the way water was dripping down her neck and chest was ridiculously alluring. The memory of her lips on his flashed through his mind, and heat suddenly pooled in his stomach, traveling all the way down to his groin. Why had she kissed him? Didn't she realize how it tied his tongue in knots and scattered his thoughts like leaves on a breeze? Did she do it just to taunt him?

He cleared his throat. "It might be a warm day, but it will take us hours to dry unless we start a fire. We should gather some driftwood. Ye take that end of the beach, I'll take this one."

He strode away from her, glad to put some distance between them. She moved to the other end of the beach and began collecting driftwood that had been washed up on the sand. It didn't take long before they had a decent pile, which they dumped in the spot where they'd come ashore.

Arran knelt and picked out a relatively dry stick and a small piece of driftwood. He didn't have his flint and tinder, so he would have to light the fire the old way. Placing the stick upright into a notch on the log, he took it between his palms and began rotating it back and forth as quickly as he could, trying to get the friction to light the wood.

Jenna watched with a slightly bemused expression on her face. Then she crouched next to him, placed her hand over the pile of driftwood, and muttered a few words. Flames flared to life in a whoosh of sparks, eagerly taking root in the dry wood.

Jenna looked at him and shrugged. "Sometimes being a MacFinnan spellweaver comes in handy."

"It certainly does," Arran agreed. "Now use yer magic to build us a boat, and I'll be really impressed."

"Sorry. I'm right out of boat-making magic."

"Shame." He stripped off his plaid, shirt, and boots, and spread them out by the fire to dry.

In only his breeches, he seated himself on the sand. Jenna hovered nearby, looking uncertain. Her shift still clung to her body, outlining her hips and breasts.

Arran's mouth went dry, and he quickly looked away.

"Come sit by the fire, lass," he said, still not looking at her. "Ye'll dry much quicker."

⇥⟫⟩⟨⟪⇤

COME SIT BY the fire? With him lounging half-naked with his ridiculously muscled chest on display? Did he have any idea what the sight of him like that was doing to her?

Jenna pursed her lips. Perhaps he was trying to get his revenge for her kissing him earlier. To be honest, she didn't know why she'd done that. It had been spur of the moment, instinctive, and she'd enjoyed every second.

Aargh! She wanted to tear out her hair in frustration. They'd agreed to pretend that their first kiss hadn't happened, so why had she gone and done it again? She didn't know. Rationality seemed to go out of the window when he was around. Oh, bloody hell.

Deliberately not looking at him, she seated herself on the sand a couple of feet away, drew her knees against her chest, and wrapped her arms around them. Arran said nothing, but she could feel him watching her. His gaze burned against her skin almost as hotly as the flames did.

"So," she said. "How long till Mal and your men come get us?"

"There are a number of islets in the bay that they'll search. Depends on which they search first."

"So we're stuck here until then?"

"Aye, lass."

It might be hours. Hours alone with Arran MacLeod. She glanced over at him and found him watching her, his blue eyes brighter than the ocean in front of them.

"I tried to fix the second anchor stone," she blurted. "It didn't work."

"Ah."

She looked at him. "You don't sound surprised."

He sat up, pulling his legs into a cross-legged position, and fiddled with a pebble in his lap. "I'm disappointed, but not surprised after what I learned today. That's why I came looking for ye. It seems there is more going on than we realized."

"What do you mean?"

Arran's sapphire gaze fixed on her face. "The men who attacked Tollman's Gate bore a strange marking. I drew it for Brother Merrick and asked him to research it, see if there were any records of what it might signify. He discovered its meaning. The mark is a symbol of Njord."

"Oh. I see," Jenna said, although she really didn't. "What's a Njord?"

"Not a what. A who. Njord is a god. A Norse god of the sea, to be exact."

Jenna blinked, digesting this. "So the raiders are followers of this god? What's that got to do with the anchor stones?"

He gave a frustrated huff. "I dinna know yet. Something. It's connected somehow, I can feel it. I just dinna know how." He scooped another load of pebbles from the beach and began throwing them into the water. Each time he did, the muscles in his right arm bulged and flexed and Jenna felt herself watching the movement as if mesmerized.

She forced herself to concentrate on the dancing flames of the campfire. Njord. A Norse god. She might have scoffed at such a preposterous idea had she not met a goddess herself only a few hours ago. She glanced at Arran. The set of his shoulders was tense and his jaw tight as he watched the pebbles go sailing one by one through the air to plop into the waves.

Should she tell him about Lir? Yes, probably. Didn't he have a right to know that the MacFinnan spellweaver he'd brought from the future was wholly incapable of doing what he was paying her for? But the famous MacFinnan stubbornness kicked in. Who said she couldn't do this? Only her own doubts. Lir had brought her here for a reason.

Do ye think I would have brought ye through time if ye couldnae do this? What ye need is already inside ye. Ye just have to find the courage to recognize it.

Trouble was, she had no idea how to do that.

"What's wrong, lass?"

Jenna blinked, startled out of her thoughts, and looked at Arran. "Sorry, what?"

"What are ye thinking about? Ye look troubled."

She waved a dismissive hand. "Nothing. Just wondering if people back at Dun Tabor will be worried about us."

Arran snorted. "Aye. No doubt Rosaline will have the whole place in an uproar. Ye know, once, when I'd just become laird, she turned out the whole castle looking for me because I wasnae in my room when she went up in the morning."

Jenna smiled. She could well imagine Rosaline doing something like that. "Mothers. Always overprotective."

"Aye. And I wouldnae have minded except I was in the privy with a bad case of the skitters when the guards burst in."

Jenna burst out laughing. "Oh no! I'll bear that in mind in future. If I get a 'bad case of the skitters', I'll be sure to pin a note on my door to let her know where I am."

Arran grinned, his eyes sparkling. "Most wise."

"You can't really blame her, though. You're all she has left. It couldn't have been easy for her after losing your father and brother."

As soon as the words left her mouth, she realized it had been the wrong thing to say. All the mirth drained out of Arran's expression to be replaced by a hollow, haunted look. He turned away, picked up more pebbles, and began tossing them again. "No," he said. "It wasnae."

Jenna cursed her big mouth. She wanted to reach out and lay a hand on his shoulder, but sensed that would not be the right thing to do. There was an old pain deep inside Arran MacLeod, one he rarely showed to the world but that surfaced at odd moments, like now. She could only guess how hard his life had been. He was twenty-seven years old, unmarried, and without children. Jenna didn't know much about history, but she knew enough to realize this was unusual in this time.

He'd forsaken having a family for the sake of guarding his people, something he'd been doing since the loss of his father and brother at the age of seventeen. Was it any wonder he could be taciturn and surly when he wanted to be?

"I'm sorry," she said softly. "I didn't mean to stir up painful memories."

"Ye didnae. All that happened a long time ago." He smiled wryly. "Families, eh? They tear ye up and break yer heart."

"Yes," Jenna said, her gaze becoming unfocussed. "They do."

Arran frowned suddenly. "Lass," he said. "Ye are smoldering."

Jenna looked where he indicated and realized that the hem of her shift was starting to singe from where she'd been sitting too close to the fire.

"Shit!" She jumped away, batting and flapping at the material until the singed bits stopped smoldering.

It was only then she realized that in her haste she'd moved

closer to Arran. So close, in fact, that she could feel his shoulder brushing hers. She turned her head to find his face only inches away.

She ought to move back. She ought to put some space between them. But she didn't move. She *couldn't* move. His blue gaze trapped and held her. She swallowed thickly, feeling a hot ache light in her belly. Oh yes, she most definitely ought to move away.

"Arran, I—"

She got no further. One of Arran's big hands came up to cup her cheek, then he leaned in and kissed her.

She gasped and Arran pulled away a couple of inches. "I'm sorry, lass. I didnae mean to—"

Jenna wrapped her arms around his neck and kissed him back, stifling whatever apology he'd been trying to offer. She didn't want apologies. She wanted *him*.

Arran's arms went around her waist, yanking her hard against his chest, and he kissed her with a fierceness that matched hers, their lips meeting in a feverish, almost desperate clash. Oh God, how she wanted him! And, if the way he was kissing her was anything to go by, Arran wanted her just as badly.

Arran lifted her into his lap and Jenna wrapped her legs around his waist, scooting so close that she could feel the hard bulge between his legs. The feel of it sent her thoughts skittering. She ran her hands down his back, feeling the ridges and contours of his muscles, moaning against his mouth.

Then, all of a sudden, Arran rolled over onto the sand, pinning her beneath him. His kisses traveled down her neck to her collarbone, his tongue tracing a line of fire across her skin. Jenna moaned, her back arching involuntarily as he explored her. His hands were on her, the hard pads of his fingers gliding across her skin, cupping her breasts through the thin fabric of her damp shift and then teasing her nipples until they hardened.

One of his hands reached down, found the hem of her shift, and slipped beneath, a finger trailing its way up the inside of her thigh. Jenna's breath hitched, a gasp escaped, and that hot core between her legs became molten. Her fingers dug into the sand beneath her and her hips bucked involuntarily as his questing fingers trailed higher, higher. At the same time, his lips came down atop hers, his tongue plunging into her mouth even as a finger plunged into the soft warmth between her legs.

Jenna gasped, but Arran did not release her lips, his kisses hard and demanding, his fingers deft and expert as they explored her. Oh God. Oh shit. What was he doing to her?

Jenna began to lose all sense of control. Her body responded without conscious thought, and she writhed under his touch as the delicious pleasure began to build. Her hands came up to tangle in his thick hair as she kissed him, wanting to taste him, to feel him, to have him on and in her. She wasn't sure she'd ever wanted anything as much.

"Arran," she groaned against his lips, the only word she seemed able to form. "Arran."

"What, my beauty?" he whispered between kisses, his fingers slowly stoking her into an inferno. "What do ye want?"

"You know what I want," she replied, her voice low and husky.

"Do I? I want to hear ye say it."

"You," she whispered. "I want you."

His eyes slid closed, and a low moan escaped him. "Then I am yers."

With both hands, he took hold of her shift and pulled it over her head. Jenna threw up her arms to help him, suddenly wanting nothing between them but hot, bare skin. As he tossed the damp garment by the fire, she began plucking at the belt that held up his breeches, her fingers fumbling in her haste to get them off. She got the belt free, and he obliged by kicking out of the clinging garment, revealing his large, muscled thighs and the whole glorious length of him standing proud between them.

Jenna's mouth went dry at the sight and as he pushed her back down, kissing her once more, she reached an arm into the space between them and ran her hands up his full, hard length. Now it was Arran's turn to gasp, and she felt goosebumps ride up his skin as she stroked him.

He gazed down at her, his face so close to hers that their noses touched. His eyes were so dark now they seemed almost black, but she could see the raw desire that burned in their depths. He wanted her. This big, powerful man who could probably have any woman he wanted on this island wanted *her*. She could feel his need coming off him in waves, hanging in the air around them like musk.

"Jenna," he whispered, the word a soft caress across her skin. "My wildcat."

She wrapped both arms around his neck. "Arran," she murmured. "My fierce Highlander."

He breathed out slowly and stared at her, unblinking, as he nudged her legs apart with his knees. Running her hands down his back, she felt his muscles bunch as he tilted his hips and thrust himself inside her.

Jenna cried out as he filled her. Delicious heat coiled up from the spot and went sizzling along her nerves. She clutched Arran's back as he began to move, slowly at first but then with increasing tempo, her nails raking him, her hips rising to meet his thrusts, their bodies soon moving in perfect synchronicity.

Her world shrank. Gone were thoughts of magic and time travel and raiders. Gone were thoughts of anything beyond this moment. It was just her and Arran, the only things that mattered.

His breath was harsh by her ear, hair falling forward to tickle her face, and his scent was all around her, a scent that smelled like the wind and the waves and the sky all rolled into one. She felt wild and reckless and... and... alive in a way she never had before.

She moved in time with him, a thin sheen of sweat sliding between their bodies, and as their tempo increased and gasps and moans of pleasure began to escape from between Arran's clenched teeth, Jenna's own pleasure began to mount. That burning ember deep in her core glowed red hot.

She threw her head back, gasping as that fire burned, burned, burned right through her until finally, finally, she exploded into tiny embers and screamed Arran's name to the limitless blue sky. She lost herself, obliterated, and was only dimly aware of Arran juddering as he too reached his climax.

She lost all sense of time and place, giving herself over to the fiery pleasure that consumed her. But finally, after what could have been a second or a lifetime, the fire slowly began to ebb and she opened her eyes.

Arran was lying on top of her, his weight pressing her into the sand. After a moment, he raised his head and looked at her. She couldn't quite read his expression, but the heat in his gaze had cooled and now it was replaced by something else, a look of sated satisfaction.

He grinned, a boyish grin that lit his face and made him even more devastatingly good-looking. "Wildcat," he murmured. "Very apt. Is there any of my back left?"

She ran her fingers over the skin of his back, feeling the gashes where she'd scratched him. "Sorry," she said. "I guess I got a little carried away."

"I consider them a badge of honor," he replied.

He dipped his head and kissed her. It was slow and gentle this time, with none of the desperation and desire of before, and it was all the sweeter for that. Jenna kissed him equally as gently and as she did so, she felt something stir deep within her. Something warm and pleasant that she struggled to put a name to. Not desire, not this time, but something else, something deeper, something that seemed to rise up from the very bottom of her being. In that instant, she realized she could live in this moment forever. With him.

He rolled away from her, lying on his back on the sand and then pulling her close against him. Jenna nestled herself against his side, head resting on his broad chest. He kissed the top of her head.

Neither of them spoke. There was no need for words, really. Everything they had been feeling had been expressed in actions, not words. Jenna didn't bother trying to explore it or explain it. For the moment, she was content. Happy even, and she was perfectly willing to leave it at that.

Arran stirred. "That was… unexpected," he rumbled.

"It was," Jenna agreed. "But not unwelcome."

A lopsided smile curled his lips, and his eyes glinted with something that made her hot all over again. "Nay," he breathed. "Definitely not unwelcome."

In one quick movement, he rolled over, pushing Jenna onto her back, and leaned on his elbow, looking down at her. His hair fell forward to curtain his face, casting his expression into shadow. All she could see was the outline of his lips and the way his eyes burned with desire once more. Slowly, she reached up and traced the outline of his lips with the tip of her thumb.

Arran took hold of her hand and kissed each of her fingers, taking them into his mouth one by one. Those embers flared to life in her core like the banked coals of a fire stirred into a blaze. Damn it, but she wanted him again already. What was it about this man that affected her so? She wanted him again, right here, right now. She wanted to—

"Is that them?"

The sudden shout was like being doused with cold water. Arran sprang away from her, uttered a string of curses in Gaelic, and snatched up one of the branches from the fire, brandishing it like a weapon. Heart pounding, Jenna sat up, grabbed her shift, and draped it over her nakedness.

She half expected to see a gang of raiders charging down the beach towards them but all that met her questing gaze was the empty beach, the bird-covered cliff, and the waves stretching out to the horizon.

"It *is* them! Ho! Over here!"

Jenna squinted against the sun on the waves and made out a small boat making its steady way towards them.

"Mal," Arran breathed, his shoulders relaxing. "He's found us." He tossed the brand back into the fire and reached for his plaid.

"Did they see us?" Jenna asked, mortified. "Did they see what we were doing?"

Arran shook his head, that dark glint of desire still reflected in his eyes. "I dinna think so," he replied. "They are too far away and the sun is behind us."

"Thank God," Jenna muttered. She would just about die of embarrassment if anyone had seen what she and Arran had been up to. She dressed quickly, pulling the still-damp shift over her body.

Arran yanked on his breeches and shirt and Jenna couldn't help but feel a pang of disappointment as his gorgeous body was hidden from view. She also couldn't help feeling annoyed with Mal and the others. Why did they have to choose *this* precise moment to come rescue them? Couldn't they have left it just another hour or so? Couldn't they have allowed her to enjoy Arran's company—and his body—a little longer?

Would you listen to yourself? she thought. *You did not come here to fall into bed with the laird!*

But she knew she'd do it again in an instant, given the opportunity. She'd never experienced anything like what she just had with Arran. It had been… incredible.

Arran strode down to the water's edge. "Mal!" he bellowed. "Over here!"

Jenna climbed to her feet and they stood side by side, watching as the boat drew steadily closer. Jenna was careful not to stand so close that they touched but she was acutely aware of his presence next to her, like a candle burning against her skin. She ached to say something, anything, but the intimacy that had been theirs only moments ago had vanished like a puff of smoke in the morning wind, and now they were the laird and the spellweaver again.

The boat was a small wooden dinghy being rowed by four

men. Mal stood in the prow, one foot up against the gunwale, and he jumped into the shallows and waded to shore as the boat finally scraped the bottom.

"There ye are!" he bellowed. "Thank the Lord! We've sent out every boat we can spare to scour the islets, and Lady Rosaline has invented at least four new swear words!"

Arran walked down to meet his cousin and pulled him into a warm embrace, the two men slapping each other on the back. "Well, I didnae want to make it easy for ye, did I? It does the men good to keep them on their toes."

"Aye, it does," Mal replied, putting his hands on his hips and looking Arran up and down. "But I wish it didnae also have to take ten years off my life. When I saw ye being pulled out in that rip…" He trailed off and ran a hand through his hair. "All is well that ends well, eh?"

Arran glanced Jenna. "Aye," he said softly. "It is."

Mal walked up to Jenna. He was almost as tall as his cousin, and Jenna had to crane her head back to look up at him. "Are ye all right, my lady? Ye are unhurt?"

"I'm fine," Jenna replied. "Thanks to Arran. I should have listened to you, Mal. I'm sorry."

Mal waved away her apology. "Dinna fash. But next time, if ye insist on going in the water, I will have ye tied ye up."

Jenna laughed. "I guess I deserved that."

Mal grinned and glanced between them both. "Right. Let's be off. I bet ye are eager to return to Dun Tabor."

She wasn't, actually. She was perfectly content where she was, thank you very much. Or she would be if Mal and the others would go away and leave her alone with Arran. He glanced at her, and she wondered if he was thinking the same thing.

In no time at all, Jenna was seated in the middle of the little dinghy, Mal on one side of her, Arran on the other, while the men cast off and began rowing back to shore. The whole way back Mal kept up a constant stream of chatter about mundane things— Rosaline's fit of temper when she discovered what had happened, the pod of dolphins they'd seen on the way here, the unexpectedly large catch of herring that one of the fishing boats had brought in last night—and his nearness precluded any talk with Arran. Not that she had any idea what she'd say if she could talk to him, mind you.

Already, what had happened between them on the beach was fading, taking on the unreality of a dream, as if it had been two different people who had shared such connection. Jenna couldn't help glancing back across the choppy waves to the thin strip of beach at the base of the cliffs. It was quickly receding, just like the fleeting closeness she'd shared with Arran.

Now that they were back among his men, Arran had snapped into the role of the laird as easily as donning a well-worn suit. He issued commands, asked questions, gathered information, and watched the shore approach with an intense gaze.

Jenna was almost glad when they landed at an isolated beach topped with sand dunes and tussocky grass. It was not the beach where she'd swum earlier. Mal explained that he'd brought them back a different route that would land them as close to Dun Tabor as possible. A band of men were waiting atop the dunes with horses, and the group were mounted and on their way before Jenna could even blink.

She found herself on a different horse but it plodded behind Mal's docilely. Arran rode next to Mal and for the whole of the ride the two of them had their heads together, discussing the business of the clan to which Jenna was not privy. He didn't so much as glance in her direction.

It did not take long for them to reach Dun Tabor and as they rode through the gates she spotted Rosaline, Ingrid, and several other people waiting for them by the doors. When the group clattered into the courtyard, Rosaline threw all decorum to the wind and came running, throwing her arms around Arran and hugging him tightly. Arran suffered his mother's attentions in silence.

"Ye will be the death me, Arran MacLeod!" she scolded him, pushing him to arm's length and looking him up and down.

"When the message came from Mal about what happened... I should paddle yer backside for ye!"

"All is well, mother," Arran replied in a patient voice. "As ye can see, both Lady Jenna and I are in one piece."

Rosaline turned to Jenna, her hands flying to her mouth. "Look at ye!" she cried. "Ye look half frozen to death!" She snapped her fingers and Ingrid came running, throwing a blanket around Jenna's shoulders.

It was a warm day, and now that her shift was almost dry, she was not cold, but she smiled and murmured her thanks anyway. It was nice to be fussed over. It reminded her of being at home with her aunts. Oh, how she could do with their advice right now!

Although, she thought, as she glanced at Arran, her aunts would give her conflicting advice where the handsome laird was concerned. Aunt Rose, always polite and proper, would caution against such a pointless dalliance. Aunt Elise, on the other hand, always the wild child of the family, would tell Jenna to let her hair down and enjoy herself. After what had happened with Alex, didn't she deserve it?

Thoughts of Alex twisted her gut and made whatever pleasantness she'd been feeling after her encounter with Arran evaporate like mist under the sun. Aunt Rose was right: Jenna should *not* have succumbed to her attraction to Arran. It would only serve to further complicate an already complicated situation.

Arran turned suddenly and met her gaze. Something passed across his features and it took a moment for her to place the look in his eyes. It had looked like... like... longing. Whatever it was, it was enough to send her thoughts scattering and the heat to flood her cheeks again. Then Mal said something and he looked away.

"Come," Rosaline said, taking Jenna by the shoulder. "Let's get ye into a nice warm bath and a change of clothes. I bet ye could do with it after the day ye've had."

Jenna nodded and didn't protest as the older woman led her into Dun Tabor. But as she walked away, it was all she could do to stop herself looking back at Rosaline's son.

Chapter Seventeen

"**D**ID YE HEAR what I said?" Mal demanded.

"Hmm. What?" Arran pulled his gaze away from where he'd been watching Jenna disappear through the doors of the keep and fixed his attention on his cousin.

Mal rolled his eyes. "I asked why ye came riding out to find us this afternoon. Ye seemed in quite the hurry when ye found us at the cove."

In all the confusion of what had happened, Arran had forgotten to tell Mal about what Merrick had discovered about Njord and his followers. He growled under his breath, annoyed with himself. Whatever else might have happened today, he was *still* the chieftain of this island, and the safety of his people came first. As his captain, Mal should have been the first to learn of this new development, not one of the last.

"Come," he said. "Let's stable the horses and I'll fill ye in."

Mal nodded, waved away the stable lads who were waiting to take the horses, and together they led their mounts into the cool dimness of the stable. As they stepped inside, the familiar scent of hay and horses filled Arran's nostrils, soothing in its familiarity.

He led Bran into a stall while Mal put his own mount into a stall opposite and the two of them began untacking the horses and then brushing them down. As they worked, Arran filled Mal in on what Brother Merrick had learned and what he thought it might mean. To be honest, he was glad of the distraction as it kept him from thinking about Jenna.

When he was done, Mal fell silent. "So what do we do?" he said at last. "Ask Lir for help? She's intervened before, so she might do again."

Arran shook his head. "Nay. I think Lir has done all she can by helping me to bring Jenna here. This is something we have to work out on our own. But Njord has something to do with why Jenna canna heal the magic, I'm sure of it."

As soon as he said her name, thoughts of her filled his head. The feel of her smooth skin, the touch of her silky hair, the soft scent of her all around him. And the indescribable sensations that had coursed through him as he'd made love to her.

He still couldn't believe it had happened. It felt like a dream. He'd known women—plenty of women—but he'd never felt anything for them like what he felt for Jenna. It wasn't just physical either. What they'd done on the beach today was just the culmination of what had been growing inside him ever since he'd met her, something he hadn't been able to put a name to, but had grown stronger and deeper the more time he spent with her.

He knew he should not have let it happen. But, by all the gods in all the heavens, he did not regret it. For the first time in a long, long time, he had felt alive. Because of her. Jenna MacFinnan. Spellweaver and time traveler. A woman he could not have.

"Are ye all right?"

Arran's thoughts snapped back, and he blinked. "I'm fine. Why?"

Mal frowned at him. "Ye seem… distracted. And ye were staring at Jenna something fierce just now."

"Dinna talk nonsense, man," Arran growled. "I wasnae staring."

"Aye, ye were. And dinna think I didnae notice how ye kept glancing at her on the ride back when ye thought nobody was looking." His eyes narrowed. "Did something happen between the two of ye?"

Arran scowled at his cousin. "Leave it, Mal."

But Mal wasn't about to be put off. "It did, didnae it? Dinna try to deny it, cousin, I know ye too well!"

Arran scrubbed a hand through his hair and blew out a breath, looking around helplessly. Was he really that obvious? Had anyone else noticed? He hoped not. He wouldn't have Jenna's honor impugned, and if any of his men should utter anything in that regard, they would soon find themselves regretting it.

"Aye," he breathed. "Something happened between Jenna and me."

Mal grinned and clapped one of his huge hands to Arran's shoulder. "So what are ye looking so glum about? I'm happy for ye! Lord knows, ye deserve it!"

"It isnae that simple, is it? I shouldnae have let it happen."

"Why not?" Mal replied, looking puzzled. "It would hardly be the first time ye've tumbled a lass."

Arran glared at him. "She isnae 'just a lass' though, is she? She's a MacFinnan spellweaver and will be returning to her own time soon enough."

"All more the reason to enjoy yerselves while ye can."

Arran threw up his hands. "Why am I even discussing this with ye? Things aren't like that with Jenna. They're… they're… complicated."

Try as he might, he didn't seem able to find the words to describe the complex tangle of emotions that was roiling inside him.

Mal blew out a long breath. "Oh. I see."

Arran narrowed his eyes. "What do ye mean? *What* do ye see?"

"Do ye really need me to spell it out for ye? Are ye really so blind that ye canna see what is happening here?"

"All I can see," Arran snapped, clenching his fists. "Is that my cousin is talking himself into a whack on the nose. Speak plainly!"

He and Mal had always been close growing up, being so

similar in age, but since the death of his elder brother, Mal had become his closest friend and confidant. He knew Arran better than anyone, and beneath his bluff exterior Arran knew Mal hid a keen mind and shrewd wit. Now, he looked uncomfortable. He shifted his feet, playing with the bristles of a curry brush.

"Ye've been different ever since ye met Jenna MacFinnan, and I'm not the only one to have noticed it. Rosaline has too. The way ye look for her when ye first enter a room. The way yer voice softens when ye talk about her. The way ye are so overprotective of the lass."

"Of course I'm protective! I would be protective of any guest under my care!"

"Not like this," Mal said, shaking his head. "When ye arrived at the beach this afternoon and saw Jenna in the water, I'd never seen a look on yer face like that."

"What look?" Arran scoffed. "I was annoyed she'd disobeyed my orders, that's all!"

"Nay, it wasnae annoyance. It was fear. I dinna think I've ever seen ye so scared."

Arran blinked, unsettled by his cousin's insights. He'd been furious when he'd seen Jenna in the water, splashing around like she hadn't got a care in the world when he'd told her time and time again how much danger they were all in. It had been anger, not fear, he'd felt. Hadn't it? But the more he thought about it, the more he recalled the cold sense of dread that had filled him at the sight of Jenna so vulnerable. Mal was right. It *had* been fear. Fear of what might happen to Jenna. Fear of losing her.

He sat down heavily on a bale of straw and leaned forward, elbows resting on his knees. What was happening to him? Why did he feel like he was no longer in control? Why did he feel like a blind man floundering his way through a maze?

"I canna stop thinking about her," he admitted, his voice hoarse. "When I should be concentrating on my duty, on defending our people, on leading the clan, she creeps into my thoughts. I canna sleep for thoughts of her. And when she's not around, I found myself counting down the moments until I can see her again." He looked up imploringly at Mal. "What's happening to me?"

Mal gave him a sympathetic smile then sat down on the straw bale, clapping him on the shoulder. "Isnae it obvious? Ye are in love with her."

Arran stared at Mal. In love with her? What a ridiculous notion! He was not in love with her. He couldn't be. Could he?

He stared down at his hands where they dangled between his knees. They were large and calloused, used to holding a sword or a scythe. And yet, when he looked at them now, all he could think about was the feel of Jenna's hair as it had run through those hands and the soft sensation of her skin beneath his fingertips.

And then he knew. Mal was right.

"I love her."

The words sounded so strange that he couldn't believe they'd just come from his lips. And yet, they felt right. He *was* in love with Jenna MacFinnan. If he was honest with himself, he'd known this for a long time but had refused to see the truth, refused to acknowledge that something could hold such power over him. But he couldn't deny it anymore. Nor did he want to. As he finally admitted it to himself, he felt his heart swell and a fierce joy unlike anything he'd ever felt before fill his chest. He loved Jenna MacFinnan. He wanted to climb the ramparts and shout it from the battlements.

And yet.

"She canna know," he said, turning to Mal. "And ye willnae breathe a word of what I've just said to ye."

Mal blinked, seemingly confused. "I dinna understand. Just tell her how ye feel and marry the lass."

"She's a MacFinnan spellweaver, man! As soon as her task here is finished, she'll be going home, and I'll likely never seen her again." As he said the words, the realization was like a knife twisting in his gut. How could he face a life without Jenna in it?

How could he be expected to go back to how things were before he met her? He couldn't. He just couldn't. But he must. She was from the twenty-first century, he was from the fifteenth. It could never be.

"Then ask her to stay," Mal replied. "Put yer own feelings before yer duty for once."

Oh, he was tempted. He was sorely tempted. An image formed in his mind: Jenna by his side, children at their feet, a land at peace, and his people safe. For an instant he wanted that future so badly he could barely breathe.

Then he shook his head. "I canna do that. How can I ask her to trade everything she has in the future for a life here with me? What can I offer her that would ever live up to what she has in the twenty-first century?"

"Dinna ye think she should be the judge of that?"

"Nay, I dinna. It wouldnae be fair to put her in such a situation. Whatever might have happened since, I still gave my word to see her safely home, and I mean to keep that promise." He fixed Mal with a hard stare. "So ye willnae breathe a word of this conversation to anyone. Do ye ken?"

Mal held his gaze for a moment and then sighed. "As ye wish."

Arran nodded. "Good." He stood up from the bale of straw. "Then we willnae speak of this again. Now, I need to see a man about a book."

He strode off before Mal could utter another word. He took a deep breath as he stepped out of the stable and into the warm sunshine outside. Following his conversation with Mal, the turmoil of his feelings had not abated. In fact, they'd gotten worse. While the realization of what he felt for Jenna filled his heart with joy, the realization of what he was about to lose felt like a cold icicle stabbed right through his chest.

Did ye know this would happen, Lir? he thought.

If so, then Brother Merrick had been right all along: the old gods were indeed cruel.

※※※

"OH MY GOD, that is amazing," Jenna sighed, sinking into the tub right up to her chin.

Ingrid had tipped a powder into the water that caused a lovely lavender scent to rise up and little soap bubbles to form on the surface. As she lounged, Jenna felt all her aches and pains and tension slowly drain away. Heaven. Absolute heaven.

"Would ye like me to wash yer hair?" Ingrid asked.

Jenna was about to decline but thought better of it. It might be nice to be pampered for once. "Actually, that would be great."

She sat up and Ingrid came to kneel behind her. The maid took a wooden scoop and began gently pouring water over her hair and then washing it with a soap made from fat and marjoram—the closest thing they had to shampoo in this time.

Jenna felt her eyes sliding closed. It was blissful to be pampered like this—but Jenna couldn't help wishing it was Arran instead of Ingrid. She wished it was *his* fingers massaging her scalp, *his* hands gently pouring water over her shoulders.

Jenna had to bite her lip to keep from groaning. Why did she have to think about Arran? Why did he have to keep filling her thoughts at the most inopportune moments?

Okay, so they'd had fabulous sex, but that's all it was. Purely physical. A bit of fun. Nothing else.

So why the hell couldn't she get him out of her head? Aargh! It was infuriating in the extreme. She had come here to earn enough money to pay off her debts and save her house. Simple. She most definitely had *not* come here to sleep with the very man who'd employed her and then moon around after him like some love-struck teenager!

Yet she could still almost feel the touch of his fingers across her skin, smell his scent in the air around her, hear his deep, rumbling voice as it washed over her.

What was he doing right now? Meeting with his staff? Discussing plans? Doing other lairdly stuff? Was he thinking about her at all? She doubted it. Arran no doubt had the pick of the ladies of Skye, and Jenna doubted she was the first woman he'd ever had a bit of fun with. Nor would she be the last.

That thought sent an unpleasant sensation sneaking through her gut, and it took a moment for her to realize it was jealousy. She pressed her lips into a hard line as Ingrid began rinsing out her hair. Ridiculous. What did she have to be jealous about? She would be going home soon, back to her normal life where everything made sense, and where people she'd never met weren't after her blood.

She'd never see Arran MacLeod again.

That little twinge in her stomach turned into a full-on ache. Never see Arran again? She didn't like the thought of that. She didn't like it one bit.

"What is it?" Ingrid asked suddenly.

Jenna glanced over her shoulder at the younger woman. "Sorry? What?"

"Ye seemed like ye were miles away. And ye looked sad."

"Did I?" Jenna asked, surprised. "I guess I'm just a little wrung out by what happened today. That must be it."

Ingrid watched her for a moment and then went back to rinsing her hair. "Ah, that must be it. For a minute there, it seemed as if ye might be thinking of something in particular. Or some*one* in particular."

Jenna swiveled to look at Ingrid. "What do you mean by that?"

Ingrid shrugged innocently. "Nothing. Nothing at all. Now turn around so I can finish yer hair."

Jenna didn't. She wasn't fooled by the maid's bland expression and feigned innocence. She narrowed her eyes. "What have you heard?"

"Nothing!" Ingrid said quickly. "Nothing at all."

"Ingrid," Jenna said, scowling at the younger woman. "Spill. What have you heard?"

Ingrid bit her lip and then put down the wooden ewer she'd been using to rinse Jenna's hair. "Oh, all right." She shuffled forward, her eyes sparkling with curiosity. "Well I'm… friendly… with one of the lads who rowed out to bring ye back. Robbie, his name is. Anyway, he said ye and the laird looked a bit… flustered when they picked ye up." She paused and bit her lip again, as if deciding whether to continue. "And that yer clothing looked a little… hastily donned. Apparently, the laird had his breeches on back to front."

Jenna stared at Ingrid for a moment longer and then burst into laughter. It was such a ridiculous image of Arran that she couldn't help herself. She hadn't noticed his slip, and neither, it seemed, had he. After her mirth subsided, she put her head in her hands and groaned.

"Oh God, Ingrid! What am I going to do? Does the whole keep know that Arran and I… that we… that we… oh, you know what I mean!"

"Dinna fash. The lads from the boat are the only ones who know, and they wouldnae breathe a word for fear of the laird's anger. They willnae tell anyone."

"But Robbie told you."

"That's only because we are… close."

"Oh, close are you?" Jenna snorted. "In the same way that the laird and I are close?"

Ingrid grinned. "Aye, something like that."

Jenna blew out a breath and then slapped the surface of the water, watching the droplets catch the light as they fell back down. "This is such a mess, Ingrid. I didn't mean for this to happen. What am I going to do?"

"I dinna understand," Ingrid replied with a frown. "Why is it a mess? The laird is unmarried so—" Her face suddenly went pale. "Oh! Ye aren't married in the future, are ye?"

Jenna laughed at the shocked expression on the younger woman's face. "No! Relax, I'm not married." *Although I was going to be,* she thought, as an image of Alex flashed through her mind.

She pushed it away. She would *not* think about him now. She would not think about him ever again.

Ingrid breathed out, pressing a hand against her chest. "Oh my. Dinna give me a scare like that! But if ye are unmarried why are ye so concerned?"

"Because I don't know how to handle this! It's not like I planned for it to happen."

"But if ye and the laird are... close... isnae it obvious how ye handle it? Ye do the same thing Robbie and I are going to do."

"And what's that?"

"Ye marry the laird, of course!"

Jenna felt her mouth drop open. She couldn't have been more shocked if Ingrid had told her she had to run naked around the island under a full moon.

Marry Arran? Was she crazy?

With an effort, Jenna snapped her mouth shut. "Um... that's not exactly what I had in mind."

"Why not? He's the laird, and a more eligible bachelor ye'll not find in all the islands. And you're a MacFinnan spellweaver. What a match ye would make! And what children ye would produce!"

Jenna recoiled, holding up her palms. "Whoa! Stop, Ingrid. Just stop. I've just had a brief... encounter... with Arran and you've already got us married with children!"

Ingrid shrugged. "It's the way things are done on Skye."

"Well, it's not the way things are done where I come from. I will most definitely *not* be marrying Arran."

Or anyone else, she added to herself. *Ever. I'm not taking that kind of risk again. Sure, Arran is gorgeous and charming and sweet and protective and hot as hell in bed, but I don't love him. I don't. I won't love a man ever again.*

"Oh." Ingrid's shoulders sagged with disappointment. "I see."

Ingrid said nothing else, and an awkward silence filled the room as Jenna finished her bath and Ingrid handed her a large cloth to use as a towel. Jenna wondered at Ingrid's reaction. It seemed that Rosaline wasn't the only one eager for Arran to marry and start producing heirs. Jenna wondered why he hadn't. Was it really because he'd been too busy defending his island from raiders as he claimed, or was there more to it than that?

It doesn't matter, she told herself as she began pulling on the clean clothes that Ingrid laid out for her. *It's none of your business, and it's not your problem. Just do the job you came here to do, get paid, and go home. And stop thinking about Arran bloody MacLeod!*

"How is Rosaline now?" she asked Ingrid.

When they'd returned to the keep, it was clear that Rosaline had been going out of her mind with worry. It must be horrible, Jenna thought, to have the only remaining member of your family constantly in danger. She didn't know how Rosaline coped.

Ingrid picked up the pile of Jenna's laundry, tied them into a sheet, and deposited them by the door. "Oh, ye know. The lady of the keep is a strong woman but still, she worries me. She's getting on a bit now and all this constant worry canna be good for her."

"Getting on a bit?" Jenna said. "Rosaline is *not* 'getting on a bit'!"

"She is too. It's her name day tomorrow, and she'll be fifty. Fifty! Imagine it! I've rarely met anyone so old. Even my old gran didnae live much past that, and she was the oldest person in her village."

Jenna blinked in surprise. "It's Rosaline's fiftieth birthday tomorrow?"

"Aye."

"Is she having a party?"

"A what?"

"You know, a celebration. Fifty is a pretty special birthday, after all."

"I dinna think so. What, with all the troubles I dinna think anyone has really thought about it."

Jenna pressed her lips into a flat line. Surely *Arran* had

thought about it? Surely he was planning something for his mother's big day? She would never dare let one of her aunt's birthdays go by without marking it. Once, when she'd been in her late teens, she'd forgotten her aunt Elise's birthday. Never again. Her aunt had sulked for a week as though *she* was the surly teenager and Jenna the adult.

An idea began to form in her head, and she grinned suddenly. "Well, if nobody else has thought about it, then it's up to us, isn't it?"

The maid gave her a puzzled look. "What's up to us?"

"Organizing Rosaline's birthday party, of course!"

Ingrid's mouth formed a little O of surprise. "Do ye think we can? Would the laird mind?"

Jenna waved a dismissive hand. "You leave the laird to me. It's just what everyone needs with all the trouble we've been having. A chance for the clan to celebrate and let their hair down."

And a chance for me to do the same, she thought. *And forget about magic and obligations and Arran MacLeod for a while.*

Ingrid clapped her hands together. "Aye, ye are right! It will be wonderful!"

"Don't tell Rosaline though—we'll keep it a surprise. Do you think you can rope in some of the other staff without her knowing? We'll need their help if we're to pull this off."

Ingrid nodded enthusiastically. "I'll speak to Cook and Chamberlain. They'll help." Her eyes sparkled. "This is going to be fun!"

Jenna nodded. "I sure hope so—as long as a certain laird doesn't throw a spanner in the works."

Ingrid blinked. "Throw a what?"

Jenna waved a hand. "Never mind." She did a little twirl. "How do I look?"

She'd donned a long gold dress with silver brocade along the hem and bodice. Her hair was still wet, but without a hair dryer there was nothing she could do about that.

Ingrid sighed, clasping her hands together over her heart. "Ye look beautiful," she said. "The laird willnae be able to deny ye anything."

"We'll see about that." She took a deep breath. "Well, no time like the present. Shall we meet back here in say, half an hour and start planning?"

Ingrid practically bounced on her feet. "Eeek!" she cried. "This is so exciting! I've never been a conspirator before!"

"Well I'm on old hand," Jenna said with a laugh. "So I'll teach you everything you need to know! Back soon."

She walked to the door and slipped out, looked up and down the corridor, checking Rosaline was nowhere in sight, then set off. She guessed that Arran would be in his study. When he wasn't training with his men or eating with everyone else in the great hall that's where he normally was, so Jenna wove her way through the corridors of the castle, nodding greetings to people she passed, until she reached the stout wooden door she needed.

She paused outside, taking a minute to straighten her hair and brush imaginary dirt from her dress. Butterflies fluttered in her stomach, and Jenna couldn't quite decide if it was nerves or... or... anticipation?

Confident that she looked as presentable as she was going to get without a pair of hair straighteners, mascara, and a half-decent mirror, she knocked on the door.

A few seconds later, it opened to reveal the young lad who acted as Arran's page. Disappointment flared in Jenna's gut. She'd been hoping to catch Arran alone.

"Hi," she said brightly. "Could I speak to the laird, please?"

The lad—Archie?—bobbed his head. "Aye. Please come in, my lady."

She followed the lad into the room and then stopped dead. Arran was seated at the polished round table that dominated his study, but he wasn't alone. Several other men were sitting with him, including Mal and Brother Merrick. They all looked up as she entered.

"Oh. Um," Jenna faltered. "Sorry. I didn't mean to interrupt."

Arran cleared his throat. "Lady MacFinnan," he said, his voice sounding stilted and formal. "We were just meeting to discuss what Brother Merrick discovered. What can we do for ye?"

Jenna met his gaze across the room, and her stomach fluttered. Despite herself, she felt a blush rising up her cheeks. "I… er… was wondering if I could have a quick word. Um, alone?"

"Of course." Arran pushed himself up from his seat. "If ye would excuse me, gentlemen."

He followed Jenna out into the corridor and pulled the door shut behind him. He glanced up and down the passage, checking they were alone before his deep gaze settled on her. Jenna tingled at the nearness of him. Her fingers itched to touch his face, to trail through his hair.

"Is everything all right, Jenna?"

"Yes," she said quickly. "I just wanted to ask you something."

He shifted, taking a tiny step nearer. His arm rose as if he would touch her, but then he let his hand drop. Memories flashed in Jenna's head: the heat of his body, the feel of his lips, the touch of his hands, the all-consuming desire that he'd sparked in her. She felt her cheeks flush scarlet and hoped the dimness of the corridor hid it.

"Oh? What do ye wish to ask me?"

So many things, Jenna thought. *Like why you couldn't have been born in the twenty-first century. Like why couldn't I have met you before I met Alex. Like why can't I stop thinking about you no matter what I do?*

"I… um… Ingrid tells me it's Rosaline's birthday tomorrow."

Arran's eyes widened and he let out a string of Gaelic curses under his breath. "Aye," he said, rubbing the side of his face. "It is. How could I have forgotten? She'll skin me alive!"

Jenna laughed softly. "Don't worry, she'll never have to know. That's what I've come about. Ingrid and I are planning on throwing her a party."

"A party? What's that?"

"A feast. A celebration. Call it whatever you want. To mark her special birthday. But I wanted to come check it's all right with you first. What do you think?"

He smiled, and his face softened into a gentle expression. "I think, Jenna MacFinnan, that is the best idea I have heard in ages. It's just what we need."

"Exactly what I thought. So I have your blessing to go ahead and arrange it then?"

He inclined his head. "Ye do. And I'll give instructions that ye are to be given whatever help ye need from the castle staff."

"Thank you."

She paused and found herself staring at him. He stared right back.

Jenna cleared her throat. "Right. Well, I'll… um… let you get back to your meeting. Er… see you at the party tomorrow?"

"Aye," he breathed softly. "Ye will."

Jenna turned and hurried away.

ARRAN WATCHED JENNA walk away from him. *Go after her*, a voice shouted in the back of his head. *Tell her how you feel! Do whatever it takes to make her yours!*

Oh, how he longed to give into that voice! How he longed to call her back, to take her into his arms and never let her go. But he could not. He *would* not. He would not be that selfish.

Taking a deep breath, he turned and pushed the door open, returning to his advisors.

"Is everything all right, my laird?" Edrick, captain of his guard asked.

"Aye," Arran replied gruffly. "Lady Jenna wished to discuss a household matter, that's all." He glanced at Mal and found his cousin watching him with a knowing look on his face.

Arran cleared his throat and returned his attention back to Edrick. He waved a hand. "Continue with yer report."

"As I was saying, the fortifications at Tollman's Gate turned back most of the attack, as we hoped they would, and most of the damage to the settlement was borne at the eastern end. That's where they concentrated their attack."

Arran thought back to the raid on Tollman's Gate. It had been so chaotic he'd taken little heed of the disposition of the raiders but now, with Edrick's report, something began to nag at him.

"What is at the eastern end of Tollman's Gate? The chapel? Wealthy households?"

Edrick shook his head. "That's what's strange. We would normally expect them to attack those sorts of places—it's generally where the wealth is—but both the chapel and all the wealthier households were ignored. And some of the defenders said the raiders didnae seem so bent on destruction as they expected either. Once they broke through, they didnae stop to fight, but ran farther into the settlement. As if—"

"As if they were looking for something," Arran finished for him.

He pushed himself up from his chair and strode to one of the bookcases against a wall. Pulling down a scroll, he rolled it out on the table and pinned it at each corner with the pottery goblets they'd all been drinking from. A detailed map of the island filled the parchment, with each settlement clearly marked. Arran leaned over it, ran his hand along the coast until he found Tollman's Gate, and placed a marker on it. Then he found the cove where his fishing fleet had been attacked and marked that too.

"Where else have there been attacks in the last six months?"

His advisors rose to their feet and clustered around the map.

"Here," Mal said, placing another marker. "And here."

In short order, twelve markers covered the map. Twelve attacks in six months. More than double the number that had taken place in the whole of the year before. The raiders were stepping up their attacks, but why? He placed his palms flat on the table and leaned over the map, scanning the placement of the markers. He began to sense a pattern, although he couldn't quite see it yet.

"Mal, where was the first attack?" he asked. His cousin pointed to one of the markers. "And the second?"

As Mal pointed to each of the markers in the order that the raids had taken place, the pattern Arran had sensed gradually became clear. His fingers gripped the edge of the table hard. Unease began to churn in his gut.

"They're not random," he said, looking around at each of his advisors. "Look. Follow the pattern of the attacks. Each one takes place a set distance and direction from the last, homing in on a particular area, like a net closing in."

Mal swore loudly. "Damn them to the hells! Ye are right! They're moving closer and closer to this spot here." His big hand came to rest on the far southeast of the island. It was the only area that had yet to have any markers on it—but it was surrounded by others.

"Why?" Edrick asked. "What are they doing?"

"They're not just here for plunder," Arran replied. "They're looking for something. That's what the attacks have been about."

He looked over at Brother Merrick. The monk was leaning over the map, studying the pattern of the markers and his lips were moving as though talking to himself.

"Brother Merrick," Arran said. "I want ye to switch yer research to the southeastern tip of the island. Go through all the land records, old myths, anything that might relate to this area. See if you can find any record of old Norse settlements or myths relating to the place. Especially anything that mentions Njord."

Brother Merrick nodded. "Aye, my laird. I'll get to it immediately."

"Good. And get as many people to help ye as ye need. Let me know the instant ye find anything." He turned his attention to his other advisors. "Double patrols in that area. If we're right, they've exhausted the other areas they've searched so that's where they'll attack next. I want to know the moment anything out of the ordinary is spotted. The raiders have always been one step ahead of us, but now we might just have the chance to turn the tables. Mal, take as many men as ye need and set up messenger relays to bring word back here as quickly as possible."

Mal nodded. "Aye, my laird."

Arran's gaze returned to the map. He ought to feel pleased that they'd figured out their enemy's strategy, but all he felt was a dark sense of foreboding. He stared at the south-eastern tip of the island. *What's there?* he thought. *What are ye looking for?*

He had no idea, but one thing he knew for sure. Whatever it was, he had to stop them finding it.

Chapter Eighteen

"ARE YE SURE they canna sort this out themselves?" Rosaline asked as she and Jenna wove through the castle towards the great hall. "They aren't children, ye know."

Rosaline sounded uncharacteristically grumpy, and Jenna didn't blame her. She'd probably feel the same if everyone forgot *her* birthday.

"I don't think so," Jenna replied. "Cook looked pretty angry. Last I saw, she was waving a wooden spoon at the chamberlain like it was a sword. Ingrid said I best come find you before they come to blows."

Rosaline harrumphed. "And where is Arran?"

"Out training with his men."

"Of course, he is." Rosaline muttered something under her breath in Gaelic and while Jenna couldn't understand the words, she suspected it was not polite.

The corridors of the keep were unusually quiet for early evening—just as Jenna knew they would be. Rosaline, luckily, didn't seem to notice, and stomped towards the great hall with a scowl on her face that would have curdled milk. Jenna tried to hide her smile as she followed the older woman.

Finally, they reached the doors to the great hall. They stood closed, which again, was unusual. Rosaline grabbed the handle and shouldered them open.

"I dinna know what the two of ye have been arguing about now but ye—" she began.

She trailed off as she caught sight of the crowd waiting inside. Her eyes widened as she looked around at the rows of tables laden with food and drink, at the garlands that had been hung from the rafters, at the three musicians that struck up a lively tune as she entered.

"What?" she murmured, eyes shining. "What is going on?"

Jenna came up beside her. "Surprise! Happy birthday, Rosaline."

At that, everyone burst into a round of cheering and applause and cries of "happy name day" echoed around the room. Arran was standing by the high table and as the cheers died away, he came around the table and approached his mother. He gave her a flourishing bow.

"If ye will allow me to escort ye, my lady, we can let the festivities begin."

Rosaline beamed. Tears sparkled in her eyes. "Ye organized all this?"

"Nay, I canna take the credit for that. Jenna and Ingrid are responsible—all I did was get out of their way."

"Oh my!" Rosaline said. "I thought everyone had forgotten."

"Not a chance," Ingrid said as she came up on Rosaline's other side. "Do ye like it?"

"Like it? I love it!"

"Then let's get this party started!" Jenna said.

Rosaline laid her arm on Arran's and he escorted her over to the high table, seating her in the place of honor—the chair that was normally reserved for him. Arran sat on her left side while Jenna took a seat to her right. She couldn't help glancing at Arran as they took their seats. He was smiling at his mother, both more relaxed than she'd seen them in some time.

A warm sensation stole through her. For an instant she imagined what it would be like if this was her life. If she and Arran were together and Rosaline and Ingrid and all the others became her surrogate family. If this was her home. That warm feeling increased, spreading through her like honey, and bringing with it a mix of contentment and wistfulness.

"A drink?"

Jenna looked around at the young lad standing at her elbow, holding a jug of whisky. "Don't mind if I do," she replied, holding out her goblet.

When everyone in the room had a goblet, Arran scraped back his chair and rose to his feet. Everyone fell silent, and all eyes turned towards their laird.

Arran cleared his throat. "I know times havenae been easy," he said in a gruff voice. "And I wish to thank each and every one of ye for yer courage and steadfastness. I am proud to call ye my kin and friends and even prouder to be yer chief." There were shouts and rumbles of agreement. "But tonight I want ye all to forget our troubles. My lady mother has reached the ripe old age of fifty years." Rosaline scowled and swatted his arm at this. "So tonight we celebrate. We celebrate her, we celebrate each other, and we celebrate this clan. To Clan MacLeod!"

He raised his goblet and everyone else did the same. There were cries of "Clan MacLeod!" "Lady Rosaline!" "Happy name day!"

Jenna raised her own goblet in the toast and then knocked it back in one. But as the party began in earnest, Jenna found a strange melancholy replacing the warm feeling inside. Everyone was in high spirits—talking, laughing, sharing jokes. Over in one corner, Ingrid was deep in conversation with a handsome man whom she guessed must be Robbie. Arran and Rosaline were reminiscing about family get togethers of the past, and the atmosphere was warm and jovial.

I'll be leaving this behind soon, she thought. It made her sad. Her gaze flicked to Arran. *I'll be leaving him behind.* That made her even sadder.

She called over the young serving lad and held out her empty goblet.

"Could I have another whisky, please?"

ARRAN HAD TO admit that this had been a good idea. As he watched his people eating, drinking, laughing, and dancing, he realized that they'd been missing this sort of camaraderie for far too long. Life shouldn't be all tension and worry. They had to take their chances at happiness whenever they came along.

It had taken Jenna to remind him of that.

He took a sip from his goblet and leaned back in his chair, searching the room for her. There she was, in the cleared space in the middle of the floor that had been set aside for dancing. His people had formed two lines facing each other and were engaged in one of the traditional Highland dances that his mother loved so much.

Right now, Rosaline was twirling and laughing like a giddy girl, and it did his heart good to see her happy. Lord above, she deserved it.

His gaze moved to Jenna. Her partner was old Drurie, the retired stable master. They were trying to keep up with the complicated moves, getting it horribly wrong, and laughing at their efforts.

Arran smiled. Jenna was so unlike anyone he'd ever met. Free-spirited, confident, so full of life. She made his life richer, more vibrant. How could he go back to his old life when she was gone?

All his good humor drained away. His fingers closed around his goblet, squeezing so hard that a sudden crack appeared in the pottery. He thumped it down onto the table. He suddenly felt stifled, like there was no air in the room.

He scraped his chair back as quietly as he could. Despite his size, when he wanted to, he could move as silently as a cat. He employed all of those skills now as he stepped into the shadows around the edges of the room, made his way to the door, and slipped out.

Outside, a fat moon was hanging in the sky and the air had turned chilly now the sun had gone down. Torches burned along the keep's high walls, chasing away the shadows.

Crossing the bailey, he approached the postern gate on the far side and was pleased when a voice spoke from the darkness. "Who goes there?"

Hamish, one of his guardsmen, stepped from the shadows, one hand resting on the hilt of the sword strapped at his waist.

"My… my apologies, my laird," he said when he saw Arran.

Arran clapped the man on the shoulder. "Nae need to apologize for doing yer job, my friend. I'll be going out now. I need some air."

"Aye, as ye wish," Hamish said, stepping aside. Like the guards on the battlements, those that manned the gates were used to Arran leaving the keep at strange times and knew better than to question him.

Arran lifted the heavy wooden beam from its brackets and set it to one side. Shouldering open the door, he stepped out onto the keep's far side. Here, the walls of Dun Tabor ran close to the hillside that rose behind, creating a strip of land away from the prying eyes of Dun Tabor's residents which was kept private for the laird and his family. In the darkness, Arran could just make out the rows of mounds that ran towards the hill's base and smell the night flowers that had been placed on the two nearest.

He paused, wondering why he'd come. Did he expect to find answers here? Not likely. Here there was only dust and memories. And yet, he still came whenever he needed to think.

He seated himself on a crude wooden bench set before the nearest two mounds. Each of those mounds bore a stone cross carved with the names of Arran's father and brother, but also a round stone marked with the symbols of the old religion. If nothing else, his father had been a practical man, hedging his bets by appealing to both the old gods and the new. Even in death, that had not changed.

Ten long years had passed since these graves had been dug.

Sometimes it felt like yesterday. Sometimes it felt like a century. Sometimes he struggled to remember the faces of his father and brother.

"What would you do?" he said aloud. "What should *I* do?"

He wasn't entirely sure what he was asking—whether he was referring to the raiders or the situation with Jenna, or a combination of the two. He only knew that the lairdship felt heavy tonight. The weight of responsibility felt like an iron collar around his neck, dragging him down.

"How did ye bear it?" he said to his father's grave. "How did ye carry the weight of it all?"

He already knew the answer to that. He'd had Rosaline to help him carry it. Two sons to help him carry it. But what did Arran have? Nobody. All these years he'd thought he could carry it alone, but now it was getting too heavy. He couldn't stop the morbid thoughts from forming in his mind. What if he and Jenna failed? Would he be remembered as the last laird of the MacLeods of Skye? The man that oversaw the final destruction of his people?

"Arran?"

The soft voice had him spinning around, staring into the darkness. A shadow moved and his hand went to the hilt of his dagger.

"Who's there?"

The shadow stepped into the moonlight, revealing long hair the color of midnight and bright green eyes that sparkled in the gloom.

"Jenna," he breathed.

"I... I... missed you at the party," she said softly. "The man on the gate said I could find you here."

She'd missed him. His heart thrilled with pleasure to hear that.

"What are you doing?" Her eyes alighted on the cemetery, and her mouth formed a little O. "I'm sorry. I didn't mean to intrude."

"Ye are not. I just come here when I need to think."

She sat down on the bench next to him, close enough that he could feel the warmth from her skin and smell the soap from her hair. "And what is it you need to think about?"

Ye, he thought. *About how ye have turned my world upside down. About how I canna bear the thought of ye going home. About how I canna tell ye any of this.*

But aloud all he said was, "Lots of things."

Jenna nodded then turned and stared out at the rows of graves. Her gaze traced the names carved on his father and brother's crosses, and her expression softened. "It wasn't your fault, you know."

He looked at her sharply. "What wasn't?"

"What happened to your father and brother? It wasn't your fault. None of this is your fault."

Arran's nostrils flared. His breathing quickened. "I... um... I don't know what you mean."

"Yes, you do. I recognize that look in your eyes because I used to see it in my own whenever I looked in the mirror. You have to let it go. The guilt. That nagging voice that says you could have done more. That if only you'd been better, done things differently, they'd still be alive."

Arran was shocked by her insight. His chest was suddenly heaving, stomach roiling. He'd never heard his innermost feelings spoken aloud before. He'd never given voice to the turmoil that roiled inside him ever since his father and brother had died. He thought he'd kept it carefully hidden, buried beneath the façade of the strong-willed laird.

But he hadn't. He hadn't been able to hide it from this twenty-first century woman who seemed to see him more clearly than anyone ever had.

He opened his mouth for a quip, a denial, a rebuttal of what she'd said, but instead, the words that tumbled from his mouth were, "I dinna know how."

"It's hard, isn't it? Believe me, I know. But you have to find a way, Arran, otherwise it will crush you. Nobody could have done better than you have. Not your father. Not your brother. You need to stop comparing yourself to them."

The moonlight lit the edge of her face, outlining it with silver. "How do ye see these things, lass? Yer magic?"

She snorted softly. "Not magic. Just experience. Like I said, that look on your face is one I used to see in the mirror all the time."

"Yer mother?" Arran asked softly.

She went rigid, and Arran knew he'd guessed right. She didn't answer for a long time and sat staring out into the darkness. Finally, she nodded.

"Yes, my mother. I blamed myself for her death for the longest time. She had cancer, you see, and the doctors said there was nothing that could be done. But I didn't accept that. I was a MacFinnan spellweaver, damn it! I could do anything! But I couldn't, and she died.

"For years after that I carried around guilt like a millstone. If I'd only found the right spell. If only I'd worked harder. If only I'd thought of something we hadn't tried. If only this, if only that. But it doesn't work, Arran. It just chews you up inside." She laid her hand on his arm, and his skin tingled where she touched him. "None of this is your fault, just like what happened to my mother wasn't mine. It's just... life. Bad shit happens."

Arran smiled wryly. "Bad shit happens. Ye certainly have a way with words, lass."

"What can I say? I'm a poet."

"I'm sorry about yer ma, lass. I'm sorry that happened to her. To ye."

"So am I. But the past is gone, and the future is yet to be determined. All we have is now. That's all any of us ever have." She blinked, as if surprised by her own words. "Wow. I almost sounded wise then, didn't I?"

Arran laughed softly. "Aye, lass. Careful. Ye'll get a reputation." He met her gaze. "What am I going to do without ye?"

He hadn't meant to say those words, but they were out of his mouth before he could stop them. Jenna stared at him, and he could see a swirl of thoughts and emotions in her eyes. An ache lit inside him, a deep, almost painful longing for this woman. Was this what love felt like? This almost primal need for another? Like he wasn't whole unless in her presence?

She said nothing. Then, slowly, she reached up and ran the tips of her fingers down his cheek. Then, in a swift movement, she slid closer on the bench, leaned in, and kissed him softly.

He'd dreamed of this. He'd longed for it ever since he'd made love to her on the beach. This was real. It was *now*, and Arran felt himself getting lost in this moment. Getting lost in *her*. He cupped her face and kissed her back.

But then it was over.

Jenna pulled away. "Sorry. I shouldn't have done that."

Yes, you should, Arran thought. His muscles trembled with the effort of not reaching out, not pulling her close and kissing her into submission.

"It's all right, lass," he said, his voice hoarse.

"No," she replied. "No, it isn't." She wiped a hand across her forehead. "Oh God, I promised myself I wouldn't do this! What happened between us at the beach, Arran, I... I... thought it would just be a one off. A bit of fun. That I could live with it being no more than that. But I... I keep wanting more. I keep wanting you."

"Then what's the problem? We're two grown adults. We—"

"I can't!" she said, wringing her hands. "I can't do this. I can't take this step. I promised myself I wouldn't. Never again. Not ever, ever again."

Her eyes shone with sorrow and old pain. Someone had hurt her. Badly. That was what she was trying to tell him, that she would not risk her heart again. Fury bubbled in his stomach. Not at Jenna. Never at Jenna. But at whoever had hurt her so badly.

He tamped down on the desire burning through his veins. Tucked away that awful, bone-deep longing. Shut away the feelings that were threatening to overwhelm him. It was one of the hardest things he'd ever had to do. But he'd do it. For her. For her, he'd do anything.

He leaned forward, placed a kiss on her forehead, then rose to his feet, holding out his hand.

"Come on," he said. "We'd better get back to the feast before my mother sends out a search party."

Jenna smiled wryly, took his hand, and let him pull her up. "We wouldn't want that, would we? The laird and the spellweaver being caught together in the cemetery? Imagine what the gossips would make of that."

"Nothing close to the truth, I'd wager. Come. There's a flagon of whisky inside with our names on it."

"I thought you'd never ask."

Chapter Nineteen

JENNA GROANED AS she opened her eyes. Her head was thumping something fierce and her eyes felt grainy. Drinking whisky last night had seemed a good idea at the time. Now? Not so much.

As she sat up and swung her legs out of bed, she wondered if anyone else in the keep was feeling as bad as she was. Probably not. They were all used to whisky and besides, she doubted any of them had been drinking to forget the way she had. Drinking to forget that she was a zillion miles from home. Drinking to forget the mess that was waiting for her when she returned to that home.

But most of all, drinking to forget the longing she felt for a certain corn-haired laird and what had happened between them in the cemetery last night.

She'd been so close to the edge. So close to taking that last step and falling, falling, falling. Into him. She'd only just pulled herself back from that cliff edge.

It's for the best, she told herself. *Nothing good would come of it.*

She put her hand to her throbbing head. Ugh. Her tongue felt furry, and she was pretty sure her breath was strong enough to stun a horse. With a groan, she stood, tottered over to the pottery basin, and poured in some cold water from the jug that stood on the side table. Without further ado, she dunked her head in.

The water was freezing, and she would have gasped if she didn't have her mouth underwater. It did help to clear her head a little though, for which she was profoundly grateful. She raised her head and began her morning ablutions—washing her face, scrubbing her teeth, and then brushing her damp hair.

Ingrid didn't come in to help like she usually would, but Jenna didn't begrudge the maid for taking a little time off. The last she'd seen of Ingrid, she'd been leaving the great hall hand in hand with Robbie, the pair of them seemingly oblivious to anything else around them. A small spike of envy pricked Jenna's stomach. It was all so straightforward for Ingrid. She loved Robbie so she would marry him. That's all there was to it.

Why couldn't Jenna's own life be so simple?

Moving carefully to avoid making her head pound, Jenna washed and dressed and then left her room and made her way to the great hall. When she entered the cavernous room, she saw that it had already been cleared and cleaned following last night's celebrations. It was quiet too, with only a few people in attendance, and they sat quietly, sipping from cups and eating porridge.

Jenna wondered if they were nursing heads as thick as hers.

Arran was already in the great hall, sitting at the place of honor at the high table. Rosaline sat next to him, looking a little more disheveled than usual.

As she stepped across the threshold, Arran's gaze sprang to her and she felt that familiar warmth coil in her belly. Why did he have to look at her like that? Didn't he realize that this was hard enough for her already?

"Good morning," she mumbled as she joined them at the high table.

"Is it?" Rosaline groaned. "Feels like a pretty terrible morning to me."

Jenna gave her a sympathetic smile, and Arran said nothing as Jenna took a seat. She was sure she could see a spark of amusement dancing in his eyes though. Clearly *he* didn't have a hangover.

Jenna pulled over a basket of bannocks and began nibbling on the corner of one. She wasn't sure her stomach could handle anything more—certainly not the porridge, sausages, or boiled eggs that lay in platters on the table. She ate in silence, staring at her plate, but looked up when the door suddenly burst open.

Brother Merrick came hurrying in. His habit flapped around his knees as he rushed over. He was holding a stack of books under one arm and he looked, Jenna thought, a little flustered.

"I've found something, my lord!" he blurted. "Ye need to take a look at this!"

Any amusement at Jenna and Rosaline's condition vanished from Arran's expression and he scraped back his chair and stood.

"Come with me."

Jenna stuffed the last bit of bannock into her mouth, muttered an apology to Rosaline, and followed as the two men strode off. Arran glanced at her as she caught up with them, and nodded.

"Find Mal and Edrick," Arran snapped at a servant as they strode through the keep. "Tell them to meet me in my study immediately." The servant nodded and dashed off.

Once they'd reached Arran's study, he gestured to the empty chairs around the table. Jenna sank into hers gratefully, wondering what exactly was going on. Arran was all focused and alert, like he was when he thought danger was near, and Brother Merrick looked apprehensive as he dropped into a chair and laid the books he'd brought with him on the table.

Jenna bit her lip. Mal and Edrick arrived only moments later, both panting as though they'd run all the way here.

"What is it?" Mal demanded. "Dougie said to come straight away. It isnae another attack, is it?"

"Sit down, both of ye," Arran said. "And listen. Brother Merrick has something he wishes to share with us."

The two men exchanged glances and then lowered themselves into chairs.

Arran clasped his hands together on the table and leaned forward. His piercing gaze fixed on the monk. "Well? What have ye found?"

Brother Merrick swallowed thickly. "I did as ye asked," he said. "I've scoured everything we have in the library that pertains to Norse settlements or stories about the area ye marked on the map."

He nodded to the table, and Jenna realized that a map was spread out on it. The map showed the whole of Skye, and there were markers placed all around the island except for an area in the southeast.

"At first I didnae find aught and I thought this might all be a wild goose chase," Brother Merrick continued. "But this morning I thought I might look at the land records again—after all, that's where I found our last clue, isnae it?"

Arran's jaw clenched and Jenna could tell he was working hard to keep his patience with the monk's roundabout way of explaining things. "And what did ye find?"

Brother Merrick took a scroll from the pile and rolled it out. He leaned forward, running his finger down the parchment until he found the spot he was looking for. "Ah ha! Here it is!" He tapped the scroll then turned it around and offered it to Arran, pointing at the spot.

Jenna leaned forward, squinting. It was a map. She couldn't see anything particularly special about the spot he indicated, just a small bay on the southeast coast.

Arran frowned. "What exactly are we looking at?"

"It's not marked on the map anymore because when the Norse were chased out of Skye several hundred years ago and the MacFinnan magic placed to keep them out, it was destroyed. Or so everyone thought."

"*What* was destroyed?"

Brother Merrick grinned and unrolled another parchment on the table, laying it flat next to the map. "This is a land grant from around the same time the MacFinnan magic was first constructed. It talks about several settlements in the area we're interested in, but most of them were abandoned. There's one, though, that's of particular interest to us. Here. Nordve."

Jenna sat back. As Brother Merrick said the word, a strange feeling went through her, a cold shiver, as though somebody had stepped over her grave.

"I am supposed to recognize that?" Arran said, impatience clear in his voice.

"*Ve* is the Norse word for shrine," Merrick said, practically bouncing in his seat in excitement. "So put this word together with the name Njord and what do ye get?"

"Njord's shrine," Arran breathed, eyes widening in realization.

"Aye! And the land grand lists where it is." He pointed at an empty spot on the map. "It isnae marked, but it's around here."

The cold Jenna had felt as Merrick pronounced the name hadn't left her. In fact, it was growing stronger. "That's it," she said suddenly, looking up at Arran. "That's what the raiders have been looking for. And I'll bet my last penny that it's this shrine that's been preventing me from fixing the magic."

Arran nodded. "Then if we can find this shrine and destroy it—"

"There will be nothing to keep me from fixing the magic," Jenna finished for him.

She should have felt elated. At last! Finally, a breakthrough! At last she would be able to do what she'd come here to do and go home. Yes, she should have felt elated. But as she stared into Arran's bottomless eyes, all she felt was a creeping sense of dread.

Arran's face was a carefully controlled mask as he nodded. "Why are the raiders looking for this shrine?"

"Same reason we are at a guess," Jenna replied. "Only for opposite reasons. We want to resurrect Skye's magic; they want to stop us."

Brother Merrick ran one hand down his face. "It's more than that, I reckon. After all, the raids started before ye arrived here, Lady Jenna. Centuries ago, Skye lay under the dominion of the Norse lords. What if Njord was the god they worshipped? What if that god was ousted when the MacFinnan spellweavers worked their magic?"

"And now the magic is broken, they want Skye back," Jenna breathed. "They mean to resurrect Njord's power."

Arran looked between Merrick and Jenna. "And from yer expressions I'm guessing that's bad."

Jenna swallowed and nodded. "Arran, if Njord's magic is revived, it will give him complete control over Skye. There would be nothing you could do to stop him and his people from taking your island from you."

A snarl curled Arran's lips. "Over my dead body. We'll destroy this shrine before they ever find it. We'll ride out immediately to look for it. If we—"

He cut off suddenly as a commotion sounded from outside the room. Arran's hand went to his sword hilt as the door burst open and one of Arran's clansmen came tumbling in. He was disheveled and wind-swept and brought the smell of the sea and open skies into the room with him. His chest was heaving.

"Tam?" Mal said, his brow furrowing with concern. "I thought ye were out with the eastern patrol? What are ye doing here?"

"Was… out… with… the… patrol," Tam gasped. He leaned over, hands on his knees. When he'd caught his breath, he straightened. "Was… sent… to warn ye. Raiders. A huge force. Bigger than any we've seen."

Arran's face paled. "Where?"

"We spotted them from the top of Kerrig's Fell. A fleet of them heading southeast. They were still some miles off and will take some hours before they reach us. I rode here as fast as I could. The rest of my unit are tracking them along the coast."

That cold that had been building inside Jenna suddenly intensified. She felt as though she'd been pierced through the middle with a dagger of ice. She could feel things shifting around her, the strands of fate tightening, and she knew, absolutely knew, that this force would destroy Skye if it landed. They had to stop it.

"They're going for the shrine," she murmured, looking up at Arran.

He nodded tightly, jaw clenched. "Aye, but they willnae reach it." His voice was low and dangerous, like the growl of a wolf. He turned to Mal and Edrick. "Send out the call to arms. Every man able to wield a weapon. Tell them to muster here." He tapped a spot on the map close to where Merrick had said Njord's shrine lay. "And mobilize whatever is left of our fleet."

Mal scratched his chin as he examined the map. "If we do that, we'll leave the other areas of the island vulnerable. This might be a ruse, designed to draw us out while they attack elsewhere."

"I know that," Arran replied. "But it's a risk we must take. If we dinna fend off this attack, they will take Skye and there willnae be any of us left to worry about it. Do as I say. Send out the call to muster."

Mal looked troubled but he inclined his head all the same. "Aye, my laird."

The men left. Jenna found herself alone with Arran. His shoulders were hunched, his jaw tight, and a vein was throbbing in his temple.

"Arran, I—"

"Ye will stay here."

Jenna sat back. "I'm sorry?"

Arran raised his head and looked at her. His expression was ravaged, his eyes full of shadow. "My men and I will ride out to meet this force, but ye will remain here."

"What are you talking about? I have to go! This is my chance to do what I came here to do! If I can destroy whatever power is in that shrine, I'll be able to fix the magic!"

He shook his head. "It's too dangerous. We dinna know that this shrine has aught to do with the magic at all. It could all be coincidence."

"You don't believe that."

"It doesnae matter what I believe!" he snapped. "I willnae put ye in harm's way! I willnae risk it! Ye will stay here with Rosaline!"

Jenna said nothing. Then softly, she said, "Arran, this is my chance. This is *our* chance. If I'm right, I will be able to restore Skye's magic, and those raiders won't even be able to reach the shore. Nobody will get hurt."

"And if ye are wrong?" he asked, just as softly. His blue eyes found and held hers. The expression in them almost stopped her heart. "I canna risk it. I canna lose ye, Jenna." These last words were spoken so quietly they were barely above a whisper.

That icy dagger sliced through her middle again. She felt the bands of fate tighten around her—around *them*—and she felt the future slide into place. She suddenly knew that if she stayed behind, if she didn't go with him to face this threat, then Arran would not return.

And that thought filled her with a horror so dark she could barely breathe.

"I'm coming," she said, her voice shaking a little. "I have to. And you can't stop me. Even if you lock me up, I'll only use my magic to escape and follow you. You can't win this argument, my laird. I'm sorry."

His lip curled in a snarl, and she heard a growl in his chest like the low rumble of an avalanche. His hands clenched into fists. Then suddenly, he let out his breath in a whoosh.

"Has anyone ever told ye that ye are the most vexing woman on God's clean earth?"

Jenna smiled wryly. "On occasion."

"Dear God, woman. Ye will be the death of me."

No, I won't, Jenna thought. *I will be the saving of you. No matter what it takes.*

She gestured to the door. "Shall we? It looks like it's going to be a long ride."

Arran hesitated then gestured for her to precede him through the door. As she did so, Jenna felt fate snap tight around her and knew she'd taken a step from which there was no going back.

ARRAN RODE WITH a sick feeling in the pit of his stomach. He couldn't quite tell if it was fear or dread or apprehension or a mix of all three. He was used to all of these sensations—they had been his constant companions for most of his life—but now those feelings seemed more insidious, reaching dark, twisting roots right through him until he could barely think straight.

He realized he was pushing his horse harder than necessary and forced himself to rein the beast back. He was caught between wanting to get there as quickly as possible and not wanting to get there at all.

He glanced over his shoulder. His warriors were spread out behind him in a phalanx that would drive fear into the hearts of anyone who saw them. They wore grim, determined expressions as they rode, every one of them willing to die for Skye. For him.

He hoped it would not come to that. He'd already lost too many, and each death dragged around his neck like a weight that would drown him if it got much heavier. If Jenna was right, if she could somehow destroy the shrine and restore Skye's magic, this would all be over.

Was it even possible?

He closed his eyes for a second, trying to picture a future where his people were protected, where his lands were not under constant threat from the sea, where they could plan and dream rather than living day by day. But he couldn't. He struggled to see beyond today.

As they rode steadily southeast, more warriors swelled his ranks. The call to muster had gone out, and his people were answering. If the raiders thought to catch them unawares, they would be disappointed and if they tried to come ashore, Arran would make sure the waters ran red with their blood.

Bran snorted, and Arran forced himself to relax his grip on the reins, taking steady breaths to calm the rage and trepidation that warred for dominance inside him. It was another fine day. It seemed that whenever the raiders came, the sea was as calm as glass and the sun blazed in the sky overhead. Coincidence? Or the dark power of their god?

Lir, he prayed. *If ever we needed your help, we need it now. Protect my people.* He glanced at Jenna who was riding beside him, clinging to her mare like a limpet, face creased in determination as she concentrated on not falling off. *Protect her, Lir. Please.*

If anything should happen to her...

The sun was nearing its midday zenith by the time they reached the isolated bay that Brother Merrick had marked on the map. As they looked down on the horseshoe bay, Arran pulled up his horse and gazed out. The bay was unremarkable. Enclosed on either side by rocky cliffs, it boasted a small beach and strands of kelp that waved in the water like tentacles.

Down on the beach a group of men were gathered—his eastern patrol that had been tracking the raiders along the coast.

Of the raiders, there was no sign.

Arran allowed himself a small nod of satisfaction. They had made it here before them. So far, so good.

He ordered his men to dismount and, leaving the horses picketed on the trail, led the way down onto the beach, Jenna walking at his side. The captain of the eastern patrol strode to meet them, looking over how many men Arran had brought with him.

"My laird," he said, inclining his head. "I'm mighty glad to see ye, I can tell ye."

"Alec," Arran said, taking the man's arm wrist to wrist in the warrior's grip. "What news?"

"They're coming this way all right. They've been keeping out to sea, trying to sneak up on us without us noticing. The daft bastards seem to think we are eejits. We've been using the higher ground to keep track of them. I've posted relays up and down the coast. If the force splits or changes direction, we'll soon know about it. They've not shown any signs of doing that so far though."

"Nor will they," Arran said. "Because what they want is right here." He looked around the bay. "Somewhere."

He turned to Mal and issued instructions for his men to take up position on the cliffs overlooking the bay and on the sand dunes behind. "We have to stop them from landing if we can. Have everyone keep out of sight and have fire-arrows at the ready. Fire as soon as they're in range. I want as many of their boats sunk as possible before they can land. We need to give Jenna as much time as we can."

Mal nodded then turned and began bellowing orders. His warriors hurried to obey. As he watched his people move into position, not a grumble, nor a question, nor a hesitation among them, pride swelled in his chest. This was Clan MacLeod, and they would not allow Skye to fall. Not while any of them had breath left in their bodies.

He turned to Jenna. "Well, lass? Should we get started?"

Chapter Twenty

J ENNA DID NOT like the feel of this place. Not at all. To the naked eye, it looked peaceful. Beautiful even, with its calm waters and golden beach. But that beauty was deceptive. There was something here that felt… wrong, like the stench of rotting meat hidden by expensive perfume.

The feeling had been building the closer they rode to the place Merrick had marked for them and now she was here, it was so overwhelming she felt sick to her stomach.

"Jenna?" Arran asked. "Are ye all right?"

His big hand settled on her shoulder, and she jumped. "What? Yes, I'm fine. It's just… just…" She swallowed down the bile that was trying to rise up her throat. "I'm fine."

His expression suggested he wasn't convinced. There was no sign of the raiders, thank all the gods. That meant she had time. Time to find whatever it was in this shrine that was blocking her magic, and destroy it. Time to stop the coming battle before it ever began. Time to stop Arran from getting hurt.

She took a deep breath and closed her eyes. The sun was warm on her face, the wind a gentle caress across her skin as she reached down into her magic and sent her senses questing wide across the bay, searching, searching for that sense of corruption and wrongness.

Her eyes opened with a gasp, and she stumbled. Arran was

there immediately, hands going around her waist to steady her.

"What is it, lass?"

She raised a shaky finger and pointed at the far cliff. "There. It's over there."

Arran's expression tightened. He drew his claymore, the blade flashing in the sunlight. "Let's go."

They marched down the beach towards the dark cliff and with each step, the sick feeling in Jenna's stomach intensified. By the time they reached the rock face, she was stumbling in the sand and Arran had to hold her up with one arm. A shelf of rock sloped gently out into the sea in front of them, with waves lapping at its farthest end. Arran helped Jenna up onto it and she saw that it was littered with seaweed and small pools. At high tide, it would likely be completely submerged.

Which is why the raiders are coming now, she thought. *At low tide. So they can access it.*

She turned, gazing behind to where the shelf of rock ran back into the cliff. At first she could see nothing out of the ordinary, but slowly, as her eyes adjusted, she spotted something. A darker shadow against the base of the cliff, a patch so black it seemed like a void. It was from there that the sense of corruption came, wafting on the breeze like the scent of carrion.

She clutched Arran's arm tighter and pointed. "There."

Together, they made their way towards it. Then suddenly a call went up from the cliff top above.

"Raiders!"

Jenna's heart jumped as she spun to face the horizon. There, still far out to sea, but coming this way, Jenna saw sails. Many, many sails.

Arran growled a string of curses in Gaelic. "We have to hurry."

Jenna nodded, and they hurried towards the hole in the cliff. It was a cave much like the one in which she'd encountered Lir. This one though had none of the reflected light of the waves or the smell of salt. Instead, it was as dark as a tomb and smelled of stale air that hadn't been disturbed for centuries.

Jenna halted on the threshold. The sense of wrongness thrummed on her senses like a note played out of key, a wrong chord in a vast orchestra. The back of her neck tingled.

"I'll go first," Arran said, holding his claymore in a double-handed grip.

"Wait." Jenna grabbed his wrist to halt him. She reached inside herself, grasped her magic, and used it to craft a small sphere of light, no bigger than an apple, that formed on the palm of her hand. It wasn't much, but it was enough to light their way and stop them tripping over and breaking their necks. "We'll go together."

Arran nodded. "Aye. Together then."

Side by side, they stepped forward. Jenna found herself holding her breath as they moved into the cave, half-expecting something horrible to jump out and grab them. But nothing moved, and as they crossed the threshold, her light finally chased away the shadows and revealed the interior. It wasn't large, more of a depression in the rock rather than a true cave, but the floor had been smoothed by the passage of many feet and the walls curved above them, giving the space the impression of a bowl.

And in the center of that bowl stood the thing they'd come to seek.

Rising out of the floor was another anchor stone. Only this one wasn't like the others. Instead of bearing the whorls and glyphs of Skye's ancient magic, this one was marked with spiky runes that looked like slashes carved into the stone's skin. The stone itself was not smooth but cut into sharp angles and sloping planes and as black as coal. It looked wrong, like one of those impossible objects where the lines and angles didn't quite add up. It hurt Jenna's eyes to look at it.

Behind it, farther back Jenna saw a single standing stone no higher than her knee. This one was marked with the familiar symbols of Skye's magic—the original anchor stone that had been superseded by the one placed here by Njord's followers. She could feel no power coming from this at all.

"That's what they're coming for?" Arran asked, nodding at the black, angular stone.

"Yes."

Arran's eyes narrowed. He glanced around the cave, stance and expression wary, as if expecting an attack.

"It's just a stone."

Jenna shook her head. "It's an anchor stone. Can't you feel it?" His blank expression was answer enough to that. "But it's not an anchor stone for Skye's magic. It's Njord's. It holds his magic. From here they could resurrect his power and his dominion over Skye. This is what they've been looking for."

She knelt by the stone and hovered her hand an inch above its surface. Something like electricity brushed against her skin. Closing her eyes, she sent her senses questing outwards. The golden web of energy that covered Skye flared to life in her mind's eye immediately, shimmering like a net of woven corn. The dark spots where the magic had failed were still there and she realized suddenly that the decay began here, in this cave. With the anchor stone before her.

An alien magic was emanating from Njord's stone. Instead of gold, the color of this magic was blood red. She could see it pulsing from the stone and spreading out along the golden web, weaving its way among the strands so insidiously that it was almost undetectable unless you knew what to look for. It was leaching poison into Skye's magic, weakening it, burning holes in its essence.

Jenna had no idea how long it had been here. Decades, probably. It had sat here undiscovered, eroding Skye's magic so slowly that nobody noticed until it was too late.

And now, Njord's followers were coming to finish the job. If they succeeded, it would be over. Skye's magic would be destroyed, gone forever, and there would be nothing she nor anyone else could do about it.

She opened her eyes and looked at Arran. "We don't have

much time. We have to destroy this."

Arran nodded. "Then stand back."

He pulled Jenna to her feet and pushed her behind him. Then, grasping his claymore with both hands, he swung it with all his might at the stone. Jenna flinched as it struck, an almighty clang echoing through the cave and sparks flying from the stone. But it remained undamaged. Not even a scratch marred its angular surface.

Arran growled under his breath. Picking up a rock the size of his head, he raised it high above his head and brought it slamming down on the anchor stone with all his might. The rock shattered into pieces on impact, but the anchor stone remained undamaged.

"I'll have the men bring chisels and hammers," Arran said, turning towards the entrance.

Jenna caught his arm. "That won't make any difference. Magic made this thing, and magic is the only thing that can destroy it."

He let out a slow breath. "All right. What do ye need me to do?"

"Stay with me."

He placed his hand over hers. "Always."

Jenna stared at him, a hundred things she wanted to say crowding her tongue. But she only nodded.

She risked a glance outside. The raider ships were entering the bay, inching ever closer. She saw faces lining the railings, warriors wearing leather armor and carrying weapons. So many. Too many.

"Dinna look at them," Arran said, putting his finger under her chin and turning her face towards him. "They willnae enter this cave nor touch a hair on yer head. I swear it."

Jenna said nothing. How could she explain that she wasn't afraid for herself but was terrified for him? For the people of Skye?

Taking a deep breath, Jenna knelt once more by the stone. She closed her eyes and reached out, this time laying her palm flat against the cold surface. The alien magic lunged at her like a snapping hound. It was all anger and seething rage, ocean storms and the dark, angry depths. She steadied herself. Took a deep breath. And slowly, slowly, began to push her own magic towards it.

She wrapped the anchor stone in tendrils of golden power, laying strand over strand until it was covered in a glimmering net. Then she began to contract that net, pulling the strands of magic tight against the stone and the alien magic within. But it fought her. The magic pushed back and it was woven through the anchor stone so tightly that she couldn't seem to get a good grip on it. She was soon breathing heavily, and sweat was pouring down her face.

Come on! she shouted inwardly. *Break, damn you!*

But it didn't. Jenna fought and struggled but was unable to make a dent in the magic of the anchor stone.

Weak, she thought. *You're too weak. You're going to fail!*

But then, just as her strength was giving out, she felt new vigor flooding into her. Arran had his hand clasped to her shoulder and somehow he was feeding her strength. Vitality rushed through her, pushing away the exhaustion, filling her with energy.

With renewed determination, she focused her magic on the stone. Arran's strength intertwined with hers, and she used this combined force to haul her net of magic tighter, tighter, tighter, pulling with everything she had until finally, with a retort that shook the cave, the anchor stone cracked. The top half toppled backwards and crashed to the floor in a shower of dust.

Jenna collapsed onto her hands and knees, breathing heavily, hair falling forward to curtain her face. She felt dizzy but also slightly euphoric. She had done it! Correction: *they* had done it. She pushed herself onto her knees and turned to look at Arran.

He was kneeling behind her, both hands pressed against the smooth stone floor. His hair was matted to his face with sweat and his chest was heaving as if he'd just run a marathon. He looked up at her, blue eyes bright.

"We did it?"

Jenna nodded, feeling a grin spread across her face. "We did it!"

She felt the strongest urge to throw her arms around him but held herself back. Now was not the time. They might have broken Njord's anchor stone but there was still a fleet of raiders fast approaching and she had yet to restore Skye's magic.

From outside, she heard a sudden shout and then the twang of bowstrings. The air was suddenly filled with arrows and the shouting of men. The fleet of boats had almost reached the beach and now the occupants were flinging themselves over the side, some to avoid the arrows that were raining down on them, others in a bid to reach the shore. From either end of the beach, Arran's warriors came running, a terrible, ululating battle cry coming from their throats.

The beach would soon be soaked in suffering and bloodshed. She had to stop it.

Arran was staring at the raiders too, his lips pulled back from his teeth in a snarl, the veins in his neck standing out. His biceps flexed as he strode to the cave entrance and raised his claymore, ready to fight anyone who tried to get close. But he couldn't keep fighting forever. Sooner or later one of their blows would get through his defenses and Arran would get injured—or worse.

No, she thought. *He won't. I will not let that happen.*

She had broken Njord's anchor stone. Now all she had to do was repair Skye's magic. She hurried to the back of the cave and went to her knees by the original anchor stone, taking a moment to trace her fingers along the whorls and glyphs carved into its surface. It was broken, dead. But that didn't mean that it couldn't be revived.

Closing her eyes, Jenna tried to shut everything out. The sound of roaring men and clashing steel that now sounded from the beach. The harsh rasp of Arran's breathing as he guarded the cave mouth. The thump, thump, thump of her own rapid heartbeat.

There was only her and broken stone and the magic inside her.

She reached out and laid her palm flat against the anchor stone. The net of golden energy sprang into her mind immediately and now that the alien magic was gone, it seemed to shine brighter than before, almost incandescent in places.

Yet it was still black as pitch in others. Still corrupted. Still broken.

Gathering her magic, she channeled energy out into the golden net just as she'd done twice before. And just as before, she reached the holes in the net and paused. Despite breaking the influence of the alien magic, there was no change or sign of the magic healing itself. It needed help, and she was the only one able to give it.

She began weaving her power into strands and using them to bridge the gaps in the golden net. There was less resistance this time and she wove the patches with unexpected ease, the magic melding and growing beneath her touch as though eager to obey.

A thrill of elation went through her. Yes! It was working!

When every last drop of darkness had been patched, she drew the magic into the broken anchor stone and tied it off, completing the web. Then, slowly, carefully, she withdrew her magic. The golden net thrummed through the very bedrock of Skye, right from its origin at Bail Nan Cnoc, from the darkest cave to the highest peak. The land suddenly felt *alive*. She could feel the energy thrumming in every rock and blade of grass, in every tree and flower. Even the waves lashing against the shore suddenly seemed to hum with a life force of their own.

She turned to Arran. "Arran, I've—"

The words died on her lips. Raiders were swarming outside the cave mouth, fighting to gain entrance. Fighting to get to her. They were only stopped from doing so by Mal and a group of his men and a fierce battle was raging. The clang of steel on steel, the cries of wounded men, and the stink of blood filled the air. Arran had not moved from his position by the cave entrance but from the tense set of his shoulders, Jenna could see how much he longed to go join his men, how much it cost him to hold his position while they fought and died.

Jenna's pulse ratcheted up several notches. Fear coursed through her like ice-water. What was happening? The magic was restored. Any enemy of Skye should not have been able to penetrate its magical wards. So why were they still fighting?

"I don't understand," she whispered, her voice hoarse as she stared at the carnage that was inching ever closer to where she knelt. "I fixed it. I fixed it!"

Suddenly, she felt a tremor in the rock beneath her knees, a low rumble like that of an earthquake.

And somewhere she felt something... snap.

She closed her eyes, sent her senses desperately questing out towards Skye's magic. And then she saw them. Black holes in the web. Unhealed. Corrupted. Broken.

No! she cried silently. *I fixed it!*

But she hadn't. She might have broken the power of Njord's corruption but her healing of the magic hadn't worked. Despair washed through her, black and suffocating, and for a moment she couldn't breathe, couldn't think, couldn't lift her head for the agony of defeat rampaging through her.

The sounds of fighting were louder now, echoing off the walls around her. The raiders were only perhaps twenty paces from where she knelt, blocked by a line of Arran's warriors who were fighting desperately to keep them at bay. They were so close she could make out the tattoos inked into the raiders' cheeks—the same runes that had adorned the anchor stone. Her heart began to gallop in her chest, her breathing becoming hoarse and ragged with fear.

Then, even as she watched, two of Mal's men went down, blood spurting and bodies crumpling. Three raiders burst through the line and sprinted forward with their weapons swinging.

Straight at Arran.

A scream ripped from Jenna's throat as Arran stepped to meet the first of them. His claymore swung in a blur, taking the first man in the stomach, the second in the thigh, and then catching the third's blade on his own, shoving him back with a powerful thrust of his shoulders.

But more men were breaking through the line now, first one and then another, and Arran was suddenly fighting desperately, fighting to keep them from her, fighting to stay alive.

"No!" Jenna screamed. "Arran!"

Magic gathered at her fingertips, hot and raging.

Your power must never be used for harm, her aunts' voices said in her head. *Only for the good of others.*

It had been the song of her life, the unbreakable rule. But now she didn't care. Arran was in danger, and nothing else mattered. What good was her power if she couldn't save him? What was the point of any of this if she lost him?

She raised her hands, ready to send her magic crashing into the attackers and send them flying. But there was no room. Arran was too entangled in the melee, a confusing tangle of flashing blades and tumbling bodies. If she attacked now, she would likely hit him as well.

"Give it up!" a man with a tattoo down his neck snarled at Arran. "Ye canna win! Ye think ye can stand against the power of a god?"

"Njord has no power here," Arran snarled back. "And neither do ye."

With a furious burst, he sent a stinging attack at the man, claymore swinging so fast it seemed to be everywhere at once. The ringing of steel on steel filled the cave mouth as the tattooed man desperately parried the blows, being forced back step by step. Jenna knew very little about sword-fighting but even to her untrained eye, she could tell that Arran was a master swordsman. For such a large man, he was as light on his feet as a ballet dancer, and he moved and swayed, struck and pivoted with electrifying grace.

Arran's blade caught the tattooed man's and ripped it out of his hand. The man's sword went sailing through the air and hit the cave wall with a clang. Unarmed now, the man crouched, eyes darting around as if looking for escape.

Arran swung his sword with all his might, a howl of rage and frustration bursting from his lungs. Had the blow connected, it would have taken the man's head off.

But the blow didn't land.

The tattoo on the man's neck suddenly began to glow with a strange blue light. Then he moved so fast that Jenna couldn't track his movement. One second, he was right in the path of Arran's sword, the next he seemed to flicker and reappear inside Arran's guard.

Time seemed to slow. Jenna saw the man's hand reach to his waist and pull out a gleaming dagger. She saw him lunge at Arran. She saw the blade, razor sharp and deadly, move towards Arran's heart inch by slow inch.

A scream formed in Jenna's throat. She raised her hand slowly, so slowly—and the future suddenly burst upon her with the force of falling rocks. She was driven to one knee, enveloped in visions.

She saw a world without Arran MacLeod in it. She saw *her* world without him in it. A world colder and darker for his absence. A life that fell so far short of what it could have been, a life empty of the light and laughter and warmth that could be hers if only she would acknowledge what she'd known all along.

She could not live without him. And why?

"Because I love him," she whispered.

The admission washed through her like a summer breeze and instead of bringing the fear, the vulnerability, the weakness she'd expected, it brought instead something she'd not felt in a long time. Peace.

She lifted her head to the ceiling. "I love him!" she bellowed with all her strength. "You hear me? I love him!"

Do ye think I would have brought ye through time if ye couldnae do this? What ye need is already inside ye. Ye just have to find the courage to recognize it.

Well, now she did. With the echoes of her shout still sounding around her, she twisted and slammed her palm against the anchor stone.

The effect was instantaneous.

Skye's magic flared, blazing white hot like the inside of a star. Jenna felt it rip through her hand, through her body, through the very fabric of the universe. The earth, the air, the water, blazed into life and the ground beneath her feet suddenly thrummed as if with a subterranean heartbeat.

The tattooed man's knife, which had been inching towards Arran's chest, never reached its target. A shockwave burst through the cave, picked up the tattooed man and the rest of the invaders, and tossed them away like sticks in a breeze.

Arran and his men were left untouched, as if Skye's magic recognized its own, but Njord's people were sent arcing through the air, turned over and over like tumbleweeds, and deposited on the sand at the edge of the water.

A tempest sprang up, a howling wind that raced down the beach and whipped the water of the bay into a frenzy of white, frothing waves. The ships that the invaders had arrived in bobbed and hawed in the suddenly wild water.

The tattooed man picked himself up from where he'd been tossed. "No!" he bellowed. "This cannot be! Skye is ours!"

Gritting his teeth, he bent against the furious wind, fighting to take a step forward. The wind increased, sending his hair streaming back from his face and squeezing tears from his eyes. A moment longer he fought the tempest, the tattoos on his neck glowing bright blue, and Jenna felt a silent battle of wills taking place between the power of Skye and the power of Njord.

Then the man's tattoo winked out, becoming nothing but black ink, and he and his men were pushed back, back, back by the wind, into the shallows that whipped and seethed around their legs. But still the wind did not abate. The waves tugged and pulled at them, sweeping their legs out from under them and carrying them out into deeper waters.

Jenna was reminded of when she and Arran were caught in the rip current as she watched all those screaming, struggling men, carried out to sea. Some managed to get to the boats and scramble aboard, quickly pulling anchor and fleeing from the bay. But most did not, and the last Jenna saw of them was a seething mass of bobbing heads and flailing arms being swept out into the roiling gray mass of the open ocean.

Just as quickly as it had come, the wind dissipated. All fell still. In its absence, the silence felt thick and cloying. Arran's men looked around in bewilderment, scarcely daring to believe they'd seen what they just had.

Arran turned to look at her, a question on his lips, and Jenna cannoned into him. He grunted at the impact and then, as she buried her face in his chest and wrapped her arms around him, he kissed the top of her head and stroked her hair.

"I thought I was going to lose you," she murmured into his chest. "I couldn't bear it. I just couldn't."

He felt so solid and reassuring. The rock she could tether herself to. As long as he was there, she would never get lost in the storm.

His heart beat beneath her ear, strong and steady. He pushed her back, hands on her shoulders, and looked down at her. For the first time, that shadow in his eyes, that weight that he always seemed to carry, was gone. A smile curled his lips.

"Ye did it," he breathed. "God in Heaven, lass! Ye did it!"

Jenna shook her head. "No. It wasn't me. It was *you*. You're the one who saved Skye."

His brow furrowed in puzzlement. "All I did was fight."

"Don't you see?" Jenna said, placing her palms flat against his muscled chest and staring up at him. "Lir knew all along. She tried to tell me, but I was too stubborn to listen. It was *you*, Arran. You made me whole again. You helped me to heal. You gave me something on Skye that I loved, and that's what enabled me to fix the magic."

"Something ye love?" he asked. "What's that?"

Jenna rolled her eyes. "You, you idiot! I love you! Haven't you realized that by now?"

Arran's breath hitched. His grip on her shoulders tightened. "Ye… ye… do?"

Jenna nodded then reached up and cupped his cheek. "I didn't want to, but you left me no choice. I fought against it but no matter how hard I tried, you still captured my heart. Now it's yours if you want it."

"Oh, I want it," he breathed. He closed his eyes for a moment before opening them again. "Am I dreaming? Or did that barbarian kill me and this is the afterlife? Jenna MacFinnan, ye have no idea how much I've longed to hear ye say that. Ye have no idea how much I've longed to tell ye that I love ye too. So much. Dear God, so much!"

As Arran spoke those words, it was like a knot inside her suddenly unraveled. It was like a thorn that had pricked and torn her insides for all these months suddenly worked itself loose. The tightness and pain evaporated. She felt like she was floating. Like she was invincible. Like she was a god.

"Ingrid was right," she said in a whisper. "It really is simple. You're my home, Arran."

Arran pressed his forehead to hers. "Then stay," he whispered. "I canna live without ye, Jenna. I dinna have the strength. Stay. Be my wife."

Jenna had never thought to hear those words. Not from Arran. Not from anyone ever again. But as they fell from his lips, she felt a new future falling into place. Not the empty one filled with hollowness, but the bright, rich one full of light and laughter and warmth. It was right within her grasp. All she had to do was reach out and touch it…

"Yes," she said, tears leaking from the corners of her eyes. "Yes, I'll marry you."

How had she ever thought she could resist this man? How had she ever thought she could stop herself from falling in love with him? She couldn't. She never stood a chance.

He gave a whoop of delight that brought his men running into the cave in alarm. Arran picked Jenna up and twirled her around, the two of them laughing like children.

Mal shoved to the front of the group and crossed his arms over his broad chest as he watched them.

"Well," he said. "About bloody time."

Chapter Twenty-One

JENNA DIDN'T WANT to wake. She wanted to stay here forever, nestled in this warm bed, with an equally warm body snuggled up beside her. She stretched out her toes, loving the feel of the soft sheets against her skin, and the weight of Arran's arm draped protectively across her hip. His chest was pressed into her back, warm and hard, and the only sounds in the room were his steady breathing.

Oh yes, she could stay like this forever.

But the light slanting through the window and the distant sounds of the castle waking meant it wasn't to be. The day had begun and no matter how much she might try, she couldn't avoid what was happening today. Perhaps it would be better to get it over with, like ripping off a band aid.

She opened her eyes. Arran's chambers—*their* chambers— sprang into view around her. When she'd first moved in here, they had been sparse—a warrior's rooms—but, with Ingrid and Rosaline's help, she'd done her best to make them comfortable and now they were lovely and cozy with thick rugs, warm throws, and vases of dried flowers.

She shifted and Arran mumbled something incoherent, his voice thick with sleep. She turned in his arms so she was facing him and ran a finger down the sculpted contours of his chest, watching him sleep.

She was aching this morning, her muscles sore from what she and Arran had done last night. Had done *every* night, truth be told, since they'd returned to Dun Tabor. She could never get enough of him. Even now, aching and sleep-addled as she was, she could feel the stirrings of desire begin to flutter in her belly. She wanted him to make love to her again. She wanted to stay in this room with him all day and forget what awaited her.

But she couldn't. She'd been putting it off for far too long already.

She laid a kiss on the end of Arran's nose. "Hey," she said.

His eyes fluttered open, that sapphire blue fixing on her. "Hey," he mumbled. "What are ye doing awake? It's not even midday yet."

"Funny," she said drily.

He grinned then leaned forward and kissed her, pinning her to the bed. Heat pooled in her stomach and she wrapped her arms around his head, kissing him back. Perhaps they could stay in bed just a little longer…

A knock on the door interrupted that thought. "My laird? Jenna?" Ingrid's voice came from the other side. "Ye asked me to wake ye at dawn."

Jenna stifled a groan.

"Aye," Arran called. "My thanks, Ingrid. We'll be there soon." He propped himself on one elbow and looked down at Jenna. "Well?" he asked. "Today's the day. Should we get started?"

"No," she said. "We shouldn't. We should hide under the bed."

Arran laughed. "It canna be that bad."

"You don't get it," she moaned. "They are going to *kill* me! If you think I'm bad, just wait until you see *them* in a rage."

"Dinna fash, I'll win them over with my charm and wit. Ye'll be perfectly safe."

Jenna didn't dignify that comment with an answer. She threw back the covers and climbed reluctantly to her feet. "All right. Let's get this show on the road, shall we?"

She was so nervous she didn't eat breakfast, so it was less than an hour later, after bidding goodbye to Rosaline, Mal, and Ingrid at the castle gates, that she found herself mounted on Bran, with Arran seated behind her.

It was a beautiful early summer day, with fluffy clouds in the sky high above, and the drone of insects in the flowers their only company as they rode steadily through the countryside. Arran, perhaps sensing Jenna's nerves, said not a word, but he was a steadying, silent presence at her back all the same.

They reached the beach too soon for Jenna's liking. She'd not been here since the day she'd arrived but even so, she recognized it immediately. As they rode down onto the shingle and sand, dismounted, and walked towards the rock pools that bracketed the beach, tingles of trepidation slid down her spine.

Excuses and apologies ran through her head like a litany. She'd practiced them all a thousand times but she knew they would do no good. They were going to be *furious*. Two months had passed since she'd restored Skye's magic. Two. Whole. Months. How was she going to explain that away?

They reached the rock pool and came to a halt at its edge. Jenna found herself staring down into its depths. It looked nothing special, just a run-of-the-mill rock pool that you might find on beaches the world over. But Jenna knew it was far more than that.

As she stared down into it, she felt movement at her side and looked up to see a blonde-haired woman standing beside her. The woman wore flowing robes and her hair moved of its own accord, like kelp shifting with the tide. She regarded Jenna and Arran with eyes of pure silver.

"Ready?" Lir asked them.

"Nope," Jenna said, shaking her head. "Not even close."

The goddess smiled. "Jenna MacFinnan, ye have conquered ancient magic, adapted to a time not yer own, and overcome the followers of a Norse god. Are ye telling me ye are frightened of yer own aunts?"

"Too right," Jenna replied. "You haven't met them. Give me a Norse god any day of the week."

Lir laughed lightly, a sound like rain falling on the ocean. "I dinna think ye will find it as terrifying as ye imagine."

"Ye are sure this will work?" Arran asked, stepping up to the edge of the pool. "And we can return any time we want?"

"A bargain is a bargain," Lir replied. "And by saving Skye ye have paid the price a hundred times over. Aye, the portal is yers. Ye can come and go as ye please."

Arran blew out a breath and looked at Jenna. He took her hand. "Yer aunts might be angry to start with, love, but they'll calm down. And ye want them at the wedding dinna ye?"

Jenna nodded. She and Arran were getting married in two weeks and she didn't just *want* her aunts at the wedding. She *needed* them there. She couldn't do it without them.

She squeezed Arran's hands. "I'm ready."

Together they jumped into the pool, leaving the goddess staring after them.

They emerged, coughing and spluttering in the lake behind Jenna's house. A flock of startled ducks went scattering as they broke the surface and a fisherman sitting on a platform stared in surprise, his sandwich dropping from his fingers, forgotten.

Jenna waved at him. "Hi. Nothing like a bit of wild swimming, eh?"

She and Arran paddled to the shore where he helped her out. Everything looked exactly the same as when she'd left it: the lake, the woods, the path. But smaller somehow, as if she'd grown.

"The twenty-first century," Arran breathed, gazing around. "I never expected to come here once, let alone twice. My people would never believe this."

"Well, if I'm still breathing later, I'll give you a tour of the best bits." She tapped her lip with a finger. "Let's see. The best things about this time. Hmm. Oh! I know! Hot running water. Pizza. Chocolate. And doughnuts! How could I have forgotten doughnuts?"

Arran laughed. "Lass, I think ye may be drooling. I look forward to trying these delicacies."

With a grin, Jenna took Arran's hand and together they took the path that led around the lake—but in the opposite direction to where her house lay. They would go there later so Jenna could pack some things, but right now it wasn't their destination.

Their destination was, in fact, a little white-washed cottage that stood on stilts out over the water on the northern shore of the lake. Jenna's stomach clenched and her heart did a little flip when she saw it. She clutched Arran's hand tighter.

Three steps led up to the veranda. Jenna halted in front of those steps and stared at the closed door.

"The door willnae open itself, lass," Arran said. "No matter how long ye stare at it."

Taking a deep breath, she strode up the steps and knocked, Arran by her side. She heard footsteps approaching on the other side and the door opened to reveal Aunt Rose standing there, wiping her hands on a tea towel.

"Aunt Rose, before you say anything," Jenna blurted the second the door opened. "I know I shouldn't have left without telling you first and I shouldn't have been gone so long without getting in touch, but can explain everything if you'll just listen—"

"Jenna!" Rose said brightly. "So you changed your mind about making chutney, eh? But why did you knock? Why not just use your key?"

"Eh?" Jenna stared in confusion. She'd expected Aunt Rose to be furious with her. She'd been gone for months, after all. Just disappeared without so much as a goodbye. What was going on? Was this the calm before the storm?

Aunt Elise appeared behind Rose, eating an apple. "Jenna!" she cried around a mouthful. "Come to save me from the boredom after all! Or maybe you've changed your mind about that hex?" Coming to the door, her eyes alighted on Arran and her eyebrows rose. "Who's your friend?"

"I... um... this is Arran," Jenna stammered.

Aunt Elise looked Arran up and down, an approving expression flitting across her face. "Hi, Arran. I'm Elise. Jenna's younger, cooler aunt."

"Delighted to meet ye both," Arran rumbled in his Scots burr. "Jenna has told me much about ye."

"She has?" Elise asked, her eyes fixing on Jenna. "Well she hasn't told us anything about you. A mistake she's going to rectify right now over coffee and cake. Come on in then!"

She and Rose went inside, leaving the door open. Jenna didn't follow. What was going on? What were they up to?

"I don't get it," she muttered to Arran. "I thought they'd roast me alive."

Warily, she walked through the door and into the cottage's neat little living room. Her aunts were pottering around in the kitchen, and she could hear the sound of cups and plates. She noticed Aunt Rose's phone on the sideboard. On impulse, she walked over and grabbed it, staring at the screen.

Or, more specifically, the *date* on the screen.

Her eyes widened. "I don't believe it!" she gasped, looking at Arran. She waved the phone at him as though it explained everything. "Look!"

He blinked, a baffled expression on his face. "At what?"

"The date! This is the same day I left! I haven't been gone for months at all! Lir has sent us back to the exact same day we left! No wonder my aunts aren't pissed off with me! They don't even know I've been gone!"

She didn't know whether to feel annoyed or relieved. "Lir knew about this all along, and still she let me stew! I'll kill her when I see her!"

Arran shook his head and whistled under his breath. "A showdown between a goddess and a MacFinnan spellweaver. I reckon I could sell tickets to that."

"Are you coming in or what?" Elise's voice came from the kitchen.

Jenna let out a long breath, feeling tension leak out of her, along with all the excuses she no longer needed. All this worrying and there had been no need! Aargh! If this was a goddess's idea of humor, she did *not* appreciate it!

Taking Arran's hand, she led him into the kitchen. The countertop was piled high with jars of chutney and the kettle on the stove was just beginning to boil. It was all so familiar, so homey, that for a minute Jenna felt her chest tighten with emotion. Oh, how she'd missed these two.

"Coffee or tea?" Rose asked, turning to face them with a coffee pot in one hand and a teapot in the other.

"Chocolate cake or lemon drizzle?" Elise said, balancing a cake-topped plate in each hand.

Jenna couldn't help herself. She burst into tears. With a sob, she threw her arms around each of her aunts in turn.

Aunt Rose blinked. "What was that for?"

Jenna wiped at her eyes. "I've just... missed you guys, that's all."

"Missed us?" Elise said. "We only saw you this morning."

Jenna took a deep breath, glanced at Arran. "You'd both better sit down," she said. "And you might want to put something stronger in that coffee. We have a lot to tell you."

THE END

About the Author

Katy Baker was born in London to an English mother and an American father. She grew up a stone's throw from Hampstead Heath which remains one of her favourite places in the world. During her twenties she spent several years living in San Francisco where she developed an abiding love of bagels before returning to her beloved London. She lives in south London with her husband and a very grumpy bulldog.

Katy's books explore the intricacies of human relationships with plenty of spice thrown in. What would life be without a little spice?

Website:
www.katybakerromance.com